To Nancy,
Rebecca says hi.

Joseph Bebo

Thank you!
Hope you enjoy the book!!

Rebecca
(Amber)

My Terrible Mistress
Copyright © 2017 Joseph W. Bebo
Copyright © 2001, 2010 Joseph W. Bebo
Published by Joseph W. Bebo
(An imprint of JWB Books Publishing)

Joseph W. Bebo
PO Box 762
Hudson, MA, 01749
Email: joewbebobooks@gmail.com
Editor: James Oliveri
Interior and Cover Design: Elyse Zielinski
Model: Amber Lynne Doe
Hair and Make-up: TaraLyn Rose
Photographer: Cynthia Veld Burns

Library of Congress Cataloging in – Publication Data
Joseph W. Bebo
My Terrible Mistress /Joseph Bebo – First Edition

ISBN: 978-0-9982182-4-3
Thriller; Horror

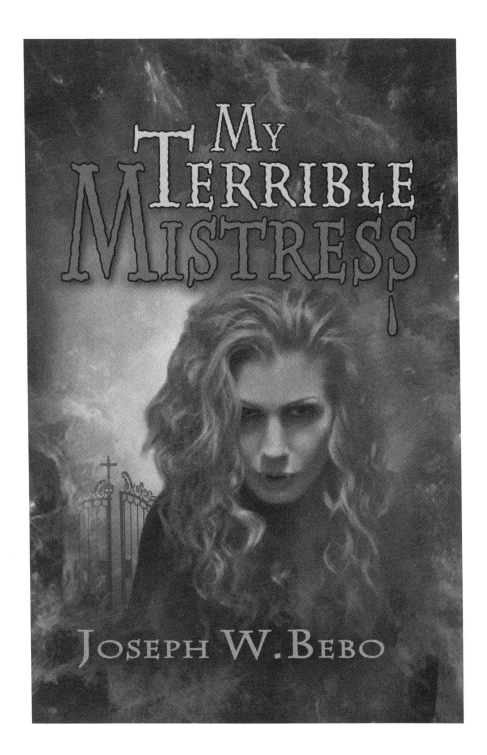

MY
TERRIBLE
MISTRESS

JOSEPH W. BEBO

Chapter 1

This abomination has gone on long enough. It's time to tell my story even though it may be the death of me, time to put a stop to the madness that has been my life for these last hundred years. I have a very singular occupation, a job only I can do. A task so horrible, so perverse, so filled with evil it makes me shudder just to contemplate it, for I am the servant of a vampire, my terrible mistress.

Perhaps you think I exaggerate, maybe stretch the truth to enhance my tale. After all, I look normal enough, rather tall and distinguished, well-preserved for my age. You might mistake me for a mild-mannered professor or your neighborhood pharmacist, but I'm a man of a thousand faces, a man without a soul.

My master, who I can hardly bear to name, is an ancient thing so corrupt that evil permeates from her very pores, over a skin so smooth you'd think it was made of alabaster. Her claws and teeth, however, are very sharp, and she uses them with a joy that is hideous to behold. She is my beloved, my obsession. I cannot live without her, yet to live with her is to live a hell on earth.

If you know anything about vampires, you know they tend to sleep during the day to avoid the dangerous rays of the sun, and stalk their victims at night seeking their blood, which is the only thing that can quench their endless thirst. That's probably all you know about them, in spite of what you may have read or seen. Yes, they are real. They are here with us and have always been, hunting the innocent and guilty alike from time immemorial, but they are nothing like you imagine.

You may find this all hard to believe. It's only going to get more difficult as we go on. For the things I'm going to tell you defy credibility, though I know them to be true, know it all too well. No matter how much I wish I could drown my knowledge in forgetfulness, it haunts my every waking moment. Alas, I doubt I will ever be free of this curse. For I could no more leave my beloved than I could leave my own skin. She owns me like darkness owns the night. I am her slave.

My thoughts hover between fear and longing, love and hate, like a moth between a flame and the night. I am tied to her, my soul and body, tied to an unspeakable horror the thought of which consumes me.

I, of course, must attend to her every whim, her every wish, sometimes I think to her every thought. For she is in my head, a constant presence, that although it does not speak, directs me like a conductor silently leads an orchestra.

This is not a diary, a daily recording of events more or less as they transpired over time. No one is interviewing me. No, this is more like a retching, a spewing out of some noxious poison. I have kept it in too long. I can no more hold back what I am about to write than I could hold back the sea. She thinks I am writing her story, but it is my tale I tell, a tale of misery and woe. .

I met Rebecca shortly after the turn of the century, the 19th century that is, January 11th, 1902 to be exact. As you may know, a hundred years is not long in the reckoning of a vampire, although it makes me rather an oddity. In the realm of the undead, such things are merely side notes.

Yes, I have been her faithful attendant for this past century. That's about as long as they can sustain us humans with their vampire ways, a combination of scientific knowledge and magic honed through millennia of practice. Her beginnings stretch back to a far remote time, back to the mists of pre-history.

Contrary to popular myth, it is not possible for a vampire to create another of their kind. They can kill you and drink your blood. They can kill you without drinking your blood. They can drink your blood and not kill you. They can keep you going in the peak of health for a very long time, like me, but they cannot make a vampire out of you. No, they were spawned when the world was still young, when older things walked the earth and the spells to bind them to a human vessel were still known. Once created, as far as I know, they can never be destroyed.

My story is short and pitiful. I was still a boy when she found me, one of many homeless waifs running loose in the streets of Berlin.

In those days Germany was the center of the industrialized world. We had caught and surpassed England in manufacturing output and urbanization. It was truly an impressive sight, my city of Berlin - building piled upon building; smoke stacks and steeples towering into the sky; trams and steam cars moving about on the varying levels of road and track - a great productive metropolis.

I guess that's what brought her there, from whatever pit she had been hiding in these thousand years. I lived in the Hochbahn area soon after it was opened in 1902, where the 'Menschenmasse' lived, in the steaming, smoke-filled slums below the train tracks that circled the inner part of the city. There I scrounged a living along with several other street urchins, orphans of neglect, poverty, and disease. My mother died before I was six. My father I never knew. Until I was ten I was brought up by a sour old spinster aunt who beat me and abused me when she wasn't using me to peddle her meager wares on the street. When she could no longer afford to board me, she abandoned me and moved to Düsseldorf. I'm sure finding me diddling myself in the stairwell had more than a little to do with it. We grew up fast on the streets of Berlin.

There must have been hundreds of others before me and there will be hundreds after I'm gone, keepers of the damned, for her life is long and her needs are great. She has told me of some of them, her ghouls, her servants, her slaves. Their stories, both good and bad, are meant to teach me some lesson. But this is my story, my confession. It will only teach you despair.

To be the slave of a vampire requires special qualities - a certain malleability, a will to follow, a pronounced weakness of character. One must be a liar, a thief, and a cheat, born and bred without love, like me on the streets of Berlin at ten years old.

It was soon after I was on my own that Rebecca appeared. Life was hard, but you get used to things when you're young and don't know any better. Life on the street was not much worse than life with my brutish aunt. At least I was my own boss. That is as long as I did what the bigger kids wanted, and that was everything, including servicing them sexually, but I was surviving, part of a gang. Then one night I became part of something far worse.

Just because I was low-born, a mongrel roaming the streets, doesn't mean I don't aspire to the better things in life. Just because I grew up an uncouth, illiterate waif doesn't mean I couldn't attain a certain level of culture and refinement. I always had a natural kind of intelligence, though never any schooling to channel it and help it grow, just a mean ability to survive and stay one step ahead of the law and the other guy.

It was late, about the time we usually prowled the neighborhood for easy marks. Some foolish tourist lost and disoriented. Or a poor fool who took the wrong turn coming home from work. Perhaps someone who thought they could sneak from a subway car to their home without being caught. We usually caught them, whoever it might be careless enough to be out on our streets at night.

The streetwalkers all knew to stay away from our neighborhood. It just wasn't safe there with all those sadistic adolescent boys, boys who would rather rob you and slit your throat than buy your wares. That was why it was unusual to see an unaccompanied female walking slowly down the empty sidewalk. We'd been watching her sauntering down the street for some time. She seemed unconcerned with the dark and menacing night or the reputation of the place. She was dressed like a prostitute, short skirt hiked up to her hips, blouse open to her naval. Medium in height and slim, she had sharp symmetric features, and seemed only a few years older than myself. If she was looking for customers, she wouldn't find any in this neighborhood, only trouble.

We surrounded her in silence, closing the net so she wouldn't get away. Being one of the smaller kids, I stayed in the background, not knowing quite what to do. This wasn't exactly my first hunt, but I had been told more than once to stay out of the way, so that's what I did. I thought she was awfully pretty, and was scared of what they would do to her. I thought about my mother and how it could have been her there, walking into danger.

I was about to yell out a warning, in spite of what the others would have done to me, but it was too late. They rushed in upon her, tearing at her clothing and punching her about the head and back. Before long the whole pack was on her, all nine of them. Still I hung back, uncertain what to do, watching in fascinated horror.

Soon she stood naked in front of us. I had never seen a woman completely undressed before, especially one so beautiful and close at hand.. Even the older boys held back not sure what to do with this unexpected gift. Suddenly, the leader of our group, Teddy, a large, freckled-faced boy from Bavaria, grabbed her from behind. Putting one hand around her throat, he choked her and roughly pinched her nipples with the other. All the boys, who were crowding around them, laughed with glee.

There was a high-pitched scream, but it was not coming from the woman, who seemed to be smiling mischievously. No, it came from Teddy. He went down with an ear-piercing cry as the demon woman ripped open his throat and drained the blood.

Before any of the gang had a chance to react, to scream, to fight or run, she mowed through them like a saw, removing body parts and fluid with ghastly speed. In a moment they were lying on the ground in withering heaps, all around me.

I stood there unable to breathe, still as a statue, in a state of shock. It all happened so fast. My companions, some of them quite big, were armed with clubs and knives, and hardened with years on the streets. A gang even the German police feared and avoided was destroyed in a heartbeat by a single, tiny unarmed female, almost too fast to comprehend. This could not be happening, though the groans and cries of my friends told me it was all too real.

She turned and looked at me, this demon girl with the flying, tangled hair and penetrating eyes. I heard her speaking in my mind, telling me that she would be my mother and take care of me until the end of time. For some reason, I started to cry. Something I had never done before, not when the bigger boys beat me or raped me, not when the police arrested and interrogated me, not even when my mother died. Now I was bawling uncontrollably, like a baby. It certainly wasn't because of what had happened to the other boys, none of whom I cared that much about, except perhaps Teddy, who used to protect me from the worst abuses of the others. No, it was because for some reason, I felt my mother had come back to me. I had finally come home.

She came to me and put her hands around me, pulling me gently to her and laying my head on her bare breasts. I could feel the stickiness of the other boys' blood as I rested my ear next to her heart, but I could hear no heartbeat. I couldn't tell if she was actually speaking or talking to me in my head, but it didn't matter, for I knew sure enough what she was saying. She started to caress me, moving her hands over me. I stood stiff as a board with my arms straight at my sides. I must have been a funny sight, for she laughed, a haunting, hollow, chilling laugh that left me weak and nauseous. My mother had never touched me like this. It all seemed like a dream.

That's all I remember. The next thing I recall, I'm dragging the lifeless, mutilated bodies of my comrades down into the sewers where the rats would devour them. What I was doing seemed ordinary enough to me at the time. I was in her spell, you see, compelled by her magic, and that made everything seem normal even though it was the most abnormal thing I could have done.

That which would have sent me screaming into the night only moments before now seemed quite natural. It was merely a play, like those stories of murder and mayhem you read in a dime novel, not real, only make-believe. As soon as I dragged them out of sight they would get up and laugh at the joke, and go their merry way. At least that's what I told myself as I pulled Teddy down the sewer pipe and laid him next to all the rest, their arms at their sides, all in a perfect line as if at attention. Then I followed my mistress into the night. That was the end of my life and the beginning of my nightmare.

Chapter 2

As I write these lines, she stirs below me in one of the downstairs rooms, even though it's not yet five in the evening. In this part of the country, in November, it's dark enough for her to be up and about, though it's still a little soon for her to venture out. In the summer she'll stay in her box until eight or nine. Oh, that it were summer again.

We live on the edge of the North Atlantic as it hits the shore of Massachusetts near Manchester by the Sea. A large, sprawling house filled with a collection of art and furnishings beyond value. I am her butler, her maid, her chauffeur, her gardener, her keeper, her accomplice, her lover. All those things I am and more, as I am her slave.

How do I describe Rebecca? How do I characterize something, someone beyond description? I hardly know what she is. All I know is that she's evil and I am bound to her with a passion so intense it drives me insane. Am I happy? Do I enjoy life? Yeah, if you call a living hell with no hope and no relief a good time, where every breath makes you nauseous and every thought makes you want to scream. I would gladly die, if only I could take Rebecca with me, but that can never be.

Still young and vibrant, the epitome of womanhood, Rebecca is hard to ignore in a crowd and harder to resist when alone. Of medium height with a lithe body, she has not changed much from when she was a girl 3700 years ago. Her silky gold hair is long and wild, laced with black. Her lips are full. Long lashes adorn large oval, green eyes. She's a lethal mixture of innocence and sexual attraction. Add to this her demonic powers and strength, her vast endless knowledge and limitless experience, and you have an idea of her danger. She is an awesome creature, with one purpose and one purpose only, to kill and feed on the blood of humans. She is as purely evil as she is beautiful.

Contrary to modern legend, only human blood will satisfy a vampire. Rebecca cannot abide the blood of another animal. For her, killing and sucking blood is more akin to having sex than a simple act of feeding, although that is a big part of it. The food must be of the right quality. Only human blood is sweet enough and full of the right nutrients, the correct proteins, the desired fragments of glucose and amino acids, to satisfy her. She would no sooner drink animal blood than have sex with one. It's a complicated process, being a vampire.

I've learned quite a bit about it over the years, more than I care to know and a lot I've kept secret. No more! Now is the time to tell it all, though it may well be my undoing.

I am happy Halloween has come and gone. Rebecca, my sweet, is no respecter of age or gender, killing men, women, and children indiscriminately, although she prefers mature males of a certain blood type. Does she have a conscience? I wonder if she ever had one. I doubt she even has a soul. She was only a spoiled child when she was taken, in a brutal time before anyone cared about human rights or moral laws, except perhaps a few Israelites wandering in the desert.

I do not think she feels bad about what she does, for she does it from necessity. She must eat, after all, quench the burning thirst that drives her. So far, she has only killed what she has had to for survival, like a simple animal. Let there be no doubt about it, though, she is evil. For her, killing is a pleasure, as it probably is for a wild cat in the jungle; something about hot blood and adrenaline-pumping stimulation. Still, no matter how evil she is or what she has done, I am drawn to her more than life itself. That is my dilemma. No matter how much I loath her, I crave her even more. She is an abomination, a monster, but I am tied to her like a child to its mother. I must break this chain that binds me or I will go mad, if I am not already so.

Do I know how it began? Do I know her story? Why yes, as if it were my own. No, better than my own. My story gets more vague and misty as the years go by, while hers builds in strength and intensity like a relived traumatic memory. She has told it to me many times. I know it sounds impossible, but there are moments when I can feel what she feels, see what she sees, when she wants me to. Her tale is not a pleasant one. It is full of death.

The moon hung low over the lush ruins of ancient Samaria, a thousand years old even in that ancient time, between the rise of Gilgamesh and the Hittite invasions from the north, in the reign of Hammurabi, the Great Law Giver. He came to power in 1792 BC, and ruled the land to the northeast of the center of the world, when the Middle Kingdom dominated mighty Egypt. Soon after that, the Great Law Giver founded the flower of the civilized world, Babylon.

Princess Ibihil, the niece of Hammurabi, looked out from her porch over the great palace and temples of Mari, with its walls and courtyards, and complexes of countless stone rooms, in anticipation of the coming evening. Her Caucasian slaves did her bidding day and night, high-flood and low. Human beings born to undying servitude, taken for granted by the Amorite inhabitants that ruled the land from the Persian Gulf to the upper part of Mesopotamia.

The beautiful young princess possessed everything life had to offer. She was pampered and preened, her every whim catered to. Yet she was unhappy. For despite her privileges and position, the only future she had in store for her was being married off to some foreign king's brutish son. And since most of the cities and towns outside the great metropolis were not much more than a collection of pig hovels, this meant spending the rest of her life in drudgery, raising some poor and lazy prince's screaming brood, a hard lifetime of thankless toil, lucky to have even one or two old slaves.

Hoping to change her destiny, despite her parent's warnings, Ibihil had of late been visiting the Chaldean seers, hoping to learn their wisdom and the secrets of the stars. After all, were not the Babylonians the best astrologers in all the world?

At the temple of Marduk, the greatest of the gods, on one of her too frequent visits, Ibihil came to the attention of the high-priest, Urammu. A man of immense power in the city, second only to Hammurabi himself, Urammu was both ambitious and ruthless, and would not be satisfied until he held ultimate power in the empire. He plotted to rule Babylon all the hours of the day, and dreamed of it while he slept at night. Still, he had time to pursue more personal pleasures, such as seducing young women and employing them in his dark rites, his quest for immortality.

Over the years, from many sources, Urammu had pieced together the sacred Texts of Ur, some contained on cuneiform cylinders a thousand years old, some from the mouth of living soothsayers who carried it in their heads alone. Only he knew the meaning of the strange designs and patterns, and even more importantly, how to pronounce the sacred words, words said to have the power of eternal life.

Urammu had instinctively known Ibihil was the one as soon as he laid eyes on her that day in the temple - the insolent, almost immoral, way she sauntered through the holy precincts; her manner of dress, rich but whorish; the scorn with which she gazed on the other worshipers and priests. The way she looked him straight in the eye, both challenging and inviting, was certain to attract his attention. He asked who she was, and on being told she was the Great Hammurabi's niece, decided he had to have her for his secret ritual.

Seducing her was easy. She was ripe for the plucking, and he had all the needed assets - charm, riches, looks, and unlimited powers. Ibihil saw him as the way out of her predicament. No matter that he was already married to the daughter of a great Babylonian family. Ibihil would make him her husband and rule the city at his side.

He promised to initiate her into the mysteries of the Chaldeans, to give her knowledge of arcane mathematics and magic, but first she would have to submit to his desires and prove herself worthy. That first night, in the confines of the Temple precincts, he took her like an animal in his lust.

Urammu was surprised at her strength, and how she reacted to his rough caresses, her body seeking his in mutual passion. He had never seen the likes of this kind of woman before. Was what the ancients of Ur said true, that through the sacred mantras and the proper sacrifice life could be extended beyond the grave, so that those that walked in the land of Ra could walk forever on the earth instead? If so, than she was one that could make such magic happen.

He told Ibihil that she had indeed proved herself worthy, and arranged to meet her again, to initiate her into the sacred rites at the temple vault on top of the Ziggurat, just after the setting of the sun on the day of the Festival of Fertility. There he would reveal her destiny.

Ibihil was uncertain what had happened on this last visit. Unsure if she had carried the gods' favor or their disapproval. In either case, things were going a bit fast for her. Certainly, obeying the high priest and yielding to his advances must be the right thing to do. What other choice did she have? Perhaps once was enough. Did she really have to go and see him again, alone, at the top of the Ziggurat? People were known to climb the 500 steps to the top and never be seen again.

That night at the palace she watched her many siblings dance and prance in front of their parents, each child clamoring for attention, each one competing for their parents' limited supply of love. She realized that her only hope of advancing, her only chance of avoiding the fate of her older sisters and being married off to some ignorant, penniless son of a foreign king, was to go to Urammu. This was Ibihil's chance and she wasn't going to let it pass without grabbing for it.

The promise of initiation into secret knowledge, into the mysteries of the Chaldeans, the mathematicians and astrologers of Babylon, was too much for her to resist. Not to mention the memory of the forbidden passion she had shared with Urammu, a man of such power and vitality, a man that might soon be hers. Soon after nightfall, after the feast of the Festival of Fertility, she went to him.

He took her hand and slowly guided her up the 500 steps of the Ziggurat, chanting something in another tongue as they climbed. At the top of the monument was a wide, flat area of stone with a small cave-like temple in the middle. Its door yawned at them like a wide black mouth.

High over the slumbering city, in the dark, dank, temple of stone, Urammu cast his ancient spell. It was not what Ibihil had expected. She was being initiated, all right, but into something unholy and horrifying. Suddenly, she was shoved from behind, her face pressed against a stone altar that smelled of dried blood and gore. She could hear him muttering ancient chants and spells, and wondered what was happening. This was not the way it was supposed to be.

Urammu stood over her. Chanting the secret words, building his power to a climax, he pulled the sacrificial knife from beneath his robe and spoke the ancient words of Ur, "Iskiel, ishnash, Astoth glimmering-esch nonnimo esto." Saying these words, he brought the sharp blade slashing down at Ibihil's naked back.

The obsidian point struck deep, piercing her heart in mid-beat. Ibihil's eyes stared wide in surprise, but the spark of life remained. Her forbidden passion had turned to terror, yet she did not die. For as the blade pierced her heart, the ancient words, uttered in the dead of night at the moment of ecstasy and death, brought forth a demon. It was a spirit from an older time, from the netherworld, one who still wandered the earth in search of a soul, an evil entity lurking in the mists and shadows of Ur.

Ibihil's body began to shake, as if in an epileptic fit, and with it the temple shook as well. Urammu looked up in surprise. The whole building was shaking around him. Plaster was falling upon his head. It looked like the heavy stone Ziggurat itself was going to fall down around him. In terror, he turned and fled the temple, down the steep steps to the large square that surrounded the complex.

Men and women ran in terror around him. Even the broad surface of the square was moving back and forth as if being shifted by an angry giant. The earth, which had always been so sturdy and firm, was now shaking like a fat man's belly. People ran out of their houses in alarm, screaming as buildings toppled on top of them. Urammu fled to his palatial dwelling at the edge of the city.

As he ran into his house, the walls started falling down around him. To his horror, a large stone slab fell on his wife as she ran to him with their baby in her arms, crushing them right before his eyes. He had no time to mourn, no time to cry. For out of the dust and debris came a menacing form, moving slowly but inexorably toward him. It was Ibihil, or what once had been Ibihil.

She was alive, more than alive, she was animated with a spirit of a superhuman being, an Espiritus, or as we would call them, a vampire. Her eyes blazed with a fierce, frenzied light. Her hair glowed with an iridescent sheen. She was more beautiful than ever, with the pure beauty of the dead.

Urammu froze. Had something gone wrong? The ancient texts spoke of immortality, infinite power, knowledge beyond measure for the one who uttered the words. Yet he felt no different. He certainly didn't feel immortal, not now, not facing this demon from beyond the grave. Ibihil was supposed to be the key, his secret passport. Her violent death, while the sacred chants were being uttered, was supposed to transform him into a god. What had happened? Why was the sacrifice standing there before him? Why did she look so dangerous? Would Marduk have played so cruel a joke on his faithful servant?

As if reading his thoughts, what used to be Ibihil of Mari, spoke through the gray, air-choked dust.

"Urammu, why do you look so surprised? Do you think you can utter the sacred words of Ur like you would a child's rhyme? You have done the unthinkable. You have cast an ancient spell long forgotten and longer forbidden, even by the old ones of the Chaldeans. You have brought forth a demon to inhabit my soul. You have unleashed a plague upon the world. It is the one who dies that is to obtain immortality, not the one who utters the words. You have condemned me to a living hell on earth. The heavens shake for me. The ground moves with my agony. I may have lost my soul. I may be destined to roam the earth forever in search of a peace I can never find, but an even worse fate awaits you. My destiny for the next 4000 years is laid out before me like one long sorrowful song. But you will pay for all eternity for what you have done! Your retribution is at hand!"

Urammu stood transfixed, even though the very sky was falling down upon him. Frozen to the spot by the sight of the undead Ibihil, he muttered something like, "Forgive me" or "Spare me", but it was of no avail.

The blood pulsing through Urammu's veins was like a giant cataract to Ibihil, each pumping rush through the arteries a scream for action. Her soul had been merged with a demon, a creature from the pits of hell, in whatever dimensions of time and space that may be; a slithering, evil, formless thing from the early mists of creation.

Urammu had no time to understand the implications of his actions for humankind or himself. For in an instant, Ibihil was upon him, with a speed that surprised even her. Ripping his arms and legs from his body, she slowly drank the blood from his still living torso. It took him a long time to die.

Ibihil took sadistic pleasure in Urammu's weak struggles and pitiful cries as he died in her arms, a feeling of power she would quickly become addicted to. For she now shared her soul with a demon.

The ground shook and shuddered around her. The sky was convulsed with lightning and thunder as she stalked off into the night. It was as if the earth itself knew that another soul had joined the damned and trembled in horror.

The secret spells and text has been lost now for thousands of years, so no new vampires have been created as Urammu had unwittingly done. My mistress, thank God, was the last. I have the impression, however, that the ancient lost tablets still exist somewhere. If these were ever found, the scourge would be raised once again.

Over time, the legend of those few spirits who made the transition to vampirism grew, although only a few hundred or so actually existed. These ancient legends got mixed and matched with later medieval myths, until finally they came down to modern times as fictitious stories of vampires. The reality behind these tales, however, lives on to this day, a reality of terror and death known only to a few, like myself. Urammu had brought forth not only the last of these creatures, but the most terrible - Ibihil of Mari. Now you know the truth, but will you believe it?

Chapter 3

So here I am, writing my confessions. Of course, she knows what I'm doing. I can do nothing without her knowledge and approval, without her willing it. For I am in her power, let there be no mistake about that. I could no more do something against her will than cut off my own arm. In fact, cutting off my arm would be easier, and I'd gladly do so if only it would end my curse.

I have been with her a long time, and the span of my artificially extended years is running out. Once she stops sustaining me with her blood-potion, I will dry up and die like the mummy I really am. Although I may appear to be in my late forties or early fifties, still robust and athletic, I am over a hundred, as crafty and wily and mean-spirited as anybody fortunate enough to live that long can be. I still have all my facilities and then some, but I might as well be a stone for all the pleasure I get out of life. What little joy I derive is from being close to Rebecca, watching her as she sleeps her sleep of death, or as she's about to go out on the prowl, luscious and seductive; or as she lounges about the house after a kill like a great cat, satisfied and sedated, with half-lidded eyes and parted lips, still excited from the hunt and blood-climax.

My Rebecca is such an impulsive creature. Oh, how she excites me, though I shudder at the sound of her name. If I am to survive this ordeal, if I am to pull off this impossible task, I will need a pact with the devil, for God will have nothing to do with me. I am an abomination in His eyes. But I dare not even think about these things, for if she knew, if she caught wind of my plan it would be the end of me, no matter how critical I am to her existence.

She depends on me for everything, her finances, the management of her property and estates, travel arrangements, banking, shopping, housekeeping, I do it or see to it. I also clean up after her when necessary, disposing of the remains of her meals when they would otherwise prove an embarrassment.

Those first years after she found me, when I was still a boy and it was all new and thrilling, she taught me the wiles of her craft, as well as general knowledge about the world and universe, information that would make me a leading academic and scientist, if only anyone but I knew about it. I was her apprentice, her disciple. I fell in love with her instantly that first night, when she took my friends one by one before my eyes. Even if she hadn't had some fiendish power over me, I would have done anything she asked, only to be near her, to behold her image each night.

There were plenty of victims in those early days, unwatched children, unwary streetwalkers, and females of the night, lazy, drunk-dumb men who practically invited their deaths. Then the war came, the war to end all wars. I was twenty-two by then, draft age, ripe for the slaughter, but she protected me as I protected her, in a sick symbiotic relationship of mutual benefit.

She thrived in the carnage of the war, when young men went to their deaths by the millions, whole generations gone before they had a chance to begin. She skimmed from the top, the healthiest, the most robust, the best bloodlines, for her own demonic pleasure. Sometimes she'd pose as a nurse and suck them dry as they lay bleeding and broken from the battlefield, rushed to her medical facility only to be fodder for her everlasting hunger. Sometimes she would roam the fields of carnage and feed off the dying or recently dead. It made no difference to her if their hemoglobin was warm or cold, only that it was human. Of course, the blood of the dead would stay good for only so long, after which even she would not drink it. Sometimes she would seduce her victims as they rested in winter quarters or spent their meager pay in the local taverns or whorehouses. Often she would simply grab them off the street as they walked by a dark alley or doorway. Berlin was filled with such places for the unwary.

When the war ended and the defeated armies came home to confusion and derision, she had even more victims. Things were good in the Weimar Republic. The roaring twenties were a time even I remember fondly. I was in my prime, and took advantage of my newfound wealth and power, wealth and power owed directly to Rebecca. I enjoyed myself to the full - wine, women, fine foods, palaces and yachts. I wanted for nothing. But the good times did not last, and the twenties gave way to the terrible thirties, when everything seemed to fall apart at the seams. Not that the rise of Hitler and the Nazis hampered Rebecca's activities. Just the opposite, she thrived under their regime.

She found employment in the early Gestapo political prisons, where she legally tortured and killed suspected communist plotters, and later in the concentration camps where she did that and much worse to the hapless Jews, Russians, and Poles that happened to cross her path.

She would become one of the most notorious and feared of all the Nazi war criminals, only to vanish on the eve of the armistice that ended the Second World War.

By then I was thoroughly disgusted with her. I had seen enough barbarity and cruelty to last a lifetime, although my journey was but just begun. I was sickened each waking moment with the horrible memories of the concentration camps, where her boundless depravity and sadistic cruelty knew no bounds. There I truly saw her for what she was, a spawn of hell, a child of the devil, so evil even Lucifer himself would pale in comparison. Yet I serve her till the grave.

Like my master I need very little sleep, and cat-nap, an hour here, twenty-minutes there, whenever time permits, which is rarely. For tending to Rebecca's needs would be a full time occupation for an army of servants, yet I serve her alone.

The genetic alterations she's made to my cellular make-up, the nutrition and vitamins I obtain from her blood-potion, which she lets me have three or four times a month, keep me alive and healthy. I have never been sick, not even a cold, since meeting her, and I have the strength and stamina of two men twice my size. As you know, I have lived far longer than the normal span of human years without growing old. I'm a regular Dorian Gray, except my alter ego resides on the canvas of my soul.

Lately, she has had me busy doing some special research for her. For some reason I cannot fathom, she has become interested in archeology and ancient scrolls. It's bad enough the house is a museum filled with the bric-a-brac of a thousand years of draining the living and stealing their possessions. Now she has me digging it up as well. What am I to do, but that which I am bidden? So I spend my free time sitting in musty buildings filled with books and old manuscripts searching for the Text of Belamarca, whatever that is.

All day long I read these dusty tomes, while the sun slants in one window and crosses the sky to another to finally be replaced by small desk lamps, in search for that elusive reference to some arcane text. I know better than to ask the meaning of her quest. I will know soon enough, I fear.

It is almost dawn. The sun is a hint of pink barely visible behind dark clouds. She came home a couple of hours ago. She was not alone. Usually she'll do her dirty work far from the house. It is nothing for her to travel several hundred miles an evening to hunt for choice prey. Occasionally, however, if the situation permits and the prey exceptional, she'll bring them home. Apparently tonight is one of those times.

My love for Rebecca is mixed with a loathing, a hatred so strong sometimes it's overpowering, but I must never let her know. Even the mere thought of it would be dangerous. So I hide my feelings and bide my time.

I can hear her in her love-making, if that's what you want to call it, the foreplay she employs to get her victim's juices flowing. From the sound of it, it's a male, probably a business type, picked up in one of Boston's nightspots, some place dark and out of the way where a guy can disappear in anonymity.

She's laughing now, that seductive, haunting laugh. She's probably removed her clothing to expose her lovely lithe body. Poor guy doesn't stand a chance. It should be over soon.

Yes, just as I thought, the first scream, followed by loud banging and more screams. He's probably trying to get out of the room. Lot's o'luck. You aren't going anywhere but an early grave. I wonder if he has a wife and kids. Well, daddy won't be coming home.

She's taking her time with this one. The screams and banging have gone on for awhile with still no let up. Her victim must be in great shape, strong heart, pumping lots of blood. Rebecca is having fun.

As usual, she left the whole mess for me to clean up and dispose of. Her most recent victim was a well-groomed male with expensive jewelry and clothes. As usual in such circumstances, I cut up the body in the bathtub and burn the pieces, along with the clothing, in our massive furnace, built just for such occasions. The jewelry we'll keep to add to Rebecca's large collection.

From the wallet, which I also burned, I learned that his name was Harvey Dane, thirty-two years of age, 6 foot 1 inch, 180 pounds. He worked in the investment firm of Riley, Hancock, and Liebnitch, at Copley Plaza in Boston, and had two little girls and a lovely wife. He would be missed, but then Rebecca always did go for the choice cuts.

As I said, I've seen her kill many times, in many different ways, sometimes slow, sometimes fast, seen her kill them young and old, robust and sick, weak and strong. Sometimes one, sometimes two, sometimes dozens at a time, but every time I see it or its aftermath, I'm sickened to the core. When I think about the lives ruined, the pain and torment it must have caused, the bereaved loved-ones and family members, the loss and sorrow, the guilt overwhelms me, although it is not my doing. I could not stop it if I tried.

As I've said, none of these things disturb Rebecca. She is no more bothered by it than a hunter after shooting a prize buck. They're going to die anyway, sooner or later, perhaps from starvation or disease, or some stupid careless accident. Better to weed out the weak ones early, keep the herd strong. Anyway, she does it out of necessity, as I who do her bidding.

She's in her box now, a large marble sarcophagus hidden deep in our cavernous basement. Sometimes I sneak down there to be with her, to lie with her in her casket. She doesn't seem to mind, although such a thing would not be possible during her active periods. To have sex with a vampire is to perish horribly, to be bitten and torn apart, to be sucked dry and mutilated beyond recognition. No, it's much better when she's asleep, lying still as stone.

Rebecca is young as vampires go, those creatures who measure their lives in thousands of years. From what I understand, which is much, she is one of the last of her kind to be made, the last to emerge from the pits of hell. The oldest ones that still walk the earth were created before the pyramids in Egypt, before man knew of bronze or metals, before the art of cultivating wild grains and domesticating animals was known. They were spawned in the pre-dawn of history, back when man still worked the skins of animals brought down with spears and clubs, with stone choppers and knives, when they still drew their magical pictures on the walls of caves. Some of these drawings tell of these creatures of the night, who suck the blood of the living, evil forms from the abyss born when hardly a flame flickered in this vast expanse of earth.

I have never seen one of the ancient ones, but she has spoken of them from time to time. She is unbelievably powerful compared to humans, virtually indestructible. Yet she is a weakling, both physically and mentally, compared to one of the old ones. She told me how one of them tutored her in the ways of their kind, and how others persecuted her because of this knowledge. Nothing will make us pick up and move faster than the fact that an old one is nearby. That is why we finally left Europe.

It's almost four. She will be up soon. She'll probably still be excited from last night's kill. You'd think after a hearty repast like that she'd be satiated, at least for a couple of nights, but no such luck. She could have an even dozen and still be hungry the next evening. It's her curse, to never be satisfied, to always need more blood.

I can't take many more nights like the last one. Somehow, someway, I've got to end it. She's promised to let me go soon. The thought both thrills and terrifies me. If there is an afterlife, I'm doomed to eternal damnation, but I'm an atheist through and through. I dare say a part of me even enjoys her ravages, her tortures and seductions, in a sadistic perverse way that fills me with guilt when I think of it. Besides, most of the time, when I'm not working on her behalf, I'm thinking about her, fantasizing it's me she's killing and my blood she's drinking.

Yes, ever since that first night in Berlin, as she slaughtered my companions before my eyes, I wanted to be one of her victims. I want to be helpless in her arms and feel her teeth sink into my flesh, while her eyes burn holes into my soul.

She'll be up soon. I dread the moment, but wait for it each day like my uncaught breath. Each morning is a malignant curse that I dread to look on, each moment a hideous nightmare. Yet the night is even worse. I live to serve my terrible mistress.

Chapter 4

She has woken. I hear her approach, her steps like whispers in the air. She is here.

"Henry, why so pensive? Have something on your mind?" She is all smiles, everything but her eyes, which burn into me like red-hot coals.

"No, Mistress. I was only thinking of the old days."

"Why dwell on the past, Henry. We have an eternity ahead of us."

"Maybe you do, but not I."

"Ah, is that why you are so sad, you see your puny lifespan coming to an end. Do not despair. There may still be hope for you yet, Henry. I still have need of you. Your time is not yet up."

"I am tired, Mistress. You promised to set me free. I have served you long."

"And well. Are you tired of me, my pet? Do I bore you?" She said these words right next to me, where she appeared from across the room as if popping out of thin air, so fast and silently she moved, her lips inches from my ear. I jerked back involuntarily, but caught myself in an instant.

All these years of living with Rebecca I am never really comfortable in her presence. No, I'm always in fear when she is near, as you would be in a room with a man-eating tiger, no matter how well-trained they're supposed to be. You just never know what she's apt to do.

"You will never leave me, Henry. There can be no freedom for you, not until the end of time. You are mine. I have great plans for you. You will serve me forever."

"But Mistress, you said yourself my time is running out, my days are few. I am already old beyond human years. You cannot sustain me forever. What do you talk of, Master?"

"Do not concern yourself, Henry. Just continue searching for the manuscript as I have instructed you. All will be well."

I wanted to protest, keep her to her promise to release me, but knew better than to plead to a soulless creature like Rebecca. She would only take perverted pleasure in my entreaties, maybe lead me on sadistically only to disappoint me in the most cruel way in the end. No, better to bide my time and hide my true intentions in a mist of false thoughts.

"Are you going out tonight, Mistress? If so, could you take your pleasure elsewhere? I'm tired of cleaning up after you. You will attract attention to us. Anyway, the furnace needs to be cleaned or it will get clogged with your leftovers."

She looked at me with her wicked smile, a look that would unsettle a Genghis Khan. One squeeze in her arms and I would be crushed. One flick of her nail could slash my throat like a shard of glass.

Then she's gone. I'm alone again.

That's how it is with her, moments of intense excitement and suspense, each second suspended between life and death - that's the slender thread that holds you from oblivion when you're in her presence – followed by lonely boredom, where nothing matters except her return.

Ah, but what a life it has been.

After the war we drifted around the continent, working our way slowly to the coast of Portugal. With my long acquired expertise in forgery and my knowledge of disguise, it was easy for us to change our identity, as well as our appearance, and move from country to country. From Portugal we boarded a steamer to England.

The pickings were easy, the homeless and the dispossessed, the deserted and lost were everywhere, good blood cheap. Always she seemed driven by some inner impulse, some drive that left her never satisfied and always searching for more.

In England my heart was broken for the first of many times, a kind of game Rebecca used to indulge in when I was naïve enough to go along. We were living just outside London in a sprawling country house once owned by the duke of Salisbury. Rebecca was in her prime, the center of a just recovering London social scene, her home the location of many gala and important events. Naturally, she took her victims from the seamier side of the city, from the docks and wharves, the dancehalls and bars, never from her small circle of elite friends and admirers.

Back then, in the late forties, I still went out looking for companionship, nothing serious, just something to take the sting of loneliness out of my life. I started to frequent one of the nearby taverns, a warm, old fashioned, friendly place where they played darts and had group sing-along's. There was a young waitress at the bar who immediately attracted my attention. She had a face like an angel, with short blonde hair. She was wearing a low-cut, revealing outfit that showed off her long legs and ample bosom to advantage. I stared at her like a dumb schoolboy until she noticed and came over.

"Eye'in me are ya," she said in an Irish brogue. "Me boyfriend's liable to take offense, if'n you keep that up, don't you know."

Rebecca had done much to wean me of my German accent and manners, and had been strict in her endeavors to teach me other languages, which I picked up readily - Italian, French, Spanish, English - long before the war. Although I had an accent of sorts, depending on the language, it was hard to pinpoint. My English easily allowed me to pass myself off as Norwegian or Swedish.

I told her my story, carefully crafted to snare innocent maidens, of my travels and travails as a decorated underground resistance fighter. She was impressed, and when I came back the next night, she made it a point to wait on me personally. Her name was Caroline. That evening after leaving the bar, we went to her mother's house, where I made love to her on the kitchen table while her mom slept upstairs.

For a brief moment, for a miraculous instant, I forgot all about Rebecca and actually felt something for another human being. It was overwhelming. All I could think about was living the rest of my life with this pretty young barmaid.

Obviously, such a thing could not be. Rebecca would no sooner set me free than set her hair on fire. I am hers. She owns me body and soul. For a moment, however, for a brief span of time, I forgot all this, or discounted it, and truly believed it could somehow be. I was to be brutally awakened.

I did not then know the art of concealing my intentions from Rebecca, a lesson learned only after many painful failures. Thinking I could hide my thoughts from her, conceal my true purpose, I naively plotted my escape. Rebecca must have known all the time. She must have strung me along just for the fun of it, to see my disappointment in the end. It's just a game to her.

One bright, long, sunny day in the middle of July, Caroline and I made our way to Liverpool, where we boarded an ocean liner to New York City. What better place to disappear in than a metropolis of five million.

When we arrived it was Sunday in New York. I was amazed by the size of the buildings and the masses of people that crowded the sidewalks, sidewalks the size of roads where I had come from. Berlin at the turn of the twentieth century had been a remarkable place, but these buildings were towers in themselves, dwarfing the smokestacks and steeples that rose above my home.

I felt safe, normal for the first time in almost a century. My passport and identification, which I had meticulously fabricated, said I was John Holstein from Sweden, decorated war hero and exporter, here in New York on business.

I knew without Rebecca feeding me, my hundred or so years would start to show, but I still felt robust and strong, and believed my new love would keep me young. Caroline and I planned to have a family, and immediately endeavored to do so. Staying in the small hotel room near Time Square that we had rented soon after arriving, we probed each other's bodies like teenagers doing it for the first time.

Those first blissful nights and days went by exceedingly fast. We were married by a Justice of the Peace and honeymooned right there in New York, picnicking in the park, going to Broadway shows, playing the young newlyweds to the hilt. Then one day, it happened, the inevitable occurred, my true fate overtook me like a Greyhound express, although the first indications were subtle, not much more than a blip on the radar screen.

Caroline and I were at the zoo, in a place called Bronx. We were standing in front of a giant buffalo, which had been peacefully grazing near the fence. Suddenly, without warning the giant bull reared its head, looked at us, and charged. The fence separating us from the giant animal only a few feet away was constructed of wire strung along some thin poles. It certainly didn't look strong enough to hold the beast, which came up short of it in a cloud of dust, stamping the ground and snorting angrily. What had we done, looked at it the wrong way?

Soon all hell broke loose. The zoo became loud with a cacophony of animal sounds. Monkeys and apes screamed. Lions and tigers roared. Hippos and elephants trumpeted, while the zebra and gazelles stampeded in their pens. It was pandemonium. We made our way out amongst a throng of worried visitors as the park was suddenly closed. I couldn't help wondering if Rebecca wasn't somehow behind it all, but tried to dispel the thought as quickly as it occurred. Had she found us?

Despite the freedom I was experiencing and the apparent normalcy of my life, I couldn't shake the feeling that it was all on borrowed time. I started to remember, at first slowly, then with more urgency, the power that Rebecca had held over me, and wondered how it could have been so easily overcome. Then I slowly began to realize, it couldn't be overcome, not unless she wanted it to be. With that it hit me that she had found me. No, had probably known where I was all along.

That night I hastily moved us out of the little hotel we had been staying in across town to an even shabbier place and changed our identities. Checking in under assumed names, we hunkered down for the duration. I told Caroline that some of my old enemies from the resistance days, ex-Nazis and criminals, were after me, and that we'd have to stay in hiding until I could figure something out. She went along like the true-blue loyal trooper she was.

I couldn't help wondering why Rebecca had not shown herself. What could she be waiting for? Then one night Caroline told me she was pregnant. Now I knew what my mistress wanted - my firstborn child. Or was I just being paranoid?

For a time nothing happened and all went on as before. Lulled into a false sense of security, I was again able to forget about Rebecca. It was much harder to track people in those days, the late forties and early fifties, before computers were in every agency, institute, and business in the world. I convinced myself that Rebecca hadn't found us, that it was just my obsessive fear.

It was relatively easy for me to get a decent job teaching in the public school system under my assumed name. Soon we were able to move to a little two-family brownstone in Brooklyn where my daughter, Emily, was born.

Life was good. I was in bliss, raising a family, being a part of the community. On my daughter's first birthday, it all tumbled down like a rockslide. Caroline and I were in bed, working on a little brother for baby Emily, when we heard a cry coming from her room a short way down the hall.

"Wait a minute, honey, I think I hear our baby cry'n," said Caroline. "I should see if she's all right, now." It was just like Caroline to put the baby before herself. I would have let it cry all night to make love to her one more time, but her mother's instincts would take over at the most inopportune time.

She left our bed and tiptoed down the short hallway, across the freshly polished old-wood floor. I thought nothing of it, and turned around to rest my eyes in the darkness. I must have fallen asleep, because when I opened them again, it was much later and Caroline had not returned. The house was deathly still. The white drapes stood limp and heavy like the air. Not a breeze stole through the open windows.

Getting out of bed, I moved down the hallway as if in a dream. The door to baby Emily's room stood shut. I opened it and entered. It was dark and quiet inside. Not a sound disturbed the stillness. The baby's crib was empty.

Looking into the far corner of the room, my eyes began to adjust to the dim light. Caroline was sitting on the rocking chair in the corner. I called her name, but she did not answer. Thinking she must be sleeping, I moved closer, calling her name again. As I did, I heard a child cry behind me and looked back in that direction. I could vaguely see the baby crawling on the floor near the far wall. There was something else there, something indistinguishable, but which stopped my heart all the same, for my mind saw it before my eyes. It was Caroline, lying face up in her half-torn nightgown, the baby crawling around her body and starting to wail.

I screamed and turned back to the figure in the rocker. Now I knew who it was sitting there, who I had seen but denied the sight of, Rebecca, come back in my moment of happiness to destroy my world. She laughed in her low, cold voice and said my name several times.

"Henry, Henry, Henry. How could you ever imagine you could leave me? And to go and have a family? Why, Henry, I didn't know you had it in you. Although I am glad you did. I haven't had this much fun in centuries!"

My mind let loose its hinges and I threw myself senseless to the floor on top of the lifeless body of my dear Caroline. I could taste the dry blood that still clung to her motionless form.

"My dear sweet Caroline, oh God, what have you done to her?" My scream of anguish only increased the gleam of joy in Rebecca's eyes.

"Oh, she was sweet, my dear Henry. She had nice sweet blood. Such ample breasts, the blue veins visible just beneath the ivory skin. Ah, yes Henry, she was very good!"

I grabbed baby Emily and ran for the door, determined to save my daughter from the clutches of the fiend. I did not get far. An invisible force threw me against the wall, almost crushing the child in my arms. She fell to the floor with me, howling in pain.

Before I could gain my feet, Rebecca was on me, pinning me to the floor with her foot. Grabbing the baby from my hands, she raised her arms to the room's low ceiling.

"If I could make your child a demon, walking the earth, eternal, undead, I would, but the ancient words and secret spells are lost, gone to the world forever. I am the last of the Espiritus, the last of the ancient ones, they who were old even when the world was young. But I can kill this child and drink its blood, and show you the futility of all you do without me."

I struggled uselessly beneath her heel, as she held the child aloft above me.

"Please," I said. "Don't harm her. I'm sorry. I'll never leave you again, I promise, only please don't hurt her."

My pleas fell on deaf ears, and only served to increase her mirth.

"Oh, you will never leave me, Henry, not until I send you away, not until I'm done with you, and that won't be for a very long time. I just want to give you something to remind you what will happen if you try to deceive me again."

With those words, she brought the baby to her mouth and was about to suck its blood.

I struggled vainly beneath her foot, and yelled out at the top of my lungs, "I will give her to you! You can have my firstborn as your slave forever. I will raise her to serve you, Mistress. We will serve you together. Take her. She is no use to you dead."

Rebecca stopped and smiled at me.

"Very good, Henry. I like that idea. You will raise her as my slave and teach her as I have taught you. But if you cross me again, she will be the first to feel my fury. Now clean up this mess." She pointed to my poor Caroline.

"Yes, my master," I said kissing her feet.

My mind has been numb ever since that terrible night when Rebecca took my love and smashed it upon the shores of despair. Before then I had only been her faithful servant, now I became her slave, a slave of hate and despair. I could see no way to save my baby but to give her away to Rebecca and a life of terror and abuse. What could I do, watch Rebecca drain her blood? I knew it was the only thing that might stay her hand. It worked, kind of. At least Emily is alive and safe for the moment.

Being the prime suspect in the gruesome murder of my wife and the kidnapping of our child, I was forced to flee New York. My alter ego, John Holstein, was avidly being sought throughout the northeast for the horrific killing and abduction. An alert had been issued for the one-year-old. I wasn't about to stick around even if I'd had a choice, which, of course, I didn't.

Rebecca took me to Los Angeles and crafted a new identity for us, so that I could once more serve her in the manner she has become accustomed to. The child was placed in an orphanage run by the Sisters of Mercy, along with a considerable sum of money donated by a distant but concerned elderly relative of the infant. As usual when it comes to Rebecca, no one asked any questions.

So, I have served her ever since, as my child will serve her, into eternity, unless I find a way to blot out this curse, this scourge, this plague that afflicts us – my terrible mistress.

Chapter 5

I suppose I've mentioned they cannot be killed, that vampires are indestructible. I find it amusing that the modern legends insist on the ridiculous notion that these spawns of hell can be disposed of with a mere wooden stake or silver bullet. Why, the very thought of it is utter nonsense. That an entity with the power of a demon would be troubled by the likes of running water or fire is ludicrous. If it was simply a matter of cutting off her head, I would have done it years ago. Sure they don't like light, and it's true they tend to sleep in dark dank secret places during the day, but that doesn't mean they are harmed or burned by the sun, though it will tend to drain their power and energy.

If she has to, Rebecca can put up with plenty of sun, like she used to do regularly when we lived in Southern California. In the late fifties and early sixties, things were as fast and loose there as anywhere, and if you didn't own a surfboard and a bathing suit, well, you just didn't fit in, and Rebecca desperately wanted to fit in.

No, there is nothing on earth or beyond, for that matter, that can kill a vampire, not stakes, bullets, fire, or water, nothing. Oh, and don't think you can wave a cross in front of her nose and get anywhere with Rebecca. She'd just as soon jab it into your cranium and suck your brains out with it. Trust me, I know.

I'm not sure where these stories came from, probably part of some medieval legend, but at one time even I believed them. The thought that I and my child could be free, and I could avenge myself for my wife's cruel death by driving a wooden stake through her heart gave me hope. I was determined to do that and more to be free.

Over the days leading up to the act, I educated myself, reading everything I could find regarding vampire lore and how to kill them. I became quite an expert on the popular wisdom of the time, as erroneous as it was. I procured all the necessary implements, garlic, a stake and hammer, a cross, and a large saw.

I waited until a long summer day after she had gorged herself on six healthy young people she had invited over to party in the Jacuzzi the night before. I needn't describe what happened, but I knew she would be sleeping in late.

In the heat of the day, when the fans barely amplified the faint breeze blowing through the open windows, I crept down to her tomb. Her black marble sarcophagus lay hidden beneath some timbers in the basement of our palatial home. The room was dark and filled with junk left by the previous owners of the house, an older, childless couple seduced and killed by Rebecca when she first moved to the West Coast.

I held a large hammer in one hand and a heavy wooden stake in the other. Around my neck I had a string of garlic and a large black crucifix, with a silver Jesus nailed on it in bold relief. I was ready. I held the image of my wife Caroline in my mind, lying dead and ravaged on the bedroom floor, Rebecca laughing and gloating at me over her remains. That, and the thought at what lay in store for my baby Emily, steeled me for what I had to do.

I approached the large oblong coffin and peered in. There was no lid. Only a thin gossamer cloth covered Rebecca's otherwise naked body. She was breathtaking in her motionless beauty, exquisite in her perfection. I wanted to crawl into her coffin and curl up beside her, to feel her cool skin on my fingertips. These are the thoughts I kept in my conscious mind as I raised the hammer and placed the sharp point of the stake above her heart.

Bringing the mallet down quickly, I struck the stake with all my might, but it did not pierce her skin. It was like striking steel. The hammer reverberated violently, while the stake shattered in my hand. Then she disappeared, simply vanished from beneath me. I stood there staring at an empty slab of marble.

"Henry, Henry, Henry. What are you doing? After all I've done for you?"

Before I had time to turn, she seized me violently from behind and hurled me across the basement floor, to crash into a pile of old lawn furniture. Several cans of paint came crashing to the floor, spilling thick liquid all over me.

"Do you think you could actually kill me, you little fool? Don't you have any idea who I am, after all this time? Do you? Well, it's time you learn. I've been waiting for this. It happens every time. No matter how nice I am, no matter how much care and protection I provide, they always turn on me sooner or later. You think there's nothing I can do to you? You want to die, do you? You should be so lucky. I may not kill you yet, but you will wish I had. You will suffer for your audacity!"

She seemed to enjoy my distress as she threw me around the room like a rag doll.

"I can read your thoughts. Don't you know that by now? I know every glimmer of an idea in your head. You cannot escape me, never!"

She said these last words with her face a fraction of an inch from mine, her teeth bared, her eyes burning into me. Then she was gone. In her place I saw my sweet Caroline, still dressed in the sheer negligee she had been wearing the night she died. Caroline's face was as close to mine as Rebecca's had been only moments before, but she seemed not to see me. Instead, her face was contorted with fear. Her eyes were wide like a frightened child's. Her mouth hung opened in surprise.

Then I knew I was seeing Caroline through Rebecca's eyes at the moment of her death. I tried to close my mind to the images, but could not. It was as if my lids had been taped open, while all the while I knew what I was seeing had nothing to do with vision. They were images from the mind. I watched the whole horrible thing over and over again, unable to turn away from the scene. I pleaded, I begged, I implored for the images to stop, only to see them repeat as if in slow motion. I battered my head against the wall in my distress and lost consciousness, but those pictures continued to haunt my dreams, like they would for many days afterward. It was an exquisite form of torture that I'm sure gave her great pleasure.

When I regained my senses, Rebecca was there staring at me, her sharp nails digging into my arm.

"You are nothing to me. I should kill you now and be done with it. Though you have been a good servant, I could squash you like a toad for what you tried. Training another so soon, however, would be quite tedious. So I'm going to let you live and serve me yet awhile longer, though you don't deserve it."

"Let me die, mistress," I pleaded, beside myself with grief and guilt. "Let me know your bite. Let me know that bliss all those others have known through these long years. Please kill me. Set me free."

She replied with her wicked, blood-chilling laugh and bit sharply into my shoulder. The pain was excruciating. My vision clouded, but I refused to cry out. She kept her teeth in me for a long time. I was getting woozy when she removed them with a jerk, taking a piece of my flesh with them. This she spit back in my face, along with my blood.

"You slug! You aren't good enough to eat. You're only good enough to do my will. And be sure you know, you and your child will be mine until the end of time."

.

Our life together has become rather routine since then. I do her bidding and she keeps me alive to suffer again another day. I see to her needs and she keeps the terrible images out of my head. Like I've said, it's a symbiotic relationship, much like a shark and its attendant nurse fish.

After that mention of my child, Rebecca has spoken nothing of her. I have never seen the girl since that horrible night. I thought Rebecca might fetch her on her tenth birthday, since that was the age I was taken, but nothing happened. I doubt she has seen the child either. Perhaps she doesn't want a kid to deal with during these uncertain times. Maybe she has something special in mind for her. I know Emily is still alive because I continue to send checks to the orphanage in her elderly aunt's name. So I live in limbo as far as my daughter is concerned, who must be approaching womanhood by now. Perhaps Rebecca is waiting for her twenty-first birthday, which is approaching in a few months.

Over the years, I've learned the hard lesson of avoiding human contact, for as soon as I would become fond or attached to someone, Rebecca would kill them. Friend, lover, acquaintance, no one was safe. It's hard enough seeing perfect strangers die horribly at Rebecca's hands, but to see it happen to someone I know and care about, like Caroline, well, that's just too much to endure.

Without relationships, without friends, my life has become a lonely wasteland. Old age is hard enough, even without physical infirmary, but this loneliness is more oppressive than any sickness. Taking up the long hours of the day with meaningful and enjoyable occupations becomes more difficult as time passes. There are only so many books to read or symphonies to listen to or plays to see, and I could no more sit through what passes for modern entertainment than I could sit through my own electrocution. Time hangs heavy on the old, especially with no friends or relatives, no loved ones, not even an acquaintance to share it with.

Of course, much of my time is taken up in managing the rather large estate, along with Rebecca's many properties and financial holdings. I've become quite an expert on modern stocks and bonds, mutual funds and money markets. I not only handle all Rebecca's substantial investments, which equal those of a large corporation, but also those day to day chores which would normally be done by, let us say, someone with much less talent and sophistication. But then nothing is too good for Rebecca.

She has lived under many identities since I've known her, and from what she tells me, has assumed many more in the millennia before that. She's currently posing as a wealthy Bostonian, a widow, who lives with her secretary and business manager – yours truely – in a rather sprawling mansion right on the ocean, on Boston's North Shore. She is known as a recluse. Although this is by no means the only role Rebecca can play, it does simplify things if I am her only contact with the outside world.

I'm sure most people that know of her assume that Mrs. Rebecca Perry is at least seventy years of age, for she has lived in the big house for many years and is never seen in public. I deal with the occasional workmen and contractors that have to visit the premises. All the other business is conducted over the phone or the computer.

Yes, computers are a big part of Rebecca's adaptation to the late 20th century. They keep her up to date and abreast of what's going on around the globe. She's quite a globetrotter, our little bloodsucker. She thinks nothing of hopping the Concorde to have a late lunch in London or Paris, or spending the weekend in Rome or Egypt. She has lived and killed in all of these places for centuries, and knows the cities and slums of the Old World as well as the veins in her arms.

The hour of nightfall too fast approaches, as if the sun and moon are conspiring to speed up their motion across the sky. She will be up and about soon. My pulse quickens with anticipation. My heartbeat escalates with the thought of her presence. I hear her stirring below.

Things have been quiet since the night Harvey Dane, the 6'1" 32-year old investment broker for Riley, Hancock, and Liebknecht supped with Rebecca. I have a feeling things are about to heat up again. It must be that time of the month. While most women get moody with the lunar cycle, Rebecca gets downright homicidal. I dread these times of excessive bloodletting.

Now she's roaming from room to room through the great house like a sleepwalker, preening herself in front of the mirrors. Oh, yes, Rebecca loves mirrors - full-length ones, round ones with golden frames and silver finishing, hanging mirrors and wall mirrors, bathroom mirrors and closet mirrors - the house is full of them. I don't know about other vampires, but Rebecca can look at herself in a mirror for hours. It's one of her favorite pastimes - so much for another vampire myth. Rebecca may have no soul, but her corporeal body reflects back her image sure enough.

I got a glimpse of her as she descended the outside wall at the back of the house. She moved like a large insect down the building and across the darkened yard, the sea crashing among the rocks below her. She has many of the powers attributed to her kind in legends and myths, super speed, super strength, the ability to crawl up the sides of buildings and leap over rooftops. She can materialize as if out of thin air. She can talk to me in my head. She is a phenomenon extraordinaire.

Just the presence of Rebecca in a room is intoxicating. She can put you under a spell in subtle ways with her voice and words, though she is not above using drugs and poison to get her way. While Rebecca treats most of her victims in a tenderly and lovingly way as she kills them and sucks their blood, when she's angry or roused she's been known to tear them limb from limb like a raging primate.

They say you have to invite vampires in, that they can't enter a dwelling unless asked to do so. Well, that may well be true, but I know no one alive who could keep this demon wench out. She is so beguiling, so alluring, that no one can resist her, man or woman.

She seems invincible, and she's one of the weaker ones. Human beings would be exterminated easily if these creatures stopped showing a prudent level of restraint or could create more of their own kind, for they are the top of the food chain. We humans would not stand a chance. For some reason the old ones seem to be very territorial, and tend to keep to themselves. This is a good thing, for Rebecca is no match for one of the old ones.

What does the evening bring? Where will she hunt tonight? In the streets of Back Bay? Along the Fens? In the sleazy alleys downtown? Government Center? Or will she prowl some college campus looking for coeds and 4-letter men? The city is at her disposal, laid out at her feet like an over-filled buffet table.

I know someone is going to die tonight and that I will be the agent of that death. This is the worst part of my job, leading innocent victims to their demise, usually comely females I would rather lead to my bed. But then she likes it that way. She loves to see me in distress. I must go. Rebecca calls.

Chapter 6

She summoned me. Even before the daylight faded, she called me silently to her lair. I went to her like I always do on these occasions, with a combination of fear and dread, anticipation and joy. It is never without consequences that I am summoned, so she can more easily communicate her instructions to me. To call me down to be in her presence while it is still daylight is rare, but bodes no good for the world or yours truly.

She lay in her coffin when I first arrived, covered by a gossamer cloth of white. I lifted it gently from her and gazed at the ivory purity of her skin. Her eyes stayed closed, but her mind commanded me. She looked as if she were made of white marble, a stark contrast to the black stone of the box that surrounded her. Dark blue veins, filled with the blood of her recent victim, ran outlines across her breasts. I leaned into the casket to take them in my lips when she stopped me.

"Not tonight, Henry," she said rising from the crypt like a mist. "That is not what I had in mind. You must drink of the cup tonight."

"But, Mistress, it is not my time," I stammered.

To my utter joy and happiness she wanted me to feed from her blood bowl. I eat just like other people, although because of all the carnage I've witnessed, I'm a strict vegetarian. I would no sooner eat meat than suck blood, which is all that Rebecca feeds on. I can cook just about anything when the occasion arises. But I need her potion to live beyond the normal span of time, and she makes sure I take it at least once a month. Tonight is different. This is not my usual time, but an extra boost to prepare me for something. She needs me at my peak this evening.

Rebecca stood before the great fireplace and took a sharp knife from an oblong cedar box. Cutting her wrist, she drained the blood, which flowed steadily, into the bowl. To this she added her secret concoction, a combination of old-age magic and new-age science, which enhances my body's strength and longevity. It comes out as a thick, dark-red milky substance, sweet as honey, which may be one of the ingredients. I've never learned. If I understand it correctly - and I have given it much study - it actually alters my DNA to create the necessary proteins.

I drank it and was instantly overcome with euphoria; my senses heightened, sharpened to a razor's edge; my brain enlivened with pulsating alpha waves; my body activated as if with electricity. How could there be so much bliss in one cup?

I knew that it was for her own selfish ends that she fed me, to strengthen me and make me younger looking, but I didn't care. I'm addicted to her blood-potion, pure and simple, and would not want to live without it.

From time to time, Rebecca has need of my services. Tonight I am bait. Despite my years, I am not unattractive, and show a certain level of sophistication and elegance, and of course, I exude wealth, dressed in the clothes and baubles Rebecca buys me. She likes to show me off occasionally, but all my charm is wasted in the places we would be hunting this night, strip clubs on the combat zone.

We cruised along Washington Street shortly after eleven that evening. It was a drizzling, misty, otherwise humid night. I was not quite sure what she was after, as she sniffed the air like a large carnivore - man or woman, young or old - except that it was warm-blooded. Then shortly after midnight she signaled for me to park in front of a seedy strip club on the edge of town, where barely legal-aged girls danced on the bar and tables. She didn't have to tell me what to do. I would naturally attract the best and most beautiful women in a place like this. She'd be happy with whatever went after this worm, for that's what I am. At least I keep it to only one. That's the implicit deal.

This girl wasn't dancing on the bar or a table, but in a guided cage above the bar. She attracted me immediately and was easily the most stunning woman in the place. She had on a small black bikini, which contrasted nicely with her dark skin and raven hair. She had to be twenty-one to dance in the place, but didn't look a day over sixteen, with an innocent pretty face topping a knockout body.

My eyes were drawn to her as if she were the only person in the bar, as were every other male's in the place, despite the variety of other women prancing about, all in various states of undress. This one was special, the way she moved, the texture of her skin, the way her long-lashed eyes looked down modestly than up at you so provocatively. She gave the impression of being extremely sexual, the way she'd lightly touch herself here and there, but at the same time she looked innocent and pure, a half-child in a full-grown body, just as turned-on as those watching.

Silently, inaudibly, in my mind only, I could hear Rebecca's voice.

"She's the one, Henry. Take her." I knew what I had to do.

It took me a long time to realize that you don't have to be dangerously handsome to pick up women. Oh, it helps if you don't look like Quasimodo, but the important thing is how you treat them, how you talk to them and listen. It also helps if you're rich or at least have the trappings of wealth, and with Rebecca's resources at my disposal I have more than enough bangles and baubles to impress the most jaded gold-digger, let alone a poor young girl fresh from the boondocks.

I've learned nothing in my extended lifespan if not how to carry on a decent conversation. I can hold my own on almost any subject. History, art, science, literature, music, wine, food, sports, you name it, I can talk about it. I'm also not a little versed in simple psychology and the knowledge of human nature. For instance, I know that nothing will bother an attractive, attention-crazed post-teen more than being ignored for some other girl. So I refused to look at her, even though every fiber in my being wanted to. Instead, I watched the rather unattractive, bored-looking, overripe one on the stage in front of me, and sipped my beer.

I immediately sensed the caged one's eyes on me as she gyrated above the bar. She seemed to move faster as she tried to attract my failing attention. I flaunted my expensive wallet and watch as I paid for my drink, making sure to flash a few hundred as I left an overly large tip. Within minutes half a dozen bikini-clad girls were milling about me, all looking hungrily at my back pocket. Lolita, or whatever her name was, began dancing even more energetically, calling out with every hormone in her being for my attention. Still, I resisted, and started up a conversation with another young lady, this one a poor man's imitation of the dancer in the cage. I glanced her way again, and was struck by the perfection of her body. The exact symmetry of her features, the way she moved, her eyes pleading for love, each feature a work of art. I looked away with a bored expression.

A small dark-eyed dancer with little-girl boobs sat on my lap and played with my collar, cooing something in English but totally unintelligible all the same, into my ear. All this time, Rebecca had remained in the car, parked a short distance down the street from the strip club. She had sent me here after sniffing the air like a hungry wolf for a few moments. I knew what I had to do - seduce the girl and bring her to the hotel where we had rented a penthouse suite.

Now is a good time for you to heap your scorn on me, to unleash all your contempt and all your fury. It won't be one tenth of the hatred and shame I feel for myself, for I am the lowest of the low, the vilest of the vile, the scum of the earth. Yes, I deserve all your scorn and more, for I am a cursed thing. My only defense is that I have no choice. I could no more disobey my mistress than I could breathe underwater. It is an impossibility. No matter how horrible the command, no matter how terrible the task, I must fulfill it as if it were my own, for she owns my very soul, and owns it for eternity.

The DJ ended his set. Lolita sauntered out of her cage and toward the bar where I was sitting. I saw her eye my expensive clothes and shoes, my Rolex and diamond cufflinks, saw her size me up in a Chinaman's minute. This was obviously a girl who, although young, had been around, and knew what her looks could get her when it came to men. She was obviously not going to be denied. In a place where the best you'd usually do was a biker with a windshield, she wasn't going to pass up a good-looking stranger worth a couple carats at least. Anyway, she saw the way I was looking at her. She hadn't been out on the street since she was fourteen not to know when someone was interested, even when they tried to hide it. She'd seen that look plenty of times before and it always meant the same thing.

Christina - which is what her name turned out to be - was in fact not legally old enough to work in the club, but that didn't bother the gangster who owned the place, or Rebecca. Christina was all of eighteen going on thirty, a neglected child of a single mother, who was practically a child herself. She'd been abused by her mother's lovers and men in general for as long as she could remember. Now the abusing was on the other foot. Christina always got her way. In fact, she was made for getting her way.

Her current boyfriend, a biker named Ronny, was out on the road, robbing some convenience store or other, his usual occupation when he wasn't humping Christina.

I continued my conversation with the buxom blonde and thin brunette, knowing Lolita would overhear me, using a tired but effective line that was sure to work under the circumstances.

"We're looking for real girls, you know, women who know what it's like to work in these clubs. You'd be dancing in the background as Sly and Wesley act their lines."

As Lolita came up, I turned deliberately and looked her in the eye. She stared back boldly.

"I enjoyed your dancing," I said. "You move very nicely. I bet you'd photograph well. You have such lovely skin, looks just right under the lights."

"Thank you," she said.

"Would you join me for a drink? I'd like to find out more about you."

Of course, she joined me for that drink and a few more at the end of the night. I told her I was interested in showing her to one of my backers, a wealthy woman producer who was staying right here in Boston. I wanted to bring her just as she was. The look was perfect, just what we were seeking. We might even have a bigger part for her, she was just so stunning. The camera would love her.

My story and credentials were impressive. The young dancer was overawed. I spread enough money around the place to make all of them consider taking the month off. No one seemed to mind or notice when I escorted the bikini-clad Christina out of the bar wrapped in my suit jacket. I still didn't know her name at that point. I learned it in the car as we drove the short distance to the Four Seasons Hotel and took the elevator to the recently rented penthouse. Rebecca was there waiting for us.

Lolita or Christina or whatever you prefer, was full of questions and tight with information. She was already quite drunk on tequila, her favorite drink for dancing, before we left the club.

"You're quite handsome," she said suddenly, as we were in the hallway, almost to the room. "For an older guy, that is. You look real cute in the suit. You married?"

"To my job," I answered, sensing her excitement at what was happening to her all of a sudden. She wasn't worried because I had given my card and name to everyone in the club. I couldn't be a sex murderer or anything if I gave my business card out, could I?

She was even more impressed when we entered the penthouse suite, elegant and large, with the skyline of Boston reflected in the wall-to ceiling windows. I almost started feeling sorry for her, even though I saw through her cunning, manipulating, attention-seeking ways. She was just naïve and disadvantaged enough to be pitiful. I felt bad for her, but there was nothing I could do. She was here for one reason and one reason only. She had the right blood type.

During the short ride to the hotel, along the drizzling streets of downtown Boston, I told Christina about the movie we were making, about a poor dancer in the combat zone, and how she meets a rich

41

promoter and makes good. The woman I'm taking her to meet is supposed to be Mrs. Barbara Stein, heir to the Steinway fortune and producer of many Hollywood movies and Broadway shows. Christina a.k.a. Lolita, took it all in and was suitably impressed. By the time we got to the suite, she was practically eating out of my hand.

I moved behind the bar and fixed her a drink. She sat on a white leather sofa. At that moment, Rebecca stepped into the room. My hands were shaking so I had to put my glass down

"Why, hello," Rebecca said in her husky voice, as she moved quietly to the sofa where Christina sat lounging luxuriously. "Henry here says he's found the star of our next movie. Can this be true? Right here in little old Bean Town? Henry says you dance very well. Could you stand, please?"

The Lolita lookalike stood unsteadily to her feet, as if the booze she'd been consuming all night had finally hit her. This was just the vampire spell, the hypnotic state they put their victim in just by their stare and smile. I've long since grown immune to it, but I remember when just having her in the same room with me would send me on an acid trip that would last for days.

Lolita blinked once or twice, trying to get her eyes back in focus. "I don't feel so good," she slurred, peering at Rebecca. "I thought you'd be older. You're practically my age."

"Oh, I'm a lot older than I look," answered Rebecca truthfully. "Can we see you dance, my dear? I know it's late, but I'm going back to LA in the morning, and I'd like to take you with me, if we can wrap this up tonight. Let's see what you've got, honey."

Lolita downed her drink, while I selected some music on the sophisticated sound system, courtesy of the Four Seasons Hotel.

Lolita started swaying to the music, a soft rock tune featuring some instrument called a soprano sax. I'll never get used to modern music, especially this stuff they call jazz, though it seemed to be to Christina's liking. She danced around the room as if she had no inhibitions, just like she had in the gilded cage above the bar.

I stood watching from the corner of the room unable to take my eyes off her. It was like I was ten years old again watching Rebecca dance among my street mates as she drank their blood. I was captivated by the scene, in suspended animation, as if none of it was real. But it was!

I thought if I could break the spell with a few words, interrupt it somehow, I could still save her, I who had brought her here in the first place to be slain by the vampire. What a cowardly slug I am, but at that moment I found enough courage to speak up.

"That's good, honey. We'll call you if anything comes up." I grabbed her and ushered her to the door, but I could not open it.

Rebecca shouted, "No! Stay!"

I froze in mid-motion, my jaws snapping shut so fast they made an audible click.

"Stay," she said again quietly. I could feel Lolita's naked body tremble in my arms.

"Come to me," said Rebecca. Her green eyes blazed. Her golden hair shimmered as if electrified. She no longer looked human, but distorted and enlarged with her fierce blood-lust. She crouched on the side of the bed like a giant cat.

Christina moved toward her, languidly. When she got close to her, Rebecca reached her hand out like a large paw and grabbed her around the waist. Pulling her to the bed, my terrible mistress sank her teeth into the girl's neck. I turned and hurried from the room as if in a state of shock. Although I knew all along what the outcome would be, seeing the young girl's pleading eyes at the moment of death was too much for me.

I ran down all twenty-flights of stairs and out into the night as if it were my Caroline that had just been murdered again. To think that I was the cause of it drove me mad, and fueled the sorrow and anger in my heart. I walked deep into the night, through the worst, most dangerous parts of the city, seeking my release, but knowing I could never be free. Standing on a bridge overlooking an eight-lane highway that passed beneath, I contemplated throwing myself over. There was still a lot of traffic rushing past below, even for this late hour, and many large trucks. Then I heard her voice. It wasn't in my head. Rebecca was standing right behind me.

"Here you are, Henry. I wanted to thank you for what a great job you did tonight. You were wonderful. I am never going to let you go. I have something for you, a little reward. Come…"

With that she whisked me away in her arms. Oh, to be loved by a vampire!

So it goes, night after night, year after year, a dismal string of lonely deaths, a litany of meaningless sorrow. When will it end? Soon, I hope. Fast, I pray. Never, I'm afraid.

It ended that night as it always ends for Rebecca's victims, with death. Of course, I had to go back and clean up. Nothing elaborate. Mrs. Stein had arrived at the Four Seasons Hotel with several extremely large and heavy traveling chests, in one of which I simply stuffed the still pliable body of poor Lolita.

It helps if I don't use her real name. As long as I can stay impersonal about it, I can maintain my composer, which is pretty hard considering. But what can I do? Like that day many years ago when I dragged my friends into the sewer, it is just a play.

But I vow I will make up for my crimes, and redeem the guilt that I carry with me through time. Somehow, someway, I will avenge them all, O-negatives and B-positives, the innocent and the guilty. I will avenge them and save my child, so help me. The days of this soulless scourge, Rebecca, are numbered.

Chapter 7

As I may have mentioned, I have been doing some research for my mistress recently, searching the libraries and museums of the city for references to some medieval tract she has recently become interested in for some reason only known to her. She tells me little, only what I need to know to do her bidding. I have recently found an obscure and indirect reference to the document she seeks, but I am loath to tell her about it for fear of what it might lead to. Whatever it is she is looking for, it can only bring me and the world misery and grief, yet I search on.

I keep my thoughts away from my real intent. I hide my intent in thoughts of a thousand other sundry things. Mostly I fill them with fantasies of Rebecca - Rebecca sleeping, Rebecca walking, Rebecca bathing, Rebecca eating. She must know nothing.

You may wonder how I can write these words, put my true thoughts down on paper for anyone to see. Certainly wouldn't Rebecca be liable to come upon these pages and read them, and thus know what I intend to do? Yes, that is if she could read, but she can't. Rebecca, with all her brain power, all her years of experience, all the things she knows, can't read one word, not one syllable. There's something about it, I don't know, maybe it's a vampire thing that prevents her from seeing anything but meaningless scribbles. It's funny because they say writing was first developed where she was spawned, ancient Sumer and Babylon.

So you see, writing it all down is actually quite safe. Ah, but you may object, how can you even think to write this down without her reading your mind? After all, you told us that she is inside your head. This is all true, I've already admitted as much. I have developed a little trick over the years of living with Rebecca, the ability to think one thing while I perform or write another. Just call it a bit of adaptation for my own survival, accomplished by a compartmentalizing of mental images.

She stirs. A subtle change in the atmosphere signals her presence like the coming of rain.

"Ah, Henry, what have you been thinking about? Your mind is always such a jumble. Do you have any news for me? Have you found what I have been searching for?"

"Not exactly, Mistress, but I have almost ruined my eyesight reading those old manuscripts and tomes of reference materials. I never thought I'd spend my days in dreary, dank buildings filled with dust mites and mildew."

"Don't complain, Henry. There are worst places you could be. What have you found?"

"There is a an obscure reference in a French Treatise of the early sixteen hundreds that mentions an order to King Edward IV of France from the Holy See to take a condemned medieval text to the New World to dispose of it so that it can never be used for evil again. The text is not named, but it could be the one you seek. It is worth investigating further. There is more information at a University Library in Providence, Rhode Island. I will go there tomorrow and find out what I can. Now are you going to tell me what it is exactly I am looking for?"

"I told you all you need to know."

"It's like looking for a needle in a haystack."

"Try the place you mentioned. It may have what I seek. Ask me no more questions."

"Yes, Mistress, but I am stretched as thin as I can get. Any more and I will break. Set me free as you promised. You have said yourself, there is not much more you can do to sustain me."

"You have a few good years left in you yet, Henry."

"I grow weak and weary. I have lived long enough."

"You think your mere hundred years lays heavy on you, try living three thousand!" She hissed these words, her hungry mouth just inches from my ear, after rushing at me in anger. "Try living an endless series of days and nights that string to eternity. Then you can tell me how tired you are. Until then, let me hear no more complaints. Besides, I have big plans for you."

"You can't keep me forever, Rebecca." I hardly ever call her by her chosen name to her face. The last time I did she knocked me across the room for my insolence. Not this time. Now for some reason she tolerated my outburst. "What is it you seek?"

"You will know soon enough, Henry, you will know soon enough. In the meantime, find out what you can. It is important to me, to both of us. I will need your daughter soon."

With that she is gone.

What could she be up to? What could be so important for her to keep me working day and night to find it? And what plans does she have in store for my daughter? I must find out before it is too late.

Rebecca has been gone for several days now. She does this from time to time, disappear for an extended period. You'd think I'd enjoy the time alone, the freedom from her depravations. But no, I am morose and empty when she is away and long for her return. My greatest fear is that she will never return and I'll wait here forever, an empty hulk, a hollow reed, a useless shell that might as well be dead.

I have contemplated suicide several times, and have even attempted it once or twice, but on each occasion she appeared at the last minute and taunted me in my misery as she prevented the fatal act. Sometimes I think she only toys with me.

I sit by the phone and wait for word. In the old days she would send telegrams or messengers, but with modern worldwide instantaneous communication so widely available, you'd think she could at least make the effort to let me know where she is.

As I said, she uses a combination of genetic engineering and magic to keep me alive and uncommonly healthy. Yes, Rebecca has tampered with my genes. At one point I vaguely remember her giving me injections and skin grafts, during her tenure in the concentration camps, when she had plenty of material to experiment with.

I say genetic engineering because that's the only thing I know that comes close to describing what she is actually doing to my cells, but it is not science, not the kind practiced in the light of day. It's more like ancient alchemy, the art of turning base metals into gold, or God forbid, humans into vampires.

Rebecca has lived through many times and civilization. She has seen the rise and fall of countless empires and far-flung dominions. Her story is a long one, but hopefully the remaining years will be short, for her evil life has brought enough suffering and sorrow upon the world to last until the sun ceases to shine.

You cannot tell her story without walking through history, for she comes from the mists of time. And though I was not there, would not be for thousands of years, I know her tale as if it were my own, see it in my mind's eye as Rebecca has told it to me countless times, whispered it to me in the night, and burned it into my soul.

For the first few hundred years after she became a vampire, when she was still known as Ibihil of Mari and walked the sands of Babylonia, she learned about herself and her newfound powers as a baby learns its boundaries, what is me and what is not.

She learned that she was indestructible and could not be harmed. She learned that she craved human blood and had to obtain it by whatever means possible. She learned that no human being could resist her power, but that there were old ones, vampires such as she that had greater power than her. She has kept on learning throughout the endless years. Luckily for our species, she never learned the sacred spells and words that changed her into a vampire, for those things had been long hidden.

Slowly, over the centuries, she roamed northward through the lands of Mesopotamia, always in search of new victims. Sometimes she lived with the Hittites, sometimes with the Israelites. Other times she resided with the Assyrians or the Phoenicians, until eventually ending up in the empire of the Persians in the time of Darius. She was already over a thousand years old when they fought the Greeks in their famous wars.

From Persia she wandered west along the shores of the Mediterranean, the Middle Sea, stealing souls from Rhodes to Corinth, from Sparta to Athens. Sometimes she lived in the great City States themselves, other times on the periphery of civilization, where people still followed the old ways.

Roughly 1500 years after her birth, Ibihil reached the Italian peninsula, during the slow rise of Rome, in the years of the Punic wars between that city and Carthage. She roamed the growing empire for her sustenance from Spain to Gaul, to the very gates of Rome itself.

To hear Rebecca talk of these times is truly remarkable. To realize this creature walked the earth with such ancients as Hammurabi, Darius, Alexander, and Caesar, is truly humbling. Of all the past times she has seen, however, it is obvious to anyone who hears her speak that Rebecca was especially fond of Rome.

Now life in 200 BC was no more brutal and barbaric than life in Babylonia in 1700 BC or Persia 1200 years later. Even Rebecca will tell you there is little in the history of man to rival the brutality of the Assyrians of 700 BC. However, Rome in the time of the republic and after, holds a special place in Rebecca's heart when it comes to human suffering.

If you were one of the fortunate, of good family, with land and wealth, then Rome could be quite a comfortable place. But if you were the other eighty-percent, peasants and slaves, the poor and destitute, than life was one long misery.

Rebecca feasted on the fat rich Romans and their well-cared for, pampered slaves, the hard-bodied soldiers and scarred gladiators. The Pax Romana enabled her to travel far and wide as never before over the land and taste the flesh of alien northern races - Germans, Danes, Brits - dim mythic peoples only spoken of in whispered tales. She had them all. Their blood mingled with hers in a mixed-up frenzy of death and ecstasy.

This was when Rebecca really came into her own. She became exceedingly wealthy even by the standards of later times, owning villas and palaces and hundreds of slaves. Emperors came and went, tyrants burned and rebuilt Rome, but Rebecca stayed the same, young and vibrant, beautiful and evil. The ancient world was her lunchbox, its people her sandwich meat. She had legions at her disposal, and sucked the blood of the pick of the Praetorian Guard. Julius Caesar and Pompey, Nero and Tiberius all paid her tribute. Yet the history books are silent of her, as well they should be of one so evil.

She speaks naught of the birth of Jesus or the rise of Christianity, as if these things never were. When I ask, I get nothing but a demon stare and hot breath from her nostrils. Her experiences of those times are from the eyes of a rich Roman for whom the Christians were but an entertainment at the Forum. Even when Rome was Christian, during the time of Constantine, there were still many who held to the old religions, and more, like Rebecca, that held no religion at all.

Then the Goths came, and after them the Vandals, to rule in Rome, filthy barbarians with the crown of Caesars' on their heads. It was all the same to Rebecca, although one by one her slaves and villas disappeared in the barbarian mist that was to follow the fall of Rome. She lived in caves and sod houses, straw huts and fur tents. She never got cold, needed no fire, but fed contentedly on the huddled masses and tribesmen in the deep forest holds and steppes of Dark Age Europe.

Tiring of this hard life of sleeping in forests and feeding on thick-blooded, barbarous peoples, she traveled east to that greatest of ancient cities, Constantinople, the center of the civilized world at the time, with its massive stone and pillared buildings. She took the name Pulchia, and blended in perfectly with the gaudily dressed denizens of the great metropolis. They hardly noted her walking among their illustrious houses of marble with their many steps, nor did the poorer of them as they begged for bread on the river bank. She lived as one of the elite, in a palace with borders that fell down to the sea.

The walls of the city were her undoing, that and the well-run and tightly managed supervision of the city. She was eventually discovered by the vigilant night watchmen, who guarded the wards after dark. Rebecca had to flee to the wastelands along the shore of the Black Sea, where the children of Attila the Hun had been scattered across the barren land for decades.

From there she worked her way slowly north, through lands untouched by any Christian saint or teacher, lands still living in a pagan past, an age of stone and darkness, until she arrived among the homes of the Norsemen.

The year is 800 AD. The Norsemen have begun sallying westward into the British Isles, and the Atlantic coast of France. Nothing was safe, no monastery or church, no village or hamlet, not town or city. Even those far inland from the sea knew the scourge and terror of the Viking hoards, as they sailed up the rivers and streams in their shallow-draft longboats.

Wherever the destruction was greatest, the death tolls highest, the suffering the worst, Rebecca could be found. She sailed with the cursed crews as the fierce shield-maiden, Regofin. She went from shore to shore across the North Sea. Feeding among the Norsemen and women, however, was not easy. Blood feuds and vengeance rained down upon the head of anyone who killed kin and everyone was kin to someone in the Norse camps. So she concentrated on their victims, soft Saxons and Slavs, or Irish churchmen and monks.

Eventually she left the Norsemen during one of their inland forays to again roam the night alone. There were plenty of isolated communities to prey on nestled deep in the black forests that covered the northlands. In this way, she slowly made her way back to civilization, where once again she set herself up in comfort and splendor in the middle of Europe, in what was slowly becoming Germany.

Here, during the time of the great crusades, she again found the world ideal for hunting. The vast movements of people across Europe from West and East as they made their way to the Holy Land and back, provided ample opportunities for Rebecca to ply her trade. Many a Crusader, who failed to reach Jerusalem or make it home, did so due to

Rebecca, as she stalked the roads and forest trails like a great wolf, fanged and deadly. She preyed on the children, the little ones, boys and girls, as they roamed unattended in large gangs through the land, sucking their blood by the thousands.

It was here that she acquired the first of her servants, the beginning of a long line of slaves, who would serve her with dog-like devotion through the endless years so she would never be alone. The first of these was a young peasant boy much like me, who with other homeless waifs had joined the Children's Crusade. They had become disorganized and disorientated in the wild and dangerous country on the way to the Holy Land. And like so many other armies before them, had succumbed to Rebecca's seductive charms.

To a child, Rebecca is like a long lost mother whose memory haunts their dreams, the mother they cry out to in their fear and pain. To a child she is also the promise of forbidden pleasure, pleasure only hinted at in childish games. He, like me, belonged to a gang, well-armed and mean, as dangerous as they were sadistic. They, like my group, had been intent on brutally gang-raping her, as they usually did with any unprotected female they came upon, young or old, pretty or ugly. She took them all in a blur of severed limbs and a spay of red. The lone boy standing amidst the slaughter was a six-year old named Brevin, who was to become a phenomenon in his time.

This was all new to Rebecca, an experiment she came upon naturally as a result of her need to adapt to a changing world and a loneliness that had been growing more acute near the millennium. It was a loneliness that drove her to kill even more. If it wasn't for the disruptions of the times and the Holy Wars, her depravity and the attention it attracted would certainly have caused her to flee long before.

She nurtured Brevin with her blood and milk, and magic herbs and plants mixed in to give him more strength and suppleness, but she did not have modern science and genetics to increase the span of his life much beyond the norm. It wouldn't matter. She taught him her ways until he grew into a man, one so big and formidable that all who saw him gave way. He was the perfect servant. Those who came after were measured by Brevin and most found wanting. Strong as he was intelligent, he was a bodyguard any king or Oriental potentate would have coveted, but one which Rebecca had no need for except for show.

She had trained him well. His feats were legend in their own right. What depravity and abuse she had subjected him to none would know.

In his fiftieth year he turned against her and had to be destroyed – a task I might add she took great pleasure in even if it deprived her of her first and best servant. She would find others.

Brevin plotted with a number of others to take Rebecca and burn her at the stake as a witch. Despite his knowledge of her strength and powers, he underestimated her and was destroyed along with the force he sent against her in the middle of the day as she lay confined in her sarcophagus. He evidently didn't know all of her secrets. It was his undoing, as it was almost mine.

Rebecca has returned. She entered the room as silent as the windless air. I did not notice in the shadows creeping about me that night had fallen, and in it, unheard, crept my Rebecca. My pen stops in mid-word. She watches from the doorway.

"What are you scribbling, Henry? What is it you write?"

"A letter, as you well know. I can keep nothing from you."

"You keep something, little brother. Your thoughts are strangely fragmented and mixed with some others I cannot fathom."

"You see into the depth of my soul, Mistress. You know everything."

"You were thinking about Brevin, my first servant, the one who betrayed me. You're not thinking of betraying me are you, Henry?"

"Brevin was a fool, like I once was, but I have been a loyal servant since then. Anyway, my service is coming to an end, you promised."

"I promised no such thing, and even if I did, what of it? Are you going to keep me to it, my little Henry?"

I changed the subject, as I tucked my secret even further into the folds of my mind. "I have found something, in the university library in Providence while you were away, a reference to that which you seek."

"The Text of Belamarca? What? Tell me!"

"According to a treatise of the Sieur De Chaste from Dieppe in Normandy, the Pope instructed Henry IV of France to hide the text you seek in the New World. At that time a Spanish convoy was heading to Puerto Rico in New Spain. The Sieur De Chaste was instructed to have the manuscript taken on a French ship that sailed with them in 1600. It is uncertain what happened after that. The records are partly destroyed. The French is ancient and hard to decipher, but there is some hint of another manuscript in Colombia that might offer a clue to what happened to it. The French Treatise also mentions a great evil that resulted from the use of the Text and instructed it be destroyed so that it may never cause such evil again. What evil is this they speak of? Is that why you seek it, Mistress, to cause evil?"

"Evil? What do you know of it? It's all relative. You should understand that, with your knowledge of modern science. One man's evil is another man's redemption. Look at your own atomic bomb in World War II."

"I am only saying that perhaps that which you seek, that which is hidden, should remain so."

"Let me worry about that, Henry. You have done well. Now I have things of my own to do."

With that she is gone again, a phantom, a ghost. Was she even really here?

Chapter 8

I'm alone again. She's disappeared as quickly and silently as she appeared, one minute standing before me in all her terrible beauty, the next, gone as if she was never here. Oh, if only that were true and I were free.

I wonder what she could be up to, what this Text of Belamarca really is. From what I've been able to determine, it isn't good. It must have been something pretty bad for the Pope to have it sent halfway around the world to be disposed of. I wonder if it has anything to do with the ancient Script of Ur, the sacred words used to turn Ibihil of Mari into a child of the night, a Vampyre. If so, then it must never be found or we are all doomed.

Is that what she has in store for me? Is that what she has been hinting at, to make me into one of the undead? I would rather die a thousand deaths then live on as the likes of her. To walk the earth for eternity with Rebecca would be a fate worse than death, although it sounds glamorous enough to hear her tell it, especially to have lived in the Renaissance. So let me continue with her story, as sordid as it may be.

The years turned into centuries, generations came and went, and still Rebecca continued her murderous ways, feeding on her victims, acquiring wealth and knowledge like a barn gathers cobwebs. Slowly the face of the world was changing, as man began to acquire knowledge long forgotten or never known, but Rebecca never changed. She remained the same fatal beauty she had been for almost three thousand years. It was during this time, in the heart of the Renaissance, that Rebecca again found herself on a much-changed Italian Peninsula, in the City State of Florence.

The Florentine artists had been the first to render the human form realistically in painting and sculpture. Their galleries flourished in the side streets and alleys of the great Renaissance city. Their work was already beginning to show the influence of the many patrons of the arts who resided there. Michelangelo had not yet made a name for himself, but Piero Della Francesca had been well known for years for his bold new experiments with perspective.

It was here in Florence, in the fifteenth century, that Rebecca fell in love for the first and last time.

Thomas was a young acolyte, not yet twenty, destined for the priesthood when she first saw him passing in the street. She was posing as a model in the studio of one of the more innovative sculptors of the time. As I have mentioned, artists of the day were beginning to capture the likeness of the human form with ever more accuracy, since the great discoveries in the new science of anatomy were just being made public. Rebecca's finely-chiseled torso and classic beauty, together with her reputation for being completely uninhibited, made her a sought-after acquisition for any studio lucky enough to afford her.

She had seen many men in her 3000 years, a good number she had seduced to their deaths, but for some reason she was particularly affected by Thomas. Maybe it was his more than handsome face, chiseled like an angel's. Or perhaps it was the way his body filled the black, clinging tunic. Maybe the fact that he was destined for the priesthood, that he stood for all that was good and pure in the world, that attracted her. Whatever it was, Rebecca was drawn to him like she had been to no other.

She made it her single-minded purpose in life to seduce the young acolyte, but in spite of her many charms and years of practice, Thomas, who was pious and devout, proved to be a very difficult subject. It was only a matter of time, however. She visited him in the confessional and whispered sinful secrets in his ear. She saw him in the market and smiled provocatively at him as he walked by. She made sure he would see her modeling, half- naked, in the street-side artists' studios. In time, he was completely under her spell, ardently confessing his love.

I'm sure his last night on earth was a happy one. The young priest had never been with a woman before, but no one had to tell him what to do. That night she made passionate love to the boy on the cathedral alter, or at least what counts for such things with one of her kind. She had not felt like this since the night those many thousands of years before when Urammu took her on the altar of Marduk.

At some point during their lovemaking, Rebecca lost control. Her eyes rolled back in her head and her mind went numb. She sunk her teeth into Thomas's exposed neck and didn't let go. She couldn't help it. She should have known that she would kill the one she loved. It was one of the last lessons she had to learn about being an vampire. She did not take it well. Lying on top of the blood-drained corpse, she beat the body and cried in anguish. She is almost overcome again every time she tells the tale, which she does often. It's one of her favorite stories. To love her is to know despair.

For days after killing Thomas, she wandered alone, abstaining from that which drove her. If she could not have love then she would have nothing. She wanted to shrivel up and die.

It was then that she first met one of the old ones, one of the earliest of the Nosferatu, who had first walked the earth when men were still learning how to sow wild grains along the banks of the Nile. The tall female stood watching her from afar as Rebecca walked along the bank of the Tiber.

"Why do you suffer so, child?" said the old one, who in a sudden motion stood next to Rebecca along the strong flowing water. "Why do you deprive yourself when the world is at your feet?"

Rebecca was startled from her reverie, not noticing the striking female approach, and stunned by her words, as if the old woman could see into her soul. She had never felt so small and needy before, not since she sat crying on her mother's knee those many thousand years ago. It was a feeling she had long suppressed. She opened her mouth to speak but could not utter a word her throat was so restricted with long forgotten emotion.

"Who are you?" she finally stammered. "Where did you come from?"

"I have been watching you, child, since you first arrived. One as cunning and beautiful as you could not go unnoticed for long. You have much to learn."

At this, Rebecca gained more of her composure, her natural-born malice rising to the surface. Who was this old dame to think she could talk to her that way? She would teach her to be so presumptuous with a stranger, a dangerous one at that.

"You make a mistake, old dame. And for that you will pay!"

With that she pounced on the old woman only to find herself flung through the air and into the river, where she was held under until she submitted. She had never been man-handled like this before, and was partially in a state of shock when the old one spoke to her again.

"Do not resist, young one, for I am one of the Espiritus, old before the dawn of time, a demon who walked this earth when your great Sumer was but a single reed hut next to the River of Life. Be still, Ibihil of Mari."

"How do you know my name?" she stammered, in a state of shock.

"I know many things and will answer all your questions in time, but first you must walk with me and ease my loneliness."

Rebecca learned much from this ancient dame, the do's and don'ts, the rules of the game. To look at her you would have thought her no more than forty or fifty years old, and still handsome despite her age. In reality she was an ancient chieftain's daughter, and over six thousand years old. It was from her that Rebecca learned of the spell that had been spoken over her at her moment of death, and how such words must never be uttered again. She was taught how to keep humans alive to serve her beyond their short life spans. Finally, when her teacher's job was complete, she vanished into the misty night as mysteriously as she had appeared.

Over the next few hundred years, as humankind advanced in their understanding of the world around them, Rebecca moved from one great center of civilization to another - Spain, France, England, Germany - moving with the flow of culture and learning. She even ventured to the Levant, the Fertile Crescent of her birthplace, by this time controlled by the Ottoman Turks.

The lands of the Moslems were well-stocked with good-quality blood, ready victims for the taking. But the Islamic attitude toward women greatly restricted her freedom of movement and behavior, so it wasn't long before she returned to the West to settle in the lands of the German Princes again, where a short time later in the scheme of things, yours truly became her slave.

How many countless lives has she taken over the endless years? How many pints of hemoglobin has she siphoned from the living to keep the evil curse that she is alive? How many has she seduced with her cunning and charms? How long will it continue? Not long, if I have anything to do with it.

Chapter 9

Rebecca is back from another hunting expedition. I woke from an unusually long dream to find her asleep in her shrouded basement tomb. I check it every morning. I sleep normally when she's gone. She has been away longer than usual. When she's away all I do is slumber and dream, waiting for her return. When she's here I hardly sleep at all, but sit and wait for her command. My life is waiting for her, waiting on her, waiting to die.

This evening she left the house early, before the sky was fully darkened. A thin band of red still lingered in the west. It was as if she had not eaten in days, although I know she has fed recently. I have not spoken to her since.

She's returned. She came back early this morning, satiated with the blood of some stranger whose only sin was to be noticed.

She came up behind me as I sat in the upstairs den trying to read. Mostly I was gazing out at the empty street, waiting for her. I did not see her enter the house, or hear her come up the stairs, but when she put her hands over my eyes I could smell the dried blood and feces of her victims. It was as if her fingers had been deep within their bowels. I stiffened in revulsion before I had time to think.

"You don't seem very happy to see me, Henry. Aren't you glad I'm home?"

"Why of course, dear mistress," I responded, although she smelled like a flesh-eating reptile. "I've been waiting for your return. How may I serve you, master?"

"You can serve me by being my friend, sweet Henry. By talking to me and reminding me what it's like to be human."

"The only thing human you crave is our blood, mistress." I couldn't help saying this even though insulting her could be dangerous. I hoped she was in a good mood.

"Now Henry, don't be like that."

"Where have you been? You've been away a long time. I was beginning to wonder if you were coming back."

"Is that what you're afraid of, that I wouldn't come back to you, sweet Henry? Now, why would you think that? Why would I leave one so loyal?"

She stroked my chin like I was a cat.

"For the same reason you leave them all. I've outlived my usefulness. Set me free."

"No, I have great use for you still. I hope you will be serving me another century or more."

"I didn't think that was possible."

"Ah, there are more wonders in the world then DNA and modern science, long forgotten things, ancient secrets even better than our Babylonian alchemist knew of. I hate the idea of searching out and finding another man. It is such a bore. Good servants are hard to find, and even harder to keep. You have been loyal."

"Where have you been, Mistress?" I asked again with concern.

Her answer surprised me and reassured me at the same time. She wasn't looking for ancient spells of vampirism. She was up to her good old blood-letting ways.

"I've been in Colombia, feasting among the poor and ignorant masses. Ah, but it's so good to be home and taste thick, New England blood again."

She slinked across the room, taking my hand and pulling me along with her to the master bedroom, where she proceeded to change into different outfits, most of them negligees and underwear. She pranced in front of the wall-sized, full-length mirrors, priming herself like a show bird. I stood and watched in fascination.

"How does this look, Henry? What do you think I could catch in this outfit?" she asked, wearing a black, strapless bra and matching under-skirt that barely covered her nicely rounded behind.

"Just about anything on two legs," I responded, unable to take my eyes off her.

"Colombia was nice. A good change of pace, and the food supply is so abundant, so much young, hot blood. Not like North America where the average age is over fifty and everyone's overweight. After awhile, though, you get sick of that thin hemoglobin, those skinny boys and thin-skinned girls. I was getting hungry for good-old, thick Yankee blood."

"Spare me the details, mistress. It's bad enough I have to dispose of them. I don't want to hear the details."

'Oh, don't you, Henry? Don't you like it when I let you see? It gives it all a special flavor with you watching. By the way, we're having guests this evening. There will be six for a late supper. Have the dining room set with my best silverware and china, and bring up a couple bottles of that lovely red wine I've been saving from the cellar. That will do very nicely."

"Yes, Madame, will there be anything else?"

"Yes, Henry. Stoke up the furnace nice and hot."

The doorbell rang. It was half-past eleven. Dinner was scheduled for midnight. As expected, our guests were from out of town, Colombia in fact. Rebecca had recently made their acquaintance at one of the more expensive nightclubs in Bogotá when she was there last - three men with shiny white teeth and slicked black hair, and their female companions. They chattered excitedly in Spanish.

"Hola," said the tallest of the men at the door.

He was dressed in a flawless white jacket with a half-buttoned silk shirt. There was a gold chain dangling around his tanned neck.

"We are here to see Missus Olivier," he announced.

"Come in," I answered, welcoming them into Rebecca's lair with a short bow. I led them into a side room where there was a small bar set up, and fixed some drinks, telling them to make themselves comfortable.

"Missus Olivier well be down shortly," I informed them using the assumed name she was calling herself this evening.

They stood around the room admiring the furniture and the expensive artwork on the walls, talking to each other in their native tongue. From what Rebecca told me, I gathered the young men were in the Colombian drug trade and had been looking for a northern distributor with connections. It was easy for her to persuade them she was that distributor. She invited them up to check out the situation in person.

Rebecca arrived at midnight wearing a radiant black dress, low-cut and long, which showed her figure to full advantage. The three other women, although beautiful by any standards, seemed dull and drab next to her. I knew it was her vampire spell, but Fernando, Enrique, and Louis were mesmerized, and showered her with attention as they ate the six-course meal, which I cooked and served without breaking a sweat. I have done it so many times before.

After dinner Fernando opened his briefcase and took out an old manuscript.

"Here is the document we spoke of. I obtained it from the university in Bogotá."

Fernando laid it on the table next to Rebecca, who was sitting next to him at its head. "It is quite valuable and very old, but I was able to obtain it for the right price, as you asked. It is in Spanish. I can read it for you if you like."

"No, that is not necessary," she answered.

She picked it up quickly and handed it to me. I placed it in the safe as instructed, and took out the thick envelope of bills she had agreed to pay for the item. I knew I would be returning it to the safe by the end of the evening.

The group retired to the spacious living room, and spread out on the many divans and chairs, snorting coke and other powdery substances they had brought along with them for their own amusement. Under the influence of the wine, the drugs, and Rebecca's spell, it wasn't long before the girls were taking off their clothes. Not long after that the orgy began. Knowing I was no longer needed, I discreetly left the room. I'd be back soon enough, to clean up the mess.

I knew what was going to happen. I had seen it all so many times before. Drug dealers or no, they didn't deserve to die like that, but what could I do? How do you stop the maelstrom?

As I mentioned, there are very few vampires in the world, thank goodness. Contrary to popular myth, they cannot create other vampires by simply biting someone, or letting someone bite them, or by whatever means. If they could, the world would be covered with them and we humans would be extinct like the dinosaurs long ago, for there is only room for one dominant species at the top of the food chain.

No, vampires could only be created in the dawn of mankind, when demons walked the earth and the ancient rites to bind them to human form were still known. So there are relatively few of them, maybe a thousand at most, scattered around the globe. Rebecca is the youngest of these, the last of her kind, as far as I know.

They roam the earth in search of human prey much as Rebecca, each I assume with their own servants and domain. They seem to be territorial and avoid contact with each other, and except for that old dame in Florence long ago, for as long as I've known Rebecca, she has never seen nor had one word with any of them. For some reason, they seem to be hostile, for we have been driven from place to place by the threat they pose. When I ask her about them I get a hiss and a glare in response, so I stopped asking decades ago, at least directly. I have continued my research, nevertheless, for somehow I know this knowledge may be of some use.

In her more sociable moments, I've learned enough from Rebecca to piece some things together. For instance, there is one very ancient vampire, one of the first, that she fears above all the others for his power and malice. This spirit walked the earth long before the long lost civilizations of Samaria or Egypt were even a dream

When men still lived in caves and hunted the big mammals with stones and sharpened sticks, and drew their images in deep cave walls, Tikana walked the warming land. He was brought forth by some ice-age shaman. For thousands upon thousands of unchanged years he stalked the earth preying on our early humanoid ancestors, building his strength with their blood.

Over time the forests and savannas where the big game were grew smaller and dryer, while everywhere the water rose as the great northern ice sheets receded ever further. As the game grew scarce, the small bands of hunters and their families moved across the landscape after them, and so came to new lands where people had never trod before. With them came Tikana, and with Tikana went death.

Early man worshipped the sky and land, the sun and the moon, river, tree, and rock as if they were all animate things that controlled his destiny. He worshipped the great bear and saber-tooth tiger, the giant mammoth and bull, the horse, the cat, the reindeer. He worshipped nature and prayed as hard as any born-again Christian for his daily bread.

Some, however, prayed not to these things, but to another god, a god of death, for death by starvation or violence or simple tooth infection was never far away for most. The shaman who turned Tikana was such a one, one who steeped himself in evil, worshipped it, and sacrificed other humans to it. Through this malignant sorcerer, Tikana, the first vampire was born.

As I tell this story, I am reminded of another time long ago, during the early years of my servitude. There was an incident that I didn't understand. Only now, after thinking about these things does it start to make sense to me.

We were in Paris during the twenties, that decade between the great wars when everyone was gay with wild abandon and naïve optimism still flourished among fashionable Europeans. Rebecca had set herself up in style, in a lavish townhouse on the tree-lined residential boulevard, de l'Avenue Foch. I was still a young man and had not yet tasted the misery of life, still enamored with the existence I led as Rebecca's man. Taking advantage of her money and power, I was able to seduce my way through half the young women in Paris, none of whom I cared about and none of whom Rebecca bothered to feed on. Things could not have been better. Times were good for both of us. Then one night, it all came to a sudden end.

She had gone out as usual soon after dark. It was summer, so it was late by the time she left, sometime after nine. Shortly after ten she abruptly returned, a highly unusual event, for she normally stayed out until shortly before dawn. Not only had she returned early, but she seemed to be agitated, although it is hard to tell with a stone cold vampire. I only saw her for a moment as she rushed into her tomb soon after coming home. I followed.

"What is the matter, Master?" I asked. "Is something wrong?"

She was scared, on edge, unable to relax as she usually did after the hunt. She paced back and forth before her casket. To think that someone as powerful as Rebecca was afraid of something sent me into a panic. What could have affected her so?

"I do not feel well. Something has happened," she told me as she moved across the floor. "Leave me alone."

"I thought you could never be sick, Mistress," I answered confused, "that nothing could harm you."

"That is true, Henry, but I have not told you everything. There are things that can hurt me. Something happened as I was stalking a young couple walking along the Seine. They were looking for a private place to make amour. Just as I was about to take them, as they embraced under a dark archway, I was overcome with nausea, and seized with a sudden vertigo. Nothing like this has ever happened before. My head was pounding. I had a buzz in my brain. The streets were spinning like a top."

"That is odd, Mistress. That happens to me when you talk to me in my head."

"I could not continue. I had to return here without supping. You will have to get something for me."

She instructed me to bring a girl home to the house. I resented the request. It was bad enough I had to aid and abet, but to bring the prey to her while she hid in her lair was too much to bear without objecting to.

"It will be difficult to find a prostitute at seven in the morning," I replied.

"Do it!" she commanded, lifting me in the air with one hand and shaking me until I had whiplash.

Soon after, Rebecca was feasting on young Parisian blood. In Gay-Paree in the twenties anything was possible. We left Paris shortly after.

I'm sure now that Rebecca must have crossed paths with another vampire, one stronger and more powerful than her, one who she feared. Anything that could instill such fright in such a fearsome creature as Rebecca must be fearful indeed. As the years pass, and the burden and misery of my life with her grows, I've begun to wonder if there is not some way to harness this power and use it against her, although I might as well try to harness the sun.

As I finished cleaning up after Rebecca's latest repast, stuffing the last of the Colombians into our oversized furnace, Rebecca summoned me from the library.

"What does it say, Henry? Read it for me, now." She waved the document from Colombia in my face.

I have seldom seen her so agitated. She paced back and forth across the room like she hadn't fed in days, like that day in Paris seventy-some-odd years ago.

"Yes, mistress," I said, taking the document, trembling, from her hands. "But it is in old Spanish. It will take some time to translate."

"Read it," she demanded, making me shake even more, so that now I could hardly see the words.

I scanned the ancient parchment, which though maintained in good condition, had many smudged-out and undecipherable words.

"It is not the document you seek, although it does seem to refer to it. The Sieur de Chaste is mentioned, and the word Belarmaja is clearly written in several places. It could be Spanish for Belamarca."

I perused it some more, reading between the lines as much as from the ancient text.

"It speaks of a great evil that the French attempted to hide in Colombia, which was then part of New Spain near Darien. This they were not able to accomplish because the Jesuits in charge of the inquisition there refused to allow it to come to shore once they learned its true nature. It says here that the document you seek was taken back to France with one of the Treasure Fleets. I will have to study it some more to decipher it exactly."

She looked at me in silence for a long time, as if trying to determine if I was telling her the truth, peering into the windows of my soul as if they had no shutters or blinds, but were wide open to her gaze. She stood stock still now, stiff as a post, a bundle of nerves and energy about to explode. Then she relaxed and smiled.

"Good, Henry. That is good," she said finally. "I need you and your little one now more than ever. We must get her soon. Learn all you can. Our future depends on it."

Chapter 10

I have been down in the basement this cold December day, gazing on the still, silent form of my beloved, Rebecca. How can something so beautiful be so evil? How can a form so perfect bring such horror into the world? How can this possibly fit the purpose of any divine creation?

Several days have passed since the party with the Colombian drug lords. I have been checking the papers for any mention of them, not that I expected to see anything. I'm sure they were in the country illegally and probably traveling under assumed names. The authorities would never notice their disappearance, but then it's not the authorities I'm worried about.

As I sat in the den earlier, reading Mann's version of the Faustus legend, identifying with the hero in his fruitless attempt to outwit the devil, I looked up suddenly to see Rebecca perched on the back of a chair, balanced on her haunches with her knees drawn up to her chin - more like a flying reptile than a bird - watching me. Although she will often do this - sneak up on me like that - I never get used to her stone-still figure appearing abruptly, her bright, hungry green eyes watching me. Startled, I dropped the book I was reading and lost my place. Just as well, for all thought or ability to read left me instantly upon seeing her.

"You humans are so interesting," she said from her perch. "How can you read those hieroglyphics?"

"You made me lose my place. Why do you have to sneak up on me like that?"

"I did not sneak. Your human senses are so dull you didn't notice me. Do I sense anger in your voice? Do I detect recriminations in your stare, my sweet Henry? Are you upset with me for something?"

"Why are you so cruel?" I blurted out against my better judgment, but no longer able to control my words. "Why do you have to take so much pleasure in it? Why do you have to butcher them so? Why do you have to kill so many?"

"You talk of me as if I were a monster, Henry. You cut me to the bone. How can you speak to me this way after all I have done for you? You humans are far more predatory than we poor creatures of the night. I have seen your blood-splattered, slaughter-filled human history firsthand, from the Egyptians and Assyrians to the latest atrocities of the Second World War. I have seen wholesale cannibalism, human sacrifice, worldwide genocide, head-hunting, torture, murder, mutilation, and necrophilia, all practiced by mankind with their common bloodlust. Not to mention their filthy habits. You are all diseased. You all carry the mark of Cain. You are more dangerous than the deadliest carnivores, the hungriest vampire."

"And yet you prey on us. You feed on humans as if they were lambs."

"Are you so thick not to see the truth? I am here for a purpose, to weed out the chaff, to winnow the rotten, to bring you all nearer to God."

"Don't blaspheme, you wicked fiend! Don't use His name in your vain attempt to justify your murderous existence."

"Now, now, Henry, let's not get hysterical. I'm sorry I was so messy with that last bunch, but they more than deserved it. They were killers themselves and would not have hesitated to rob and kill us both if it suited them. So don't feel so bad. After all, Henry, the human lot is to live, to suffer, and to die. I am merely facilitating the process."

She seemed to float in the air as she balanced on the chair-back, still clasping her hands around her drawn-up knees, staring intently at me with blood-tinged eyes. I wasn't going to let her get the last word, not this time.

"At least we humans have the potential for good. No matter what, in the darkest human soul there is, after all is said and done, still the potential to do good, to make a decision that leads to good. You and your kind are pure evil, and have the potential for nothing but evil."

At these words, Rebecca slowly rose until she was standing full length on the back of the chair, a dark smile widening on her lips. She held her arms out wide.

"And evil shall I do, until the sun explodes in the sky. And you Henry, you will do my bidding until I am done with you."

"Yes mistress," I said, throwing myself on my hands and knees before her as she seemed to grow in size. Groveling on the ground in fear, I cursed at my own foolhardiness, my feeble attempt of rebellion. I knew what she could do when aroused. As it was, she would have more need of me shortly than she ever had before.

Several weeks have passed since Rebecca's return from South America. Things have gotten more or less back to normal, with

Rebecca making her nightly visits to various parts unknown, while I continue my research. Luckily, she has not been eating in.

I have been pursuing Rebecca's quest for the Text of Belamarca, which is mentioned in a little known treatise of the French nobleman and founder of New France, the sieur de Chaste. Apparently, the Text of Belamarca contains a great evil that the Pope tried to dispose of in the New World, in Colombia, which was then part of New Spain. But the Jesuits, who not even the Holy Father could control, refused to let them hide it there, so it was returned to France.

At Rebecca's bidding I have gone in search of the document, and have spent the last week in the north of France, in Brittany and Normandy, looking in ancient city archives and libraries for some clue to its whereabouts.

It was in Dieppe on the edge of the Normandy coast overlooking the English Channel on a fog-bound day that I finally found what I was searching for. It was in the basement of the municipal archives, where it had lain undiscovered for 400 years among a pile of old papers, a clear record of the Text of Belamarca.

I arrived back in Boston late the next evening, landing at Logan on a cold wet night in the middle of the week. To my surprise, Rebecca was there waiting for me in a rented limo. As soon as we were seated in the back, my baggage stowed and the driver panel shut, she asked me about my discovery.

"You have found it? Have you found the Text of Belamarca?"

"No, Mistress. I am sorry. I was not able to locate the document itself. However, I did discover a clear reference to it. It was among some papers of an early French explorer, which had been left in Ayma. The explorer, Samuel de Champlain, put it in the care of his friend, the sieur de Chaste, after his death. It mentions Belamarca, although in a coded manner, and confirms what we learned in the Colombian document. The Belamarca Text was returned to France. From there, the king, Charles IV, sent it back to the New World, this time to New France with Champlain on the voyage that took him up the St. Lawrence to the site of Quebec, his great discovery. There it was hidden for a time. When the English invaded in the 1620's, it was taken further down the river and hidden where it would never be found, in the present-day site of Montreal, in Canada. It may still be there today."

"Well done, my Henry. You have cracked the secret of the location of the sacred text. Now all we have to do is find it. In the meantime, your child will be twenty-one at the end of the month, if I am not mistaken."

"I do not know, Master. I have lost count of the years."

"Oh, have you, Henry? Would you like me to remind you?"

"No, Mistress, as you say. Please don't torture me."

"Then do as I say. I have plans for her."

"Why do you have to be so cruel? Why do you want her? Leave her alone. You can torture me, impale me, crucify me, but please leave Emily alone."

"Henry! You try my patience. I have tried to be kind to you and show my appreciation for what you do. Did I not let your child live?"

"Yes, my Mistress," I answered, throwing myself to her feet. "Forgive me, but please release her. Let her be. We have gone this long without her, why bother the child now? You have me to serve you."

"Oh, no, Henry. We made a bargain. I kept my end. I've been patient. I waited until she has become a woman. She is mine now, as are you. I have great plans for the two of you."

I needn't have worried. As it turned out we have been slightly preoccupied lately with things beyond our control. Whenever Rebecca brings a victim home, there is always the possibility, no matter how careful we are, that someone may come looking for them. As time went on, I began to suspect that this was the case with the six missing Colombians. Even if they were in the States under assumed names, there must have been people back in South America that knew of their intentions and destination. So I had been on the alert for some time.

Then a few days ago I noticed a car parked across the street from the house with two men sitting in it. They didn't look like the police, and they certainly weren't tourists, the way they just sat there and watched the place. It could only mean one thing. Someone had come looking for their friends.

It was only a matter of time before something like this occurred. It's happened before and it will happen again. It's a very dangerous situation and one has to be crafty and patient to survive. Rebecca and I have had plenty of practice.

Whoever was surveying us made no effort to hide themselves or their purpose, but sat in front of the house like a four-legged hound dog waiting to howl.

Then there was a buzzing between my eyes.

'Prove yourself. Do this for me.'

Rebecca spoke to me telepathically, telling me what to do. Of course, she already knew about the interlopers, had already sensed their presence and intent. Now she had formed her plan. I was to be her sword. As if on cue the doorbell rang.

"Hello," said the short dark stranger with the thin mustache. He was wearing a colorful Hawaiian shirt buttoned to the neck and a pair of light-tan slacks. He had on dark glasses and expensive Italian leather shoes.

"Sorry to disturb you, Senor. I am looking for some friends of mine who I believe may have visited you a few weeks ago, from Bogotá."

"Oh, yes," I answered, looking over his shoulder to see the other man still sitting in the car, "Fernando and his friends. What a nice group of people. Very good manners for ones so young. Is there a problem? Have you not heard from them yet? That's strange. I assumed they left town weeks ago. We haven't seen or heard from them since that night."

"No, we have not heard from them either. Fernando is the son of the man I work for. He sent me to look for them. Would you mind if I come in for a few moments? Perhaps you can help me understand what might have happened to them."

"You are more than welcome to come in, Mister…?"

"Lopez, Miguel Lopez," said the stranger.

"Mr. Lopez. But I doubt there is anything I can tell you that would help. As I've said, they visited us for dinner a few weeks ago. That was our only contact with your friends. I have no further information."

"Ah, yes. Thank you, but a few moments of your time would be extremely helpful."

I led him into the living room, the very one where his employer's son and his friends partied and perished, and offered him a drink, which he accepted.

"I don't want to waste any of your time, so I'll get right to the point," he said in perfect English, as soon as I returned with his scotch on the rocks.

"Fernando came here for a specific purpose. He met someone in Colombia, a Missus Olivier, who claimed to have certain, um, business connections that we were very interested in. Fernando and a few of his associates came to check the situation out in more detail. We know he and his party arrived in Boston on the 24th and that they took a city cab to this address. They have not been heard from or seen since."

"That is strange," I said, feigning concern. "Very troubling indeed. As I've said, they dined with the Madame of the house that evening."

I explained my position as housekeeper and butler, and told him that my mistress was not home at this time. "I drove them to the airport myself later that evening."

"Yes, I was meaning to ask you about that. We've, ah, been, ah, watching your house for several days now, and have seen no one come or go. How could she have gone out without us seeing her?"

"So you've been watching the house, have you? Well, that's very unfortunate."

The drugs I mixed with his whiskey were starting to take affect. He was having trouble focusing his eyes or understanding what I was saying. He looked at me dumbly and tried to rise, belching.

"How arrogant you people are, coming here like this," I said. "Who do you think you are? Now you're going to end up in the furnace like Fernando and his friends."

I grabbed him by the ankles as he writhed on the couch holding his stomach, and pulled him violently onto the floor, where he landed with a double thud. Without stopping, I pulled him across the carpet into the kitchen and down the cellar stairs. His head bounced in rhythm to my steps. Rebecca was waiting for us at the bottom, arms open.

I left the half-unconscious man at her feet and returned to finish my task. As I turned to leave I saw her rip off his bright Hawaiian shirt and sink her teeth into the side of his neck. Reaching the top of the stairs, I heard his screams turn to gurgles then stop altogether. It was just turning dark.

Taking off my shoes and socks, and grabbing a wire coat hanger from the closet, I silently crawled out of one of the darkened windows at the back of the house. Keeping to the shadows of the many shrubs and bushes surrounding the place, I crept to the front of the building. I could see the other man parked a little way up the street, just out of the glare of the street lamp illuminating this end of the block. Quietly, in silent bare feet, I crept up behind the car to get a closer look. I could see the single occupant, a large man, anxiously looking out the side window up at the house where his friend disappeared a short time before.

This man appeared to be quite a bit larger than the late Mister Lopez, with wide shoulders and massive biceps. The silk fabric of his sports shirt was stretched to the ripping point over his large frame. I would have to move fast and surprise him. Otherwise, I would have a problem. Then there was always the chance of someone coming by and seeing the struggle. No, that would never do.

It's funny that I would be so quick to follow Rebecca's orders to dispatch these two. You might think this a perfect opportunity to be rid of her for good. Fat chance. If I thought for a moment it was feasible I would have jumped at it like a fish at a fly. But no, such a thing is not in the realm of possibilities. She would have just taken care of things without me, then punish me in some horrible way. I have to think about my daughter. I will have to bide my time and find the right moment and instrument. Until then, I'll do her bidding come what may.

As I watched, the man in the car, obviously tired of waiting and concerned for his friend, stepped out into the warm night air and made his way furtively across the street to the side of the house. I followed, keeping low and in the shadows, soundless in my bare feet as we moved to the rear of the building.

It was perfect. I couldn't have scripted it better myself. Here in the dark, behind the house, hidden from view of the street, with the sound of the surf washing up on the rocks below drowning out any noise was a perfect spot to dispatch the intruder.

The man moved smoothly for one his size. His bull neck and thick body looked built for knocking down linebackers. Even with the extra strength given to me by Rebecca's blood-cocktails, I was afraid this Neanderthal's strength would be too much for me. In any case, I wasn't really up to garroting someone, despite my fear of Rebecca. Then I saw the shovel, left in the yard from the previous day's gardening. Grabbing it, I brought it down on the back of his head as he peered into one of the first floor windows. He went down with a groan on his hands and knees. I hit him again, harder, this time on the back of the neck. He went down on his face with a grunt, out cold.

Rolling him onto his back, I stuck his ankles into the noose of the coat hanger, and began dragging him by his feet to the basement. Rebecca was there waiting for us. The body of the first Colombian lay on his back at the foot of the basement stairs. Rebecca eyed the second man as I deposited him at her feet like she hadn't eaten in days, although it was obvious from her red-smeared mouth and chin that she had recently dined quite profusely.

She was on the second man in an instant. I looked away in disgust, and tried to block out the horrible sucking, slurping sound of a vampire feeding.

Chapter 11

That night, after disposing of the bodies in the usual way and taking care of their car as well, we prepared to leave our home of the past twenty years. It was decided that we could stay here no longer. Whoever sent the two unfortunate thugs would send others or come themselves. Regardless of the outcome, which would certainly be in Rebecca's favor, unwanted attention would be attracted. Vampires, no matter how powerful and invincible, cannot long abide attention. So we fled. We packed up our belongings, put the house up for sale, assumed new identities, and moved to Montreal, Canada just across the border from New York State. Despite the inconvenience, I welcome the disruption of our lives, for it allows my child, Emily, some respite. She will be safe from Rebecca's plan, whatever that is, until we are resettled in our new home.

Long before the necessity occurred, Rebecca had made arrangements for the disappearance of one set of identities and the fabrication of another. She assumed that of a wealthy young American fashion designer, who had come to Quebec to learn from the great French masters of modern clothing design.

The move has gone smoothly and we are now comfortable in our new home on the slopes of Mount Royal, a vast two-story granite and sandstone mansion with high ceilings and dark-wood floors. Its grand crenellations and arrow-slit windows dominate the heights of the city. In spite of my rusty French, we are getting on well

The city of Montreal is a colorful blend of old and new, steel and concrete, glass and brick. Bilingual and multi-ethnic, it's a blend of cosmopolitan and provincial, religious and profane, all jumbled together in one river valley nestled between low hills in the west and the St. Lawrence Seaway in the east. Rebecca thrives on the rich, mixed blood coursing through the veins of the inhabitants, young and old alike.

Rebecca has apparently disturbed something. The space-time continuum has been distorted. She has encroached on some hidden secret, violated a long-standing taboo. It feels as if we have intruded on some evil entity's private domain. It happened on our first night in Montreal.

Even though the ostensible reason for our leaving New England was the attention caused by the missing Colombians, I sensed that there was another purpose for our departure. There were dozens of places we could have gone - New York, Chicago, LA - why here, across the border into another country? It only added to the difficulties already inherent in changing identities, even for someone like Rebecca. No, she must have had a good reason for picking this city. I found out the reason that first evening.

Without even stopping at our new home, she led me to the old part of the city. It was not like Rebecca to play tourist, for she had been here many times before in the past. We walked the streets of Old Montreal perusing some of the first buildings in the area, dating back to the 1600s. We were the only tourists out this evening on the dark, empty streets, well after midnight.

She was moving with a purpose, searching for something. I followed her down one cobbled street and up another. Approaching a low, stone building with shaded windows, dark and shuttered, she stopped and stared at a sign. It was hanging on an iron gate in front of the place and written in French. It informed us that the building was a museum, but had once been the province's first City Hall. It held many of the early archives, some from before Montreal's founding. Another sign posted in front indicated that it was also the location of an archeological dig. Someone was apparently excavating the basement of this old building to uncover an even older structure laid when the site was first settled 400 years ago.

Without hesitation, she moved to the rear of the building along a dark back alley, where she broke in through a strongly-reinforced door, pulling it from its hinges as if it were cardboard. The unfortunate night watchman was dispatched just as quickly, Rebecca not even stopping to sup. Once inside, I followed her to a dark staircase leading down into the basement of the old edifice. A sliding iron grate stood in front of it, blocking the entrance from floor to ceiling. This she ripped away as easily as she had the rear door. I followed her into the darkness as we descended the steep steps.

A locked door at the bottom stood barring the way. That door also was no match for her superhuman strength, as it was cast aside like so much papier-mâché.

At the site of the dig, the basement walls had been replaced with clear plastic sheets, which surrounded a large, empty pile of dirt. Stone foundations and wooden beams that had once been a structure of some kind could be seen within. There were large spot-lights shining on the area and workers' tools lying about in various places.

"It is here, hidden in the vaults. Dig," she ordered, pointing to a corner of stone and dirt, which had not yet been excavated.

I dug for some time in the spot she indicated, while she perused the premises.

"What are we looking for, Mistress?"

"A scroll, hidden by those Jesuit devils many years ago, of which you told me. It will be here. "

"What is it? Tell me. I have a right to know:"

"Yes, Henri, it is time you know the truth. It is not surprising the church fathers tried to bury it where it would be safe from prying eyes forever, for it is nothing less than the ancient Scroll of Ur, the very words spoken over me at my moment of death, the sacred text to bind a demon to a human soul, secret words to create an Espiritus."

"It was copied from the ancient tongue of Ur, the words of the great Babylonian priests, against all our laws, by the renegade vampyre Belamarca. It was he who copied the text from the original cuneiform tablets. I was the last to hear those words. I will be the first to utter them again, and with them I will have ultimate power."

I stopped what I was doing and looked at her as the full import of her words struck me.

"What do you have in mind, Mistress? What are you going to do?"

She stared at me hard for a moment from across the room.

"What I should have done years ago, Henri. Just do as I say. I have told you enough. It is here. Dig!"

"How do you know?" I asked.

"I feel its presence. Its power calls to me."

I knew then what she was after, what she was going to do. I knew I was to be the subject of her mad schemes. There could be no doubt now, not after what she had told me. I had seen her work on human guinea pigs before in the concentration camps. I knew what she was capable of when it came to us homo sapiens. She was searching for the spell to turn me into one of the living dead, me and countless others. She would build an army of us to follow her. She would never have to hide from the old ones again.

"Have you found anything?" she asked as I continued my digging. It was just turning light outside, the hint of sunlight tinting the sky.

"Only this," I said, prying a small metal box out of the earth, where it had been buried for almost half a millennium. As I held it up

76

to her, she snatched it from my hands and tore it open despite the lock. Inside was a scrap of foolscap.

"What does it say?" she asked breathlessly, handing it to me. It was in Latin.

"My Latin is a little rusty," I replied, talking the scrap of paper and examining it. "It's easy enough to make out, though." I laughed at the absurdity of it.

"What's so funny?" she asked angrily.

"It says the Text of Belamarca was sent to this place long ago, but was removed when it was feared it would be found and used by the aborigines, who the French Jesuits were beginning to teach. A young Huron supposedly found the ancient scrolls and attempted to speak the forbidden words, but was apprehended before he could finish the bloody ritual, or so it says. The scrolls were taken back to France and handed over to the Holy See to be exorcized and destroyed once and for all. If it was for some reason not destroyed, it might still be hidden in the Vatican."

She made me take the ancient parchment with us as we left the building just as it was getting light. It is now hidden in the wall safe of our new home. She has not spoken of it since that night.

Last night, a warm summer evening, Rebecca insisted I accompany her on her rounds, as she prowled the streets of Montreal. It was just turning dark, around dinner time, eight PM, when we found ourselves in the old city again, near the cathedral of Notre Dame de Bonsecours. Despite the hour, the streets were crowded with tourists and locals alike, though I was somewhat surprised by all the unattended children, some no older than twelve or thirteen. Did their parents know where they were? There's a hungry vampire on the loose tonight.

A short distance ahead of us I noticed a little girl about twelve years old, apparently alone, with long blonde hair, wearing a skimpy outfit that looked much too small and sexy for one so young. She looked like an underage hooker. I sensed Rebecca watching her as well, appraising the prey.

Observing from across the boulevard, I saw the little street urchin stop to talk to a group of older boys, who were practicing their skateboard tricks on the square and being otherwise obnoxious to the passers-by. She was flirting with a tall boy who tried to ignore her as she practically danced in front of him. After a while, a group of older girls came by and they all left together, leaving our little waif alone again. Hurt and dejected, she walked slowly across the street toward us.

I continued pretending to study the architecture of the old Notre Dame Cathedral, but Rebecca caught her eye and smiled seductively, beckoning for the little girl to follow her. As if being cut out of the herd by a cunning lone-wolf, the little girl turned right and followed Rebecca down the dark alley next to the church, both intrigued and captivated by the beautiful woman.

As soon as I knew what Rebecca had in mind, I was determined to somehow stop her. If she wanted to hunt innocent children, she could do it without me. Why did she have to include me in her most depraved acts? I swore that it wasn't going to happen on my watch, not if I had anything to say about it.

I followed reluctantly as the little girl moved further down the dark alley, inviting her death. I was certain that if she continued down that road, she'd never emerge from it again. Even if I could get to her in time and somehow persuade her to follow me, I knew I'd never get her back to the street. At least there she'd have a fighting chance in the crowd. Rebecca was not likely to make a kill in public, but she was equally not likely to let us escape so easily. Then it occurred to me that perhaps there was some safety in the church. I knew that such a place was no safe haven from a really determined vampire, but I hoped that there'd be people inside and light, more than enough deterrents to dissuade Rebecca from her little game. There was much easier blood to be had tonight, and I was going to make sure this little girl's wouldn't be worth Rebecca's trouble.

The skimpily-clad child slowed down as she came to the end of the alley. I could see her clearly beneath the glare of the street lamp, and sensed Rebecca nearby waiting to pounce. In the few moments it took me to reach her, I formulated my plan. I knew Rebecca was somehow clouding the girl's mind, playing on her hurt feelings at being rejected and the need to be noticed and loved.

I saw a flitting motion in the shadows. Rebecca was coming for the girl. Quickly, I grabbed the child by the hand and led her into the church through a narrow side door that luckily was not locked. She pulled against me weakly in surprise.

"He, qu'est-ce que tu fais, monsieur? she yelled in French. "Allons y! Laisse-moi!"

We entered the dark interior of the church. To our right the altar glowed faint and blue, providing the only light in the otherwise darkened building.

To my dismay, the place was empty, not a tourist or penitent in sight. Not stopping to explain, I pulled the girl up a side aisle toward the rear of the church. Her feet scuffled against the marble floor as she resisted me and tried to get away.

"Stop it, stop it!" she screamed. "Help, help!"

I heard a door open and close somewhere behind us. It echoed through the empty cavern of the cathedral like a rifle shot. Rebecca had entered the building. A low buzzing began to vibrate between my eyes, hardly perceived at first, but building to a blinding crescendo that jarred my teeth.

'Bring her to me, Henri. Bring the child to me.'

With tears in my eyes, my feet heavy as lead, I continued to pull the now hysterical little girl up the aisle toward the rear of the building.

Another door opened and closed somewhere behind the high, blue-lit altar. "What's going on here?" someone asked in French. "Who's in here? What are you doing?"

Not bothering to answer, almost to the front doors, I continued to make my escape to the street, dragging the crying little girl behind me. I could hear Rebecca's silent tread, close now. I could almost feel her hot breath. I seemed to be running in molasses, in heavy slow motion.

Finally, without an instant to spare, I reached the massive wooden doors only to find them locked tight. I pushed on them futilely as Rebecca came up behind us.

"Bring her to me," she said audibly this time. "How dare you try to take her from me." The venom in those words stung me, freezing me in my tracks. Still I had the presence of mind to pull the young girl behind me, shielding her from the evil vampire who pursued us.

"You can't have her," I said as forcefully as I could. My voice came out in a whimper, shaking with fear. "Not this one."

"Oh, Henri, you dirty old man. Have you taken a fancy to this child? If I had only known how fond you were of children I would have brought you one sooner. Would you rather I take your child instead?"

With the mention of Emily, the air left my lungs as if hammered out by a hard blow. The bile rose in my esophagus making it impossible to breathe. I gasped and retched pitifully in the attempt. At that moment, a figure dressed all in black with a narrow white collar came up behind Rebecca.

"What's going on here? Who are you people? What are you doing in my church at this hour?"

It was all the diversion I needed to break Rebecca's spell. As she whirled on the newcomer with a hiss, I ran down the front of the building toward a small auxiliary door, hoping it would be open.

"Stop!" she yelled in a voice that almost froze what little blood I had left in my brain. Still, I willed my feet to move, now dragging the terrified girl on her fanny after me. Blessedly, in answer to someone's fevered prayers - most assuredly not mine, for I have long since forgotten how to pray - the small side door was unlocked and opened onto the still busy street.

The child's screams instantly attracted attention. To add to the commotion, I yelled, "Murder! Murder!" and pointed to the church. A crowd of good Samaritans soon surrounded the little girl. Others ran into the church. I disappeared down the street in the commotion and crossed the bridge to the new part of the city. I could hear Rebecca's screams of rage echoing in my brain.

I made my way furtively out of town and into the countryside to the west of the city. Determined to get away, I ran blindly across one field after another until after what seemed an eternity of running, I was in the mountains north of the city, surrounded by a dense forest of deciduous trees. The cool wind whispered through the leaves, a fresh-scented air from the north. For a moment I felt safe in their dark, green embrace. A bright full moon stood high in the sky, shining a silver light on the world.

Then a rustling in the underbrush, a twig breaking in the darkness, a shadow behind a tree, she was here. I ran farther, until my lungs were banging against my ribcage like a cup against steel bars. I fell to my knees, puking my meager supper onto the hard ground.

"Was it worth it, Henri?" she whispered from close by. "Was it worth loosing all the good things you had?"

"Yes," I answered defiantly. "I could not have lived with myself if I had let you kill that child. Why do you have to be such a sadistic witch? Can't you get by without the cruel murder of children?"

"No, not if it bothers you so much, dear Henri. Your concern for the little girl was very amusing, quite touching. Every now and then I need a little entertainment. Watching your blood pressure rise and your pulse race as you try to outwit me, just gives me such a laugh I can't resist it from time to time."

"I hate you, you evil monster. Why don't you kill me now and get it over with!"

She just stared at me and smiled with a malicious grin.

"Yes, hate me, Henri. Revile me. Curse me, if you will," she taunted.

After a moment's silence she asked, "Don't you want to serve me forever, Henri? Or do you want me take your daughter instead of the one you saved."

"No," I screamed, throwing myself at her feet. "Don't do that, mistress," I pleaded. "I'm sorry. I'll never cross you again, I promise, only please don't harm her. We will do whatever you say."

I was beside myself with fear and regret. As much as I wanted to be free from Rebecca's evil spell, free from her murderous lust, I feared I could not live without her. Not only would I soon die without her blood-potion, but I would whither like a rose cut from the vine without her presence, without her near me. My dilemma overcame me.

"Take me," I blurted. "Take me like you have taken all those others. Drink my blood. Suck my life. Mutilate me with your fangs. Set me free."

"Oh, my dear Henri, there's plenty of time for that. I had a lovely evening planned for us tonight, but you ruined it. You will have to pay for your transgressions."

"Yes Mistress, anything Mistress, just take me back. I'll do whatever you ask."

I groveled in the dirt before her, licking her filth and gore-covered boots. She threw something metal at my head, which cut me where it hit just behind the ear. It landed at my outstretched hands, shining faintly in the moonlight. It was a blood-splattered crucifix that must have belonged to the hapless priest. My days of relative comfort were about to end.

Chapter 12

I must have passed out, for when I awoke everything around me was pitch black. I was lying on the ground, but when I reached around me in the darkness I felt dirt. A sudden panic overwhelmed me. I yelled out involuntarily, and threw my arms up in the air. To my surprise there was nothing above me, and I was able to sit up, but as soon as I did, my hands hit something solid – the lid to my coffin. Rebecca had buried me alive!

I cried out in terror, "Help! Help! Where am I?" and banged on the wooden barrier above me. But no one answered. All was deathly silent. I went on screaming and banging for quite some time until I passed out again.

When I awoke, all was still blackness. I cried and moaned pitifully until I could groan no more. I was afraid I would use up the air, but there seemed to be air coming in somehow. I could feel it blow upon my face at times. There was water too, a small underground stream seeping through from somewhere above, dirty and putrid but drinkable. After a few days in the darkness without food, I even began to eat those insects and bugs unlucky enough to crawl on me. Then I began hunting for them.

As the days wore on, I cried to Rebecca to set me free, to let me out of this hideous hole. I pleaded with her to forgive me, but she did not respond. I do not know if she could even hear me. I could have been buried twenty-feet below the ground for all I knew. I could not even begin to budge the board above me.

At one point, when I was sinking into a pit of despair to match the pit I lay in, I had a sudden realization. Reaching into my pocket, I retrieved a pack of matches I had taken with me from a tavern I had stopped in earlier in the day. I could have kicked myself for not thinking of it sooner, but I had no recollection of them until that moment. In any case, there didn't seem much I could do with them, but I lit one anyway. Suddenly, the blackness receded and I could see my surroundings for the first time. I actually winced with the glare of the match as it flared up. Holding it aloft, I moved it along the sides of my prison until it flickered out, burning my fingers. I immediately lit another. Suddenly, the light was my friend. It made everything warm. I could see the water seeping in across the floor, and see a hose where the air was passing through. I even spotted a large black beetle, which I caught and ate. Another match allowed me to examine the large plywood lid that held me in the hole.

I turned onto my stomach and lit another, examining my confines in detail, probing for any means of escape, but there was nothing. I used up most of the matches in this way. I was loath to be plunged into the darkness again. I could just sit up, which I did and lit another. I had three more matches left. I searched the lid, pushing on it as I did, but there was no weakness or latches.

I lit the second to last match and searched my surroundings again, grabbing another bug, a spider this time. Then all went black. I sat in the darkness for quite some time wondering what to do. Should I save it for some later time, when I needed to find insects to eat, or should I use it now and relish the light just one minute longer. I lit the match.

Bathing in the brightness of the flame, I looked around one last time. Just as it was about to sputter out I noticed something long and shining lying in the corner. I reached for it and pulled it from the dirt. It was one of Rebecca's wax candles, the ones she used for her blood-bowl ritual. Quickly, just before my last match went out, I lit the candle and stuck it in the ground in front of me.

I yelled for joy, and almost jumped up. I had light, and this was no ordinary candle, but a blood-candle. I must keep one burning in her chamber at all times. They are twelve-inches long and an inch think, and burn very slowly, so that I only have to replace them once every seven days. The fact that she had left one in here convinced me she wanted me to live and would one day let me out. Although it was difficult to determine, I calculated I had spent about three days and nights in the hole. The candle kept me going for another seven days. Perhaps she would come for me then. I could only hope. It became a waiting game.

I spent my time catching insects and bugs, and trying to dig myself out. Then one night I woke up feeling something scurrying across my chest. It was a large rat, who had somehow gotten into my hole. It was the last thing I wanted to encounter.

I panicked, and trashed about the confined space as if I was on fire, almost knocking over the candle and putting it out. This terrified the rodent, who came at me with his teeth snapping. I grabbed it quickly by the scruff of the neck and sunk my own teeth into it. I could feel the blood flowing down my throat, much as it must feel for Rebecca. Hunger and savage hysteria overcame me and I tore into it like a ravenous dog, devouring it raw. It was just protean I needed to keep me alive, but the euphoria didn't last long.

I cursed that motherless daughter of a Babylonian whore, once called Ibihil, now called damnation, for what she had done to me. She is a scourge upon the land. She would let me out when she is good and ready, and only to serve her sick needs. Better I be buried alive, yet every fiber of my being cried out for liberation, for the light and the air. I would have done anything to be free, anything.

The candle was down to its last four days. I sat before it unmoving. I was cadaverous, my skin gray and wrinkled, my eyes sunken. My hair and teeth were falling out. My gums bled. My beard was long and scraggly. I no longer pounded on the lid or cried for help, but sat staring at the candle, dull and listless, waiting for it to go out

By the final day, when the candle was down to its last inch, I lie shivering and near starvation on the dirt floor of my pit. I didn't even bother slurping the muddy water that seeped into my grave. I was tired of suffering, tired of being tortured. I was sick of being a servant of the damned. I longed for peace and regretted I never had a chance to lead a normal life. Then the candle sputtered out and all was black silence again. I almost cried in despair. Then I heard the sound of a heavy weight being pulled back from the lid of my hole and it abruptly opened. The thin light of the basement flooded into my pit like a sunburst and almost blinded me.

I held my emaciated hands before my face. Rebecca was standing there at the lip of the crater encircled by the light like a goddess. I sat up and looked around. I had been buried in a four-foot deep hole, six-by-four feet in size, in the far corner of the mansion's cavernous basement.

"I have need of you, Henry," she said.

Yes, there have been many children since that night in old Montreal. The one that got away has been replaced with twenty just as young and innocent. I am slowly recovering from my ordeal. Most of my teeth have fallen out. My skin is pale and wrinkled from lack of sun and fresh air. I have grown thin and bent. My hair, which was thick and full, has fallen out. I now scare little children. This is the misery that is now my life after trying to interfere in Rebecca's quest for blood. Still, I would not change a thing of what I have done. At least I can live with myself, however despicable I have become.

The large grounds overlooking the city, not to mention the house itself, with no one to take care of them, have become overgrown with weeds and littered with debris. The neighbors must think the place deserted or inhabited by a recluse, for no sign of life is ever seen. Rebecca has withdrawn into her vampiric shell, a minimal existence of sleeping in the day and hunting a few hours at night once or twice a week, which could go on unchanged for centuries if she wanted it to. It's all the same to her. To me, however, it is a monotonous torment that makes me want to end it all, if only I could.

Rebecca used to range far and wide over the vast metropolis of Montreal with all its suburbs and boroughs to hunt, or deep into the northern regions among small villages and settlements. Now she only goes out for an hour at a time, just long enough to grab a streetwalker or nearby bum.

Slowly it occurred to me over the past few months of my rehabilitation, that this much-restricted lifestyle might be attributed to more than just the citywide alert caused by the incident at Notre Dame and the sudden increase in missing children. Perhaps Rebecca was hiding from something or someone. That thought, for some reason I couldn't explain, gave me hope and the strength to go on.

Then one day she summoned me upstairs, something she hadn't done since that night at the cathedral.

"I will have need of you soon, Henri," she announced when I entered. It was still partially light outside. "In my travels through the North Country I have sensed another presence, a power I can feel but cannot see, like a silent vibration. Sometimes it is strong, sometimes weak, fading out one minute only to come back in the next. At these times I seek to minimize the effect, only going where the presence is weakest or not felt at all, in far distant corners of the city."

So now I know why she has curtailed her movements, going out less often and later, and coming back sooner. She frequents only those places where the presence is least felt, an area which seems to be shrinking with each day. Something is out there that she is afraid of. What could it be? I fear we will soon have to move again, but Rebecca still does not trust me and I would have much to do.

I am tired of being a servant of a succubus. I never had a chance to live a normal life, not that what had been in store for me was that great, more than likely an early death from violence or deprivation on the cold streets of Berlin. Who knows, though, I might have made something of myself, done something with my life. Instead I support, aid, and abet this hideous creature of sorrow and ruin that haunts the night like a thief of souls.

There are no windows in her tomb, here below the big house on Mount Royal. It is mid-December. The cold seeps through the old stone and cement walls and chills my bones. Water and wind blow in from above, through the numerous cracks and crannies of the rotting floorboards that serve as a ceiling for her chamber. Rebecca sleeps in a large black sarcophagus of marble. It is her bed. At least the legends got that right.

I can tell she is agitated, like a cat not knowing whether to go or stay, even though she has no tail to twitch. I can hear it in the pitch of her voice, see it in the wariness of her eyes, sense it in her grim smile. Is this the end? Oh, if only it could be so.

I have become that thing in the movies, a caricature of a vampire servant as seen in the popular media, a loathsome object to be shunned and abhorred. Inside I am even worse, an abomination in the eyes of the Lord and all that's good, a sinner beyond redemption. Like Renfield, I am doomed to madness and death. Before I go, though, I am going to take this evil dame with me, so help me Satan!

Several weeks have passed, as well as a new year. Out of necessity more than forgiveness, Rebecca has loosened my shackles and allowed me to live again in the upstairs rooms. The house was in the worst state of repair, covered with dust and cobwebs. It was hard to explain after only a few months, as if time were somehow accelerated here. The electricity had long been turned off.

Then it happened. It was a cold, damp January afternoon. An early darkness had come long before the setting of the sun, which still lingered somewhere unseen and unfelt in the gray western horizon. The treeless limbs of the lifeless trees looked bleak and menacing against the darkening sky. Soon she would be up. I dreaded the look of those vacant eyes.

Because she needed me, Rebecca had been feeding me more of her miraculous blood-potion, which she had kept from me for many weeks. It was enough for me to gain my strength and weight back, although my teeth and hair, I fear, are gone for good no matter how much of her magic elixir I have. She issued no orders, not even what should be done about the house, nothing. I moped around and kept myself busy putting things in some order, waiting for her command like a good servant. As long as she didn't ask me to kill any children, I vowed to obey her. I did not want to go back into the hole.

The house grew darker, while the faint light outside lingered in the sky like a dog reluctantly dying by the side of the road. Suddenly, I saw her shadow silhouetted against the window, watching me like a black ghost, and twice as terrifying.

"Henri, I have need for you," she whispered, as if she were suspended right above my head.

"Whatever you say, Mistress," I answered in response.

"There is no time to explain, we must flee."

"I will make the usual arrangements, although I am not yet ready to venture outside. Our contacts will not recognize me in my present condition. I think with some…"

"Never mind that," she hissed. "There's no time. We must go now, tonight. It's coming."

"What? What's coming," I asked, confused, although I knew the answer to my question.

"He that was old before the birth of time," she answered enigmatically. "There is no time for the usual arrangements, Henri, no time. We must move before the night is out, before his power engulfs us. He knows why I am here and can't abide my living."

"What can he do to you, my Mistress, you who are so strong and invincible?"

"Don't be coy, Henri. Don't play games with me or ask me stupid questions. I need blood and I need it quickly. You will bring it to me, now. I want something full and rich. We may be on the road a long time before I can find another."

"Yes, Mistress, but it is not that bright outside. Why can you not go yourself?"

"Don't ask me anymore of your stupid questions, Henri! Must I tell you everything? Isn't it enough I have commanded you? Do it, now! Bring me a large man, young and strong. After I have fed, you must destroy everything."

"What about the paintings, all your fabulous clothing, the jewelry?"

"Everything!" she yelled, retreating into the basement.

Alone again, I pondered my mission. How was I to lure someone to this black house at this early hour, with this face? I sat at my dressing table and stared at myself in the mirror. This would take a lot of labor. I had to work fast. After shaving, I put on a wig I had purchased recently and inserted the false teeth I got at the same time. With make-up, the hair and the teeth, I could almost pass for human again, as I walked the wet streets of Montreal.

Staying off of the main avenues, I lurked around the parks and side lanes, quiet walkways not frequented by crowds of passers-by, where a guy could meet another friendly guy.

I didn't have to wait long. In the park at the foot of Mount Royal, not far from our house at the top of the hill, I spotted a tall young man standing by a bench smoking a cigarette. He noticed me approaching up the street. He wore a cowboy hat and cowboy boots and had on a stylish suede jacket. A long blond wisp of hair poked out from beneath his hat. He smiled and took a deep pull at his cigarette.

"Howdy," he said as I walked up slowly. "Is it always cold and damp like this around here?"

"It *is* January. This is actually a thaw," I replied in cultivated English tones.

"You from around here?" he asked.

"Yes. I live a short distance up the hill here. And you?"

"I'm from the States. Kind of relocating."

"Relocating?"

"You know, man, a change of scenery!"

"Oh, I see."

"You live alone?" he asked, eyeing me over the smoke of his cigarette.

"Well, not exactly. I take care of the house. The mistress is often away."

"Is the mistress home tonight?"

"No," I answered, looking him up and down.

"Do you like men?" he inquired without embarrassment.

"My standards are a little high, I'm afraid."

"Don't you like me? I look better without clothes. Anyway, it's what you don't see that counts."

"Hmm, I see. Do you by chance charge a fee for your services?" I asked.

"Hey, it's tough getting by in a foreign country. I gotta eat, you know."

"I'm sure you do, poor boy. I suppose with a bath and new clothes you might pass for handsome. Are you with the police?"

"No." He laughed. "Are you?"

"Most certainly not. How much do you charge?"

"500 bucks," he said. It sounded more like a question than a statement.

"That seems like a lot," I replied, not that it mattered. "You're really not my type." He was exactly Rebecca's type, 0-negative, mid-twenties, well-built, about six-foot one or two, with a rugged tough guy face softened by sky blue eyes.

"I'm worth it. Haven't had any complaints yet," he bragged.

"I'm sure. OK, young man, I'll tell you what. You take a bath and put on something decent, and you have a deal. I'll supply the bath and the clothing."

"OK, but you have to pay up front."

"Certainly," I said, sure he was going to try and rob me as soon as we were alone in the house.

I escorted the Midnight Cowboy up the side streets to my home, not much caring if we were observed or not. He lit another cigarette as we walked. I sensed his nervousness like an electric wire strung between us. I couldn't tell if it was because this was his first time, or because of what he was planning to do to me.

When we reached the house, he stopped in amazement. "Wow, some spread, man. Your old babe must be pretty rich, heh?"

"Yes, you could say that," I said, as I opened the door to the side foyer and invited him in.

We walked through the laundry room to the kitchen. The least used room in the house, the kitchen looks like it belongs in a summer resort that has been closed for a long winter. I could feel him sizing me up, weighing his chances against me, waiting for an opportunity. I didn't want to get him agitated or angry, that would foul his blood. Nor did I want to drug him or get him drunk. Rebecca wanted this one pure and unadulterated without unhealthy contaminates.

"This way," I told him, leading him up a rear staircase to the upper floors where the bathroom is. "You can shower here while I get you something to wear."

"Why don't you just pay me first," he insisted as we reached the top of the stairs. "I ain't doing nothing until you pay me."

"As you wish," I answered as we stood in the hallway. "Wait here."

"Why don't you turn on some lights, buddy? It's dark in here."

"I'll be right back."

I left him standing in the dark, while I went to the safe in the master bedroom closet. He followed as soon as I left the hall.

"You don't mind if I stick with you, do you, buddy?" he asked, as I knelt by the safe. "I wouldn't want to lose you in the dark."

Without saying a word I opened the safe and removed a wad of cash, $500.

"Here, are you happy now?"

"No," he replied scowling menacingly. The pleasant face with the innocent blue eyes turned demonic. With a snarl he yelled, "Get away from that safe, now."

He pulled a large pocketknife from his jean pocket and flipped it open. Then he poked the long blade at my face. I fell back on my behind trying to avoid it, kicking at him with my feet.

"Get away!" I yelled. Fear constricted my voice. In spite of my longing for release, the prospect of getting sliced open by this punk did not appeal to me.

"Don't hurt me. Take what you want, just don't hurt me!" I pleaded.

"Don't hurt me," he taunted. "You make me want to puke, you ugly little turd. You think I'm going to take a bath for you, you sick pervert. What are you, crazy?"

He swiped the blade a hairsbreadth from my nose. I snapped my head back to get away, hitting it on the opened closet door behind me.

"I should kill you now just for being such a creepy, stinking, little freak."

With that he jabbed the knife at my chest. I scurried away backward on my butt, moving my legs and hands like a frightened crab, as my attacker came at me threateningly with the knife.

"Take the money!" I yelled, in real panic. "Don't hurt me!"

My pleas and entreaties seemed to make him madder, to spur him on to greater heights of sadistic cruelty. There was death in his eyes.

I was starting to wonder where Rebecca was, how long she was going to wait before rescuing me and taking him. Then, just as he was upon me, about to stick me in the gut for the sheer joy of it, Rebecca came up behind him and swatted him on the side of the head with the palm of her hand. He fell senseless onto the floor.

"Bring him," she ordered, descending into the basement.

I grabbed the unconscious form by the ankles and pulled him along the hallway and down the back stairs. He landed in a tumble to lie sprawling on the basement floor. He was bleeding slightly from the right ear where Rebecca had hit him.

"Here," said Rebecca, throwing me a rope. "Tie him to the ceiling."

I threw the rope over a ceiling beam and looped the end tight around the still unconscious youth's ankles. I knew what she wanted me to do without being told.

I pulled the rope taut until his feet started to rise in the air. As I was raising him, he came to, moaning weakly as he gained consciousness. I continued to pull the rope around the ceiling beam.

"What? What's happening?" he cried, coming fully awake. He was completely in the air now, his arms dangling just off the floor. I pulled until his head was level with mine.

"What are you doing?" he yelled, twisting his body back and forth futilely. "Let me down, you fucking little creep!"

"Talk like that will get you nowhere," I answered.

Even though he had been ready to kill me not five minutes before, I was starting to feel sorry for him. I stepped aside without saying another word to reveal Rebecca in all her vampiric glory.

She was beautiful, radiant, wondrous to see in her chiseled nakedness. The upside-down, hanging cowboy stopped talking and stared dumbly at the vision, not knowing if it was real or make-believe. She was the last thing he saw.

She looked up at me as she sucked his blood with such a look of satisfaction and pleasure it made me wish it was me hanging there clutched in her arms. While he was still breathing, I cut his throat and let the rest of his blood drip into a flask, which Rebecca would use to quench her thirst on the road.

As she commanded, I doused the body, along with the entire room with gasoline and lit a match. Soon the whole house, with all its valuable furniture and artwork, was a blazing inferno. As we drove away I could see flames leaping out of the second story windows like circus performers.

We drove westward. We took no clothes, no pictures or mementos, none of the priceless paintings, nothing except the contents of the now empty safe and the clothing on our backs, some of which had her jewels hidden in them. For all we know, the authorities will blame the whole thing on satanic rites and drugs, and that would suit us just fine.

As it was, Rebecca lingered too long. Already the unseen presence that has been haunting her was near, drawn by the death frenzy like a prehistoric shark, angry that someone else was hunting in its domain. It also knows what she has found and what she is after.

It swooped in behind us just as we left. Jumping on the top of the SUV, it started pounding on the roof, making deep dents in the metal. At one point it almost punched through. Then it started ripping off the roof. I yanked the vehicle from right to left across the road at fifty miles per hour, trying to shake it off, and almost went off the road. Finally, in my mad attempt to elude our attacker, I swerved off the highway and over a ditch, flying across an embankment and onto a field, where we almost tipped over. Whatever was after us flew off into the darkness as the car bucked beneath it. Accelerating over the rough turf, I made it back to the road and sped away.

"Drive on, fool," yelled Rebecca needlessly as misshapen things whirled and thundered behind us like storm clouds. "Faster! Don't stop for anyone. Drive on!"

Chapter 13

I drove all night and through the next day, ever westward, until I could drive no longer. I had no idea where we were or where we were going. All I knew was that I had to keep driving. We had to get away.

We lived on the run, off the land much as we had during the war years in Europe not so long ago. But where before we could hide our carnage in the surrounding chaos and destruction of the war it now stood out clearly for all to see, with no furnace in which to hide the evidence.

She supped on motorists we happened by on the road or on the inhabitants of farmsteads sprinkled along our route. Single men or women, whole families at a time, it doesn't matter to Rebecca. She's an equal opportunity vampire. Before long there was a trail of blood-drained bodies in our wake, a path even a blind man could follow let alone the Royal Mounted Police.

Some inner purpose compelled her to move on even when there was no longer anyone pursuing us. It was as if she were on a quest - for the lost scroll perhaps?

We moved westward, staying close to the border, past cities like Ottawa, Winnipeg, and Regina, through Calgary, a cow-town that looked like it had just been unpacked. The landscape grew steadily whiter as we drove west and upward through the Canadian Rockies, until we were surrounded by a wintry landscape of evergreens and high, white-topped mountains.

We stopped in the western part of Alberta, at a place called Banff Springs, where Rebecca finally allowed us some respite and rest. It was the first time in weeks we felt safe. Using some of our cash, we rented a chateau on Lake Louis, a bright-red building wedged between pine-covered hills and the mirror surface of the lake. There, Rebecca feasted on well-fed skiers, while I established new identities for us.

Just when it seemed that things were getting better, our past caught up with us in the form of the Royal Mounties They had traced the series of grisly murders across the country to this very spot. They didn't know who they were after yet, but they knew whoever it was, was more than likely in this area. When tourists and skiers started turning up missing or drained of blood, things began to get dicey. It was time to move on.

Dumping the SUV for a secondhand Winnebago, we headed northwest toward Alaska, which we reached after a leisurely week's drive that brought us through Kicking Horse Pass to British Columbia and the Yukon Territory, an un-peopled wilderness of towering mountains and wide empty plains. Too bad Rebecca couldn't drink bear blood! She would have had a feast. From there we traveled to the frontier town of Whitehorse and across the border into Juneau.

With our new identities we had little trouble crossing into the U.S. again. Creating false identification is an extremely useful skill I've learned over the years of traveling with Rebecca, although it was made doubly difficult this time by the circumstances and the lack of readily convertible funds. As usual, however, I managed - nothing like a hundred years of lying and conning and eluding the authorities in as many different countries to keep you on your toes.

The further north we went, the scarcer and more difficult it was to procure her food supply, a farm here, a camp there, a tourist in one place, a local in another. At times she went days without feeding, something I have seldom seen her do before. It always leaves her sullen and angry, even compared to her usual dark moods. She rarely smiled or talked to me, and always I had to abet her and watch. I became her snare, her net, a trap for the unwary, as evil and depraved as she.

I longed for the days when we had been pursued, when she had been too busy with the thing chasing us to bother about me or even to kill. To see the fear in her eyes was truly thrilling. To know that there is something out there that can end her fiendish existence gives me hope. Then why am I running? Because I have no choice, I am a slave. At least my beloved Emily is safe for the time being, while we are on the move.

I often wonder if I could ever leave Rebecca, for as much as I hate her and detest the things she does, I am drawn to her. Rebecca is all I think about, the only image I hold in my mind. I do not even know what my child looks like, but my terrible mistress's visage is burned into my brain. I dream about her at night, and fantasize about her during the day.

How alluring she is, especially at the moment of her most dangerous, all that power trembling beneath the surface of her velvet skin. The need in those eyes, the plea on those ruby lips is all I live for. I long to serve her, to give her pleasure, but oh, how she tortures me. The more I love her, the more she turns the knife of my pain. The more she scorns and ridicules me, the more I love her. Oh, she torments me so.

She needed me those first few days as we fled the ancient vampire whose lair we had trespassed upon. If only I could bring those moments back. If only we could be consumed together in a funeral pyre, lying in each other's arms amongst the flames. Only then could I find peace.

We are now in the most heavily populated area we could find, in a rented cabin in the hills above Juneau. Times are bad here and unemployment has already forced many to leave the area. They are the lucky ones. I know our days are numbered, that it's only a matter of time before the authorities trace the murders to this place following the unmistakable trail of corpses. It won't be soon enough for me.

I hate Alaska, the interminable cold, the always damp, chilled air, the biting wind that sweeps down from the snow-capped mountains, ice everywhere. I hate every stinking permafrost bit of it. I'm tired of living like a hermit in the middle of nowhere. I long for the warmth of the sun and human company even though I would be shunned by the most depraved of humanity.

Life is simple here. We buy the food and supplies we need by catalog. FedEx delivers it every other week. My main task is to provide wood for the stove and to keep the fire going, and of course, watch over her box during the day. She keeps it in a tiny shed under the cabin where there's barely room enough to stand.

She has been feeding on the inhabitants of the city below, bringing them to the cabin where I can dispose of them in the oversized hearth. The charred and cindered bones I bury in the woods, under the waist-high snow. All in all, it's a less than satisfactory arrangement. Most of her food consists of oilmen and other frontier types, who she lures to the cabin with promises of sex and drugs.

I knew it was too good to last. It hasn't taken long for the long arm of the law to reach us in the form of two state police who arrived this morning to ask some questions. It seems a rowdy, who worked for one of the local oil companies, had bragged about a girl he had met, and about what he was going to do to her, shortly before he disappeared. He had mentioned something about a cabin in the mountains above town, so they were making a routine check of the area. Would I mind answering some questions?

Fortunately, Rebecca ate out the previous evening, and there were no bones smoldering in the fireplace on this day, or I would have had quite a bit of explaining to do. As it was, I had all I could do to sputter out answers to their innocuous questions. With my appearance – I did not have my teeth in or my hair on - and halting manner, my darting eyes and nervous behavior, I'm sure I've become the number one suspect in their missing person case.

I told them my name was Mister Henri Bouchard, and that I lived here alone. I had recently moved up from Seattle and planned to do some writing, fishing, and hunting in that order. No, I had never heard of the name they mentioned, nor seen the faces they showed me. They seemed to linger a little longer than necessary, and looked around a little more carefully than they needed to. One of them actually commented on the size of the hearth and the nice blaze I had going. Fortunately, it was just wood this time.

As they left, they took careful note of my vehicle and the yard. Neither of them smiled or waved. I got the distinct impression I was under suspicion. I made sure they were gone, following their vehicle down the snow-packed drive and watched from above as they descended the hillside into town. Then I ran to the shed beneath the house and threw myself on her plain wooden casket.

"They're here, Mistress. They have found us, I am sure. We must depart." I swooned over her box, lying atop it like a prostrate lover.

"What should I do? What shall I do?" I implored, tears spilling from my eyes.

While still on top of the casket, I started moving the plywood lid, sliding it from side to side with my arms, as I humped up and down to counter the weight, until at length I fell in on top of Rebecca, who lay there naked like a sculptured piece of marble. I kissed her still cold form.

"Mistress, oh Mistress," I moaned, overcome with anguish and longing.

Suddenly I was flung up and out of the box with a force so strong it sent me flying across the small cluttered room, where I landed with a crash amongst the hoes and rakes and shovels used to clear the land during the warmer months.

"Off me, you oaf!" she hissed, with a voice like a snake, all teeth and tongue. "How dare you touch me. Don't you think I know what's going on? I don't need to hear your sniveling whine. Do what you are told, when you are told. Do you understand?"

"But mistress, they…"

"Be gone!"

"Yes, Master, as you wish."

I was crushed and left the cabin to walk the streets in the town below. When I came back later that evening, she was gone.

Several days have passed. She left that night and has not returned. I have become frantic with worry. Has she left me, abandoned me to my fate? Am I no longer of use to her? Have I finally offended her once too often? I should be happy I am finally free, but I dread the thought of living without her. What's to become of me? My protector is gone.

The police returned in the middle of the night, this time with a search warrant. They spent extra time nosing around the fireplace and grounds, using large search lights to illuminate the scene. They must have found something, for they cuffed me and took me away in the back of a van without so much as a merci. I have sat in a cell in the Juneau jail for three days now.

This is it. This is the end of the line. What else is there to tell about except my brief incarceration, my speedy trial, and my expedient execution? What else is there to convey to the world except my guilt, my infamy, and my shame. The worst of it is I'm mad for the lack of her, going through a withdrawal that makes heroin addiction seem like a wiener roast. I need to see her again. If not, I will go mad, madder than even I have been these past hundred years.

Then tonight I awoke from a dreamless sleep to see her standing by the door of my cell, looking in at me like the grim-reaper coming to take me away.

"I have need of you, Henri. Come."

With a flick of her wrist, the steel door flew open with a clang. I thought the noise would wake the guards, but only the prisoners locked up with me at the time stirred. They clamored for attention, wanting to know what was going on. Seeing what was afoot, they all wanted their freedom as well. They got their freedom all right, freedom from their worries, freedom from all their ties to the world. So did the hapless men and woman who pulled guard duty that fateful night.

Soon I was following Rebecca's rapid strides through the starless, blustery night, as she headed for the pier and a large cruise ship anchored there like an oversized beached whale. I trailed her up the gangplank, passed the courteous steward, and into our double-occupancy suite below deck.

It has all happened so fast, I'm not sure if I'm not still dreaming. She has said nothing since breaking me out of jail. Her mouth is still wet and red from her recent feeding frenzy, at least half a dozen robust men and one woman, dispatched like tuna in a can without so much as a batted eyelash. Her power and lust for blood still astounds me, even after all these years.

Rebecca has booked us on a slow boat to the South China Sea, to Singapore, our new home and feeding ground. Hopefully here, we will be far from the prying eyes of the Canadian and American authorities - and ancient vampire bullies.

Day after day we have traveled with no land in sight. The seas warm imperceptibly as we sail slowly southwestward toward China. Because of the confines of the ship, she's supped sparingly from the two thousand or so guests and crew. She's careful to target only lone travelers. Those who will be least missed at the evening table or shuffleboard court. Or crew members after we stop at port, where it's suspected they jumped ship. In this way, she's eaten herself across the wide blue Pacific with little notice.

Wherever we stop, at an island or port, she disembarks to hunt on land, Oahu, Manila, Taipei, until finally the city of Singapore stands sparkling in the distant horizon, over the languid green water of the South China Sea. I gaze across it at the far shores surrounding us - the hazy coasts of Kampuchea behind and to the right; the dark, brooding shoreline of the Malaysian peninsula straight ahead; the tangled forests of Borneo on the left; in the hazy distance through the straights, the island of Indonesia. All these throngs of people - Chinese, Malays, Thais, Indonesians, Indians, Europeans - all the races jumbled together in one huge heap, all that blood waiting to be harvested. These should be happy hunting grounds for Rebecca.

Upon disembarking in Singapore we rented a car and drove up into the fast disappearing jungle. Over the years the city has encroached upon it more and more, until it's now nothing but a patch of green clinging to the ancient hills. Here Rebecca has purchased a mountain villa to spend her days, using a small portion of the gems and precious jewels she has acquired over the millennium and still carries with her hidden in her clothing.

Being one whose sole source of food is human, it's natural that Rebecca would seek the centers of civilization for her pursuits. Constantinople, Rome, London, and Paris, New York, and Berlin, these are the places you will find her haunting the streets at night. Boston and Montreal are about the littlest cities she can hunt in and remain undetected. Anywhere smaller, as we have seen, her depravations soon attract attention. As we have also noted, stronger creatures, more ancient vampires that seem to resent her presence with deadly malice, prowl these centers of humanity as well. Maybe here in the Far East things will be different.

We arrived at the villa just after dark. Rebecca, veiled and shaded, was well-fed from a cabin boy she left drained in the cargo bay of the docked ship. Even in the darkness, the splendor of the place is apparent. Rebecca has spared no expense this time, and is obviously intent on re-establishing herself in style. Her search for the Text of Belamarca is apparently on hold, for she has not spoken of it since we left Montreal.

The grounds of the house are large and well-tended, with gardens of wildly colored flowers and terraces of lily-topped pools. Tall palms and stately fruit trees dot the landscape. It's truly a refreshing sight after the harsh, barren land of Alaska and the monotonous infinitude of endless ocean. Not that this sort of thing has any effect on Rebecca, whose only concern is her food supply.

The dwelling itself is palatial, larger than anything we've lived in to date, probably due to the value of the dollar in these poverty-stricken lands. Surrounded by palm trees, it has pinnacled towers topping three terraced stories of teak siding and white masonry. Each of the floors is separated by a light tiled overhanging roof. The house is a mix of Far Eastern and Western architecture, designed to appear in some House and Garden magazine. Inside, hardwood floors are polished to a high sheen and covered expansively with large oriental rugs. Bamboo and teakwood fixtures and Chinese artwork adorn the walls and pillars, while soft lights, hidden in ceiling and wall panels, create a warm glow. Beneath the house is a stonewalled basement finished with the same fine-grained wood and lighting found in the upstairs rooms. In a darkened corner is her bed of bronze, a gilded coffin festooned with oriental designs and inlaid ivory finishing. A black velvet pillow adorns its otherwise bare interior.

A huge coal furnace burns in the middle of the room, hungry for human bone and skin. It will have plenty if Rebecca has her way.

It looks like things are about to return to normal, if you can call anything about Rebecca normal. Our situation has taken a turn for the better in the board game that is Rebecca's evil life. Or is this just the calm before the storm, before the forces gathering around her will send us fleeing from this place to the next until we have circled this puny globe? How far must I travel before I find rest?

Chapter 14

Singapore is a concrete jungle of towering office buildings and sumptuous hotels, with miles of highways, overpasses, and cable cars. Most of the inhabitants live in its high-rise apartments, where Rebecca does some of her hunting. The deepwater harbor full of sampans and junks, where she prowled those first few nights after our arrival, is the second busiest in the world and her favorite hunting ground. Every commodity you can imagine is available in this duty-free paradise, from antique Chinese porcelain and crocodile skin handbags, to the latest electronic equipment and French designer shirts, not to mention the exotic cuisine. Yes, the food supply in Singapore is plentiful and good.

Rebecca has her pick of the cream of the city's elite, the choicest bloodlines, the finest blood types. She travels far and wide over the land, and they travel far to see her. She's pawned herself off as a world-renowned masseur and our place as a resort. People come from around the world to literally die in her arms. Not all of them, of course, that would be bad for business. Just those that come via the advertisements she runs in the sleazy magazines, the ones bought by single men with plenty of cash and a penchant for the very kinky, who no one will miss except some waitress in a crowded city bar. They get the exotic thrills they're seeking and a whole lot more. From what I can tell they all die happy, with wide stupid grins on their faces. Oh, how I envy them, as I stack their limbs and throw them into the incinerator.

I'm beginning to get some of my color back, and am starting to look almost human again. I run the house like an oriental butler, efficiently, with an imperious manner and superior attitude. I'm even contemplating the joys of the flesh again with one of the young Melanesian beauties that grace the city. Male or female, at this point, after a hundred years of looking on flesh, it hardly matters.

This evening as I was unpacking some of her recently acquired art treasures, while Rebecca was watching the city below from our terraced balcony, I could not help reproaching her for leaving me for so long in Alaska. The pain still stings me when I think about it, which I often do.

"I suppose you have no more need of me now, Mistress, now that we are out of danger."

"I have told you many times that I have need for you still. Do not make me repeat myself or I will grow tired of you."

"Have you not already grown tired of me to treat me so?"

"You mean Alaska? I needed a diversion. You weren't in jail for long. You've been in worse places and could still be again if you cross me."

"Who was after us back in Montreal? Why are they after you?"

"Why must you ask such stupid questions?"

"I have a right to know."

"You have no rights." She said this with an expression that chilled me. "But I will tell you just the same. The old ones, the Espiritus, cannot abide me. They resent my beauty and my youth. They are very powerful, and there is more than one of them. They hate me."

"Why? Why do they hate you so, Mistress?"

"They are jealous. They want to keep all the power for themselves, but I have other ideas."

"Is that why we are here in this strange place?"

"I thought you liked it here, Henry. It's so nice and warm, and you complained so about the cold."

"Yes, but not this hot, where you sweat just sitting in the shade. I must have changed my suit six times since unpacking these crates this morning."

"You complain like an old woman, Henry. Now be a good boy and finish unpacking my new trifles. There is something I must do. Don't wait up. I won't be back until morning."

With that, she's gone.

Our lives are ruined. It has all happened so fast that I hardly have time to recount it. One minute everything was fine, the next the sky has fallen. Where do I begin?

It was New Years Eve, the first year of the new millennium, the fourth for Rebecca, but the first for the rest of us humans. Being one of the local notables, with her world-renowned resort, Rebecca was invited to an exclusive masked ball at the top of the Singapore Towers. The spiked, twin buildings rising into the clouds over the city, is one of the tallest in the world. This night it would be host to a vampire.

She wore a short red devil's outfit that showed off her well-shaped form, with a pointed tail of velvet and red velvet horns. A fitting costume indeed! I drove her to the party and sat at the bar with the other chauffeurs, sipping cognac and champagne compliments of the house.

Rebecca held this night special, as each turn of the 1000-year mark was a day of remembrance of her ancient past, her long lost humanity and youth. She had fasted for the last few nights. The bloodlust was upon her heavily. She was hunting someone special this evening, someone whose rare blood would stimulate her as once a millennium it could.

She worked the crowd, sniffing each suitor in turn, each partner she danced with, to see if he might be the one. She haunted the lady's room, smelling the stalls as the women sat, or sniffing them as they stood in close circles gossiping. Then she saw him, tall and handsome, dancing with a slim blonde who looked like she was about to faint in his arms. The woman's blood seemed drained from her face as she clung to him and he twirled her around the dance floor.

I watched as Rebecca seduced the young man, dressed like a character from some *Gone with the Wind* novel, a cross between Rhett Butler and Zorro. They were soon dancing. He was obviously under her spell, and why not? Rebecca was the most beautiful woman in the room, beyond compare even in her silly devil getup. They glided across the dance floor, the center of attention.

At midnight all the lights went out, and balloons dropped from the ceiling, while the band plays suld lang syne. With the strobe light flashing above the dance floor, things seemed to move in slow motion. Everyone was hugging and kissing, lifting their glasses. I watched Rebecca and the handsome man embrace, as if to kiss. The man's grin looked odd under the flashing lights, as if his teeth had been chiseled. His eyes had a sinister, almost demonic look. I sat up in alarm and stared harder.

It appeared that Rebecca was struggling, trying to get out of the man's embrace, which seemed odd to me. I had never seen her so agitated before. Her strength is overwhelming, but now she was struggling and in distress. I wondered how this could be. Suddenly there was a whirling motion in the middle of the dance floor as people went flying in all directions, as if they were being bowled over. A whirl of flashing colors moved across the floor and crashed into the wall, knocking over people, tables, and chairs in the process. Men yelled. Women screamed. Yet it was hard to see exactly what was going on. The commotion moved to the entrance, where the doors blew opened and slammed shut again.

Everyone stood in shock. Some were just beginning to get up. Others went to assist the injured. I rushed to the dance floor looking for Rebecca among the scattered bodies, but she was not there. No one seemed to know what happened. Some thought lightning had struck, others that it was some kind of mini-burst. A few thought there was a fight, but no one knew for sure.

I was frantic with worry, and ran out of the room and down the wide hall looking for her. Seeing a piece of red cloth from Rebecca's costume stuck in the stairwell door, I opened it and rushed down the stairs. It was over 100 stories above the ground, thousands of steps, yet I plunged on.

There must have been a struggle at some point, for I found strands of her hair and a fingernail on the stairwell, along with another patch of cloth that belonged to her red costume, but no Rebecca. I ran on, following her telepathic orders as best I could with the static interference buzzing in my head.

After what seemed like an eternity, I reached the street, and burst out among the New Year's celebrators. People were yelling and singing. Fireworks were going off over the towers. But Rebecca was nowhere to be found. I made my way through the crowds, to the side streets and then the outer districts of the city, through patches of jungle, to our villa in the hills. All the while, I expected to get some sort of telepathic command from her, some kind of psychic message, but there was nothing. At least the incessant buzzing between my eyes had stopped.

I found my way back to our villa in the hills, but Rebecca was not there. The place had been ransacked. Her treasure of ancient books and manuscripts, rare paintings and personal mementos had been strewn across the floor as if a tsunami had swept through the place. I raced from room to room calling her name. All thought gone, my mind was a complete blank.

"Mistress, Mistress, where are you?" I cried. "What's happened?"

A strange voice answered that froze my blood.

"Your Mistress is not here, puny one. She has left you to your fate."

Out of the shadows of her boudoir stepped the man from the dance floor. His presence filled the room like a huge shadow. I shrank back against the wall, but could not move a muscle.

"Who are you? What do you want?" I stammered.

"I will ask the questions here," he roared, stepping forward and seeming to grow in size.

I cringed against the wall, crouching in submission.

"What did she find in old Montreal?" he demanded. "Why is she here?"

"I do not know, Master," I answered instinctively in fear. "I am only a humble servant who obeys my Mistress's commands. She tells me nothing."

I tried to block my mind as I had trained myself to do, but felt his thought probing my psyche like icy tentacles.

I had to get away or perish.

"Oh, where is my Rebecca now," I cried in distress. "Why has she forsaken me yet again?"

I had once thought to use her adversaries against her for my own purpose, to free myself. Now they were to be the cause of my destruction. It was only fitting. At least I would finally be released.

"Your mind is a void, puny one," he said. "She has drained you of more than blood, I see. Do you know that it is taboo to speak the ancient words, to utter the sacred scripts of Ur? Even to say their name is to court destruction. Ask Belamarca what befell him. I, Marco, the youngest of the undead should know. There will be none after me, puny one. We will make sure of that. Where is Ibihil of Mari?"

"I do not know, Master. Please spare me."

"It does not matter. We will find her soon enough. Now I will take care of you, you little servile, breast-fed dog."

He took another step toward me, his large canines clearly visible in the gloom. As he did, there was a rush, as something smashed through the bedroom window and crashed into my assailant. It was Rebecca in all her fury.

She and the stranger banged from wall to wall like cyclonic billiard balls, smashing furniture and plasterboard. As they fought, several Malays with machetes and pikes rushed into the room to help her, followed by several large, fierce dogs. They threw themselves on her adversary, distracting him with a savage but fruitless attack.

It was all the time I needed to gain my feet and make it out of the villa. As I did, I heard the groans and cries of her men dying at her beck and call. Soon her mental commands were ringing in my ears again, telling me what to do. The incessant buzzing in my head began again as well. I made my way, half blind with fear, down the hillside to the city below.

In the morning, I headed to a car rental at the edge of town where I am now, still in my evening clothes. I'm soaked with perspiration and grimy from my rush down the jungle paths.

Again, our life is in ruins.

Following her instructions, I've rented a jeep and driven north out of town along the Serangoon road, past Indians in saris and dhotis, across the causeway over the Straight of Batan to the mainland. Here I wait, in a little village just north of the city.

She arrived, haggard and bleary-eyed, just before dawn.

We are on the run again. Worse than that, Rebecca has been forced to go without blood after days of fasting, and is weak from her struggle with the other vampire. She seemed to hold her own against him, unlike the earlier time in Montreal. Still, she had been forced to flee at the end, when all her minions - weak-willed men and mongrel dogs - lay dead about her. She found she could not subdue her adversary, nor he her, as neither could get the upper hand. It was all I needed to get away. She had saved me!

She needs some sustenance soon or she will get sick, and a sick vampire is something you don't want to be around. We have been forced to leave everything behind this time, even what was left of the cash and jewels, years of collecting and accumulating gone in a flash.

Although Rebecca is able under extreme circumstances to hunt during the day, what fare she has been able to obtain this morning, after our desperate departure from Singapore, was poor and sick, a far cry from the feast she had planned for the new millennium. However, there was little choice.

We're headed north now along the torturous western coast of Malaysia toward Pinang. From there we hope to either make our way northward to Bangkok or seek passage across the Andoman Sea to India, whatever Rebecca in her great wisdom decides. The past few hours, as we've traveled along the highway to Kuala Lumpur, have been one long miserable exodus. My sweat-drenched clothes stick to me, as does the odor rising from Rebecca's hot, rancid breath. The buzzing between my eyes grows weaker as we move north, only to be replaced by the constant buzzing of flies and mosquitoes, as we move to whatever fate awaits us.

Chapter 15

Weeks have passed since we fled from our home in Singapore. After reaching Pinang with no funds and limited means of obtaining more in the time needed, we made our way across the Andoman Sea and the Indian Ocean, begging, bribing, and stealing passage on steamers, trawlers, and whatever other bilge-filled barge that would transport us. We sailed from one hellhole to another along the southern Indian coast, then across to the Red Sea and up to Cairo, Egypt, where we arrived hungry and tired a short time ago.

Egypt, the land of the pyramids, has apparently been her destination all along. We have been pushing on as if we had an urgent message to deliver, Rebecca not stopping more than a day or two to feed during our headlong journey. Now that we are here, however, all I do is sit and wait, while she pursues her quest for whatever perverted thing it is she searches for. Alas, I can guess all too well what it is.

My terrible beloved has snatched me from the jaws of destruction, risked her life for mine. The thought fills me with elation and ecstasy, as if a long-sought unrequited love had suddenly given me her hand. Since that night, however, she has given me nothing but scorn and contempt.

Without our usual funds, we've had to make do with the dingiest of hovels, down in the poorest district, the teeming slums that hug the muddy Nile. Besides crawling with vermin, they throng with human blood, most of it young and sickly.

The slums of Egypt abound with people of all shapes and descriptions, all of them destitute or otherwise on the edge of survival. Many of them are children much like I was in old Berlin. It is a rich hunting ground, where many can disappear and not be missed.

I sit in our small, dank Cairo room, in the mud-brick house we call home, waiting for her to return. Her nightly travels gain us enough cash to live on, which she steals from her victims after she siphons their blood. It's a long way, however, from the fortune she left behind. It will take a lifetime to amass all that she has lost.

The city's abuzz with rollicking street life day and night, as fifteen million souls move on their appointed rounds, in honking cars, stalling buses, zigzagging bicycles, or on sandaled feet, in Arab dress and Western clothes.

This evening Rebecca summoned me and led me through the crowded streets to the cool, quiet confines of a citadel just below the hills at the eastern edge of the city. From there the great metropolis spread out below us across the Nile to the grand pyramids beyond, invisible in the western desert through the darkened, polluted sky. Hundreds of mosques thrust their thin, ornate minarets into the star-filled darkness, over rooftops crowded with peoples' laundry and open-air fires. How fitting it is that Rebecca would roam amongst the temples and tombs of these ancient parts, so unchanged through the centuries.

She stood beneath a leafy tree on an outlook where we gazed at the view, beneath the high walls of an old fort. Decorated with mysterious calligraphy, it enclosed a spacious courtyard, where a fountain played softly in the center. It was deserted for the evening of tourist and groundskeepers alike.

"These have been difficult times, Henry," she told me. "I have been hounded and persecuted even though I have done nothing wrong. My only crime is being born too late, of being young when others are so old. I have had to give up all that I love, my home, my treasures. Now I have nothing, nothing."

"You have me, my Mistress."

She did not reply, ignoring me completely as if I was not there.

"You must have done something wrong," I continued, emboldened and angered by her silence.

"No more than being born. No, I have done nothing wrong, yet. But if they keep pushing me so, anything may happen. In any case, who are you to judge me?"

"You said you would release me, that my time was up. Then you said you had big plans for me. Which is it to be, Mistress? Tell me."

She answered my question with one of her own.

"Do you know who that was back there in Singapore? What did he tell you?"

"I don't remember. It was all so confusing. I was in a state of shock. Everything was happening so fast."

"Did he mention the Text of Belamarca?"

"Yes, he said something about the Scroll of Ur and that you would never get it, about it causing great destruction."

"It is only *their* destruction it will cause. That's why they don't want me to have it. That's why they are after me."

"And you aim to find it, do you Mistress?"

"Yes, with your help."

"And then?"

"Then we will see."

"No wonder they want to kill you. No thanks, Mistress. I will not do it. I will not participate in your crazy scheme. What you are talking about must be terrible beyond all reckoning if even these evil old things object. It would be madness. They would only destroy us. Remember how it was like in Montreal. We were running for our very lives!"

She stood staring at me, not saying a word, her mouth smiling but her eyes steely-cold. She seemed to be tearing me apart in her mind, enjoying the agony of my death. It was a look that told me she would just as soon rip my head off and drink my blood as look at me.

"So, who was that back there?" I asked, getting back to the subject. "Was he one of the old ones?"

"No, just the opposite. That was Marco, the youngest of our kind."

"I thought you were the last, that's why all the old ones hated you."

"They all have their own territories, the Old Ones. I have none. I can go nowhere without treading on one of their domains. Marco is their lackey. But I will run and be shunned no more, once I learn that secret."

"Tell me about this Marco, Master. I should know."

"Yes, Henry. You should know. There is one younger than me, created during the middle-ages by the great scholar-sage Belamarca, using the very text which we seek. Marco's existence nearly spelled the end of the Espiritus, for it caused a bloody war that went on for ages and cost measureless misery and sorrow."

"And that's a bad thing? Your kind deserves no less."

"My sentiments exactly, Henry, but this time I will prevail. I am done running. You are no ordinary human. You have my blood-potion in you, which has kept you young and strong all these years. I have taught you much. You will make a very powerful servant, a very formidable ally. And you will be only the beginning. Together we will rule the world. But first you must prove your loyalty."

"Master, how can you doubt my loyalty after all these years?"

"There is one last test, but we need not talk about it now. We have more pressing concerns.

"They will destroy us, Master."

She laughed that hideous shriek of hers and looked at me with demonic glee.

"You are mad!" I cried again in despair.

"Yes, I am mad. Mad at having to run like a frightened child whenever one of them turns up. Mad at being a pawn when I am a Queen. Look at me, Henry. Was I not born to rule?"

She seemed to grow in size. Her shadow filled up the room.

"You rule me, Mistress, and any humans you deem not worthy to kill. Must you rule the world?"

"Yes, and you will be my tool."

"I'll die first."

"You have no choice."

She was right, of course. What could I do against this super-human monster? She had my daughter. I had to bide my time, learn what I could. Perhaps turn it somehow to my advantage.

"Yes, Mistress, what could I have been thinking. You have answered my fondest wish. I grew faint of heart for a moment, but I see now that this is my destiny. Thank you, my most beloved Mistress, thank you for this great honor."

I threw myself at her feet, kissing and caressing them with my tears.

"Forgive my momentary lapse. You can count on me," I assured her, feigning affection.

"These are perilous times, Henry. Until we find the scroll we will be vulnerable. From your research, we know it was taken back to Rome, but there the trail ended. I have picked up the thread of something even greater these past few days, but we must work fast, for the old ones are close."

"It is here, in the citadel where Belamarca was imprisoned during the Crusades, while he masqueraded as a great French knight. It was here that he first learned of the Text of Ur and its immense power, the key to immortality that men have been searching for since time immemorial. He made a copy, which now lies somewhere in Rome, but the original is purported to still be here. It is hidden in the dungeons below. Come, follow me."

I followed as she entered a stone blockhouse that stood in the far corner of the square, easily opening the foot-thick steel doorway that blocked our path. Following her down a flight of circular metal stairs, with only an occasional light bulb to guide our descent, we came upon a long, narrow stone tunnel that sloped gently downward into blackness. Here she lit the lantern she had been carrying and led me deeper into the bowels of the ancient citadel.

We soon came to a wooden door, half-eaten by worms and termites that had been dead a thousand years. An ancient bolt still locked it. Rebecca snapped it with ease.

"It is here, in Belamarca's cell. Come," she whispered.

"How do you know? It was not I who gave you this information."

"Marco told me when it looked like I was getting the better of him. But his superiors were close by and I had to let him go. Before I did, I made him squeal long enough to tell me of Belamarca's cell. It was here he is said to have made his translation of the sacred Text of Ur."

She led me into an empty, ten-by-ten room, just large enough to stand in. Its walls were covered with empty wooden shelves, bare except for dust and rodent droppings. An old table stood in the corner with a short bench next to it. It looked like the cell of a penitent monk, where one would transcribe verses from a bible to save one's soul. The verses copied here, however, were from no bible known to man.

"There is nothing here, mistress. The shelves are empty. Marco lied to you."

"No, I think not, for it is just as he said in his distress. Here, in the corner, dig."

"I have no shovel."

"Dig!" she yelled in a voice that almost knocked me over, so confining and closed was the room we stood in.

I quickly knelt on my hands and knees and started digging in the spot she had pointed to, using a broken shard of an old jug as a tool. Soon I had a hole about two or three feet deep and just as wide, dug in the soft dirt floor. I struck something solid. Stopping in amazement, I looked down to see an old wooden box, with flayed pieces of rope attached, long ago decayed. Pulling at the box, I yanked it free. It was heavy and sounded as if it was filled with broken flower pots.

"What is it? What have we found?" I asked her in amazement.

She did not answer. Something had moved in the corner. At first it looked like coiled up rope resting on the floor and covered with filth. Perhaps a rat had stirred. Suddenly, the thick rope appeared to uncoil itself and slither across the floor. It was a huge snake, and kept unwinding as it moved toward me. As it grew close, it opened its hideous mouth to expose two fangs.

Rebecca sprang on the beast as it reared its massive head to strike me. Grabbing it by the neck with both hands, she squeezed with all her iron might. The large snake instantly wrapped its body around her and began to constrict. I thought it would crush her. Still she held it tight, squeezing it back until she twisted its head off with a yell.

"A guardian," she observed casually, as she kicked it back into the corner it had sprung from.

She kneeled and picked up the box, which she turned around in her hands several times to examine the figures carved on it.

"This is the Scroll of Ur," she said in hushed tones filled with awe. "These are the secret cuneiform tablets that contain the sacred words, the very words Urammu spoke over me that fateful night, the ancient Chaldean curse to summon a demon and bind it to a human soul. This is what I have been seeking for so long."

My blood ran cold as I watched her open the box. As we stood in the dank and dusty dungeons of the ancient fort gazing at the tablets of Ur, she spoke of the old ones as she had not done before.

"The old ones have found us. They are gathering for the attack. That's why we have not been bothered yet. They have been waiting for us to find the tablets, and for one called Tikana, he who guards the sacred tombs, the tombs of the first amongst us. He is now here. I can sense him. We must move fast."

She ordered me to carry the box and we headed out. As we exited the door to the blockhouse, a figure appeared in the still dark courtyard, then another, then more.

"The old ones," Rebecca gasped. "Flee."

She grabbed me and carried me up the walls of the citadel to the roof. Two of the old ones gave chase. Just when they were almost on us, I panicked and threw the box I was carrying off the roof. To my utter relief, both old ones stopped chasing us and went after it. I clung to Rebecca's back as we fled across the rooftops against the full moon. There were old ones chasing us, trying to cut us off, but what Rebecca gave up in strength and power being younger, she more than made up for in speed, and quickly outran them. Running on all fours like a wolf, she bounded from roof to roof. I closed my eyes tight and hung on to her neck for dear life.

Soon we were in the desert, and still she carried me on her back. We stopped beneath the massive shadows of Giza's ancient pyramid, where I drank from an old well.

"That was close," I said, as we rested near the oasis pool. "You were incredible, master."

"Why did you throw away the tablets?"

"I am sorry, master, but they were almost upon us. What could I do?"

"No, you are right. They would have had us *and* the tablets, but there is still hope.

That was twenty-four hours ago. I have not seen her since.

Just when I need her the most, she has disappeared again. I was sure I would find her sleeping in her crypt when I woke this morning, but it was empty. She was not there, nor has she shown up today, though the sun burns high in the cloudless sky. I'm beside myself with worry. What is she up to? After what happened last night, with the old ones at our heels, I did not expect her to be away like this. Perhaps it's part of her plan. What will the old ones do with the tablets, destroy them? Or will they use them to create more vampires? The thought of more hideous creatures like Rebecca drives me to madness. Even worse, what if she has decided to replace me? One can never know with one such as Rebecca. I must find her.

Much has happened. Where do I begin?

I haven't lived with a vampire for a hundred years without learning something of her habits. I know how she thinks. I knew that if she was seeking a new manservant, she'd be looking for someone with the right type of outlook, young and hungry. I figured the docks would be a good a place as any to start. It was getting dark.

I searched the riverside, the docks and wharves where we had first washed up on this godforsaken shore, looking for her among the felucca and riverboats that plied the ancient Nile.

I saw the gang first, a group of teenage boys, street kids, dirty and scruffy, obviously unattended and up to no good. I was in a deserted district of abandoned warehouses and wharves. They seemed to be stalking someone, some unfortunate soul caught in the wrong place at the wrong time. It struck me as oddly familiar, a gang of boys following someone, a young girl perhaps. Then I saw her, scurrying along the dusty street, a tall, lithe figure in a white sundress, totally out of place in this grimy scene, more than likely a lost tourist.

Before I could do anything, the gang converged on the lone woman, pushing and shoving her into a nearby alley. There they proceeded to force her to the ground, stripping off her light summer dress with violent jerks. She made not a sound, but went submissively to the ground whimpering. Her white panties and bra, which only a moment before were just a faint image glimpsed through light fabric of the dress, were now all she wore.

I froze in mid stride. I recognized that lithe figure, huddled in the middle of the mob, the dark hard body of a vampire. I recognized the scene, Berlin shortly after the turn of the previous century. It was deja vu with a capital D.

Just as before those many long years ago, she took them as they were about to take her, tore them apart just as she did my comrades a hundred years ago. She killed them in a moment, all except one, the leader of the group, a boy of about eighteen, larger than the rest, wearing dark blue shorts and a faded polo shirt already too small for his large frame. He stood stock still in shock as his gang of toughs perished around him in a heartbeat.

Was this to be my replacement? Was it all to begin again? No, I could not allow this travesty to occur.

"Come here, it's all right," I heard her say, just like she had said to me so long ago, as she lured him deeper into the dark alleyway.

I could tell she didn't know I was there, preoccupied as she was with slaking her thirst. She did not have full control of the youth yet, and hadn't sensed my presence. I had the element of surprise on my side and little else, except perhaps for a small modern contraption - my cell phone. I though such an object might come in handy someday. After all, we live in dangerous times. There are deadly things walking about at night, like Rebecca.

The bodies of her victims were strewn across the street. Rebecca was about to lure the single survivor into an alleyway where she'd teach him her forbidden secrets. I took out my cell phone and keyed the number for the local authorities. Telling them there had been a gang war near the docks, I urged them to bring all the men they could to the address. Then leaving the line connected, I sprang from my hiding place and raced toward the boy waving my arms.

"Stop!" I yelled. "Get out of here."

I ran forward to scare him away, throwing a trash can at him in the process. He seemed to come out of a trance, and took off down the street. I could hear a dozen sirens coming our way. Rebecca sprang after the boy, but I threw myself at her legs to block her. She did not fall over me as I'd planned, but kicked me away easily, almost breaking my ribs. It was enough, however. On hearing the sirens approach, she turned and ran up the side of the building and away. My mistress hates crowds unless she's feeding on them, and she had already supped.

Later this evening when I got back home, Rebecca was waiting for me. I thought she would be angry, but she was hurt instead, if such a thing is possible, which I doubt.

"Why do you interfere? Why do you oppose me?" she asked. I was tired, spending all night eluding the police.

"I was afraid you were going to replace me."

"You fool" she replied. "Don't you understand? It is partly for you that I do this. Don't you want to join me? The boy would have made a good servant for you."

"I am still your servant, and I will remain so. You don't need another. "

Rebecca came at me in fury.

"Don't presume to tell me what I need," she growled, grabbing me by the back of the neck and pressing her forearm into my windpipe so that I could not breathe. "You don't understand. Do not interfere. I hope I have not made a mistake in you. Because of you, the old ones have the Tablets of Ur, which they will destroy. You have failed me. I will take your daughter for that."

"No, Mistress, I am sorry. They were on us. I had to divert them. And tonight I became crazy when I thought you were going to replace me. It will never happen again. Leave Emily alone."

"You gave her to me, remember, Henry. She's mine to do with as I wish, just like you. I suffer you to live because you have been useful to me. I would like to continue the partnership. I do not seek to replace you. I did not ask you to give me your daughter. You had betrayed me. I would have been happy to take the baby's blood with the mother's, but you made me an offer I could not turn down. So far I have left her untouched, but her time has come. As soon as we get resettled, we will get her. After that, we will see what happens.

"Mistress, why don't you kill me now and let it be over with?"

She stood over me, but instead of being menacing, she looked almost kind. It was a look I don't remember seeing on her face before.

"No, Henry, I need you, but don't try my patience. There are worse things I can do to you than kill you, remember."

"Yes, Mistress, but think again. Have we not been happy as we are? Why change it? Why ruin it all with your mad scheme?"

"I told you, Henry. You are either with me or against me. They will give us no rest. There is no place we can go to get away now that we have raised their wrath. They have destroyed the tablets, but there is still the text of Belamarca. We must find it before they do. Let us go."

Even though daylight was but a short time away, we ran out into the gathering light.

Chapter 16

The old ones were waiting for us, and gave chase. All that day, through the blistering heat we ran. If I had not seen it with my own eyes, I never would have believed it possible for Rebecca to move through the scorching sun like that, though it taxed her mightily. By evening her skin was black as ebony, while mine was red and blistered. It was only the daylight that kept them from pursuing us. Rebecca's youth has given her this slight advantage over her adversaries, who seem as adverse to the sunlight as old Dracula himself. Not so Rebecca, my demon mistress.

She fed on tribes-people and Bedouin races that live in the sparsely inhabited regions, shepherds and farmers, who often wander these places alone and would not be missed for many days.

Leaving the desert we headed north across the Greek Islands to the Peloponnesian Peninsula. From there we traveled through the Balkans and across the channel to Italy and Venice. From Venice we went to Rome, where we hope to find the Text of Belamarca now that the original tablets have been destroyed.

She needs me now more than ever. I have become indispensable, with my penchant for disguise, forgery, and procurement. We slip across borders like invisible agents, go into and out of cities like locals, disappear into the night like ghosts. Yet there is no rest for our weary feet.

Ah, Rome, the Eternal City, as eternal as the mistress that I serve. For Rebecca, it's like coming home. She's spent so many centuries here, watching the city grow and change, seeing emperors come and go, it's as if she never left. It's so strange to see the Coliseum and know that Rebecca herself sat there and watched gladiators fight to the death and Christians being fed to the lions. Yet she is sad and pensive. She shows no joy, none of the old excitement.

Our long trip along the shores of ancient civilizations has been exhausting. She has had no place to sleep except deserted crypts and haunted mausoleums, stolen from the long-dead. She has eaten on the run, without being selective, the sick and diseased, the malnourished and destitute, the addicted and parasite-ridden. Not the healthy fare she has known in the past.

Rebecca has seen her share of hardship and lean times. After all, she was weaned in an age of suffering and privation. This was different, however. Now she had the legion of the damned hounding her, giving her no peace or rest.

The past speaks to us here in Rome, in the mustiness of the cathedrals dim with the dust of the centuries; in the black-dressed women, their faces crabbed with wrinkles, standing on the corner beating the air with their gestures; in the mules hauling logs out of the nearby woods; in the squares and piazza much like they were when the dukes ruled. Yes, Rebecca should feel right at home in Rome. We have not seen or sensed the presence of the old ones, but we know they can't be far.

The city of Rome is a cornucopia of delight, a feast for the famished. There is no want of ripe blood, there for the taking. The very first night of our arrival, tired and disoriented, before we had even found lodging, Rebecca began her murderous pursuit. It must have something to do with the deprivations of the road, because as soon as she got to Rome, she began a killing spree the likes of which I have never before witnessed.

Rebecca would binge occasionally, but she normally only killed what she needed to slake her burning thirst. For the sake of keeping a low profile, she normally did not over-hunt the neighborhood. Now it seems all restraint has been loosened. Her urge to feed has become overpowering. She kills all night long and deep into the day, until the heat and sun drives her reluctantly into her coffin. There have been so many that my ability to dispose of them has not kept up. I am afraid that soon, if the old ones don't get us the authorities will. Even a vampire can be locked up with enough steel and bars. Maybe the Italian government could even figure out how to kill her. Perhaps this is part of her plan, to cause a diversion. If that was her objective, she has certainly succeeded.

I wish I had not been with her that first night in Rome, that I had missed the whole thing. You'd think I'd grow jaded at the sight of death these long years. I was even beginning to think I had. After all, I had not been bothered by scruples since the night in Montreal when I saved that little girl, and I had seen plenty of little girls die since then. I certainly wasn't bothered by any of the vermin-filled vagabonds she murdered on our way here from Egypt. But the plight of her first Roman victims filled me with pity.

We spotted them on the street walking hand in hand along the shops and stores, both young and female, both pretty. They gazed and pointed with excited gestures at the various window displays. They were both the picture of healthy vibrant womanhood. That Rebecca wanted them sickened me.

Over the past months, during our harrowing escape from Egypt, I have redeemed myself in Rebecca's eyes. I was the one who procured her supply of humans. I lured and seduced and otherwise kidnapped them so that she could feed while hiding. I realized that this evening was going to be a test, to see if I could be counted on. I would have to do whatever she asked. Still, I shrank at the thought of something happening to these two innocent girls.

We followed them down the glitzy street, lit by colorful lights and window displays. Well-dressed people moved back and forth all around us, each couple more handsome than the next, but Rebecca was fixated on the two girls and would not be distracted.

Following them into a clothing store, we watched discreetly as they tried on a few things, and into another where they bought some frilly undergarments. At some point I lost Rebecca in the crowd, and hoped that perhaps she had grown weary of this game and gone to seek easier prey. After all, she hadn't eaten in almost twenty-four hours, not since the old, gray prelate she had found early the night before a few miles from Rome.

Although Rebecca was no longer by my side, I watched as the two young women entered another boutique arm in arm. Stopping, I peered through the window.

To my surprise, the sales lady in the store turned out to be Rebecca, dressed in an elegant white dress with matching boots, speaking perfect Italian. Her long, gold and black-streaked hair contrasted nicely with the soft gray fabric of her blouse, obviously just taken off the rack.

I watched as she showed them outfits and dresses, subtly putting them under her spell. At her suggestion, they entered a dressing room where they could try on some of the more expensive ensembles. Rebecca then pulled down the blinds and locked the door, telling me with a gesture to make sure no one came in. Then she went into the changing room where the two young women were undressing.

I was thankful I didn't have to witness it. Instead, I listened to the sounds of the street and watched the traffic flow by. All was deathly silent inside the boutique, not even a muffled scream.

When she was finished we left unobserved. Most of the stores along the boulevard had long since closed. I expected to have to dispose of the remains, although I was not quite sure what I would find and what I would do with it. Ingenuity goes with the territory. I had been thinking of this when Rebecca came out of the store, blood-smeared and satiated. I suggested burning the place or dumping the bodies in the Tiber, but she told me to leave everything as it was, including the unfortunate sales clerk. She evidently no longer feels the need to cover her tracks, and there will be plenty of them.

This was only the beginning of her rampage, a destructive impulse so great it threatens to consume the entire city. For something has changed in Rebecca during our flight. Something has snapped in her sinister mind, and her evil has become even more menacing.

That night, after satiating herself on the blood of the two young women, she stalked the streets in search of more. I knew the dam had broken by the dull sadistic gleam in her eyes, and the world was no longer going to be a safe place, not for us humans. In their fervor to punish her, to sanction and persecute the young vampire, the Old Ones had pushed her to a place even they didn't know about.

I followed her up the dark streets, each one smaller and darker than the last, until she stopped to sniff the air. I could see two people huddled in a doorway whispering to each other conspiratorially.

"What are you doing?" I asked her, although I knew the answer well enough.

"I'm doing what my kind has always done, from the beginning of time."

"You have just fed, and we did not clean up after ourselves. If you want to stay here in Rome and recuperate, we had better not attract attention. Remember what happened in Alaska. Don't push your luck."

"You don't feel them do you, Henry? They are all around us, closing in from all directions. Rome is their mousetrap. They knew I'd come here to find Belamarca's translation. I must make the city unsafe for them."

"What about us. You will make it so for us as well. Let us go to the catacombs and hide until we can refurbish ourselves. We can search for the scrolls then."

"Didn't you hear me, Henry? There's no time to waste. We must find Belamarca's manuscript. In the meantime, I will make this place a killing field where no vampire will be able to dwell again."

"What about us humans? Don't we have a say in this?"

"No, Henry, you don't."

"Let us go, Mistress. We can leave this place. There are plenty of places we can go. We don't have to stay here."

"What? And live like beggars in the night, like we have been these past miserable weeks? I'd rather we all die than live like that. And so we shall, Henry, so we shall, starting with those two."

"Yes, Master. Tell me what I can do to serve you, Master."

"Watch, Henry. Witness the destruction of the world."

With those words she moved down the street like a padded predator. A well-dressed, older man, with wide shoulders and short-cropped gray hair, was getting amorous with a young, dark-haired woman. She had small features and a round face, and was smiling at him as she feebly tried to push him away. They hardly noticed as Rebecca stole up behind them.

The man gave a snort as Rebecca jumped him from behind and sank her fangs into the side of his neck, pinning him against the wall with her arms. The woman's screams were muffled by the man's bulk as he sagged against her. It didn't take long for Rebecca to drain him, and he to drop to his knees with his head on the woman's lap.

The lab girl froze in terror when she saw what was happening. Before she could scream again, Rebecca slit her throat with a slash of her nails and sucked the blood as it gushed from the wound. But even these two victims did not satisfy her.

There were at least two more that night, a portly, mustached man in a brown suede jacket carrying a case of wine, probably a steward from one of the local restaurants coming home late from work. The other was a short man in a white sleeveless undershirt, a vendor of some sort, carrying a large, round piece of cheese to the morning market. Then she let me take her to the catacombs, to an area of the ruins that were roped off and not accessible to the public, where we were finally able to rest.

The next night she was up and out before the last rays of the sun had disappeared, and the slaughter began again, this time en masse.

Her first victims were a group of musicians and marchers carrying statutes of the saints, some religious celebration or other. The marchers all wore black suits and hats. The musicians wore sunglasses despite the setting sun. A few passers-by bowed their heads, but most people ignored the procession. Unfortunately for them, Rebecca did not.

She followed stealthy, robed in black, staying in the gathering shadows. Starting in the rear of the group, stealthily, one by one, she took them as they marched. Slicing this one's throat, that one's jugular, strangling one, snapping the neck of another, she went through them like a silent plague, cutting a vein here, an artery there, until the music stopped with a jagged halt. It was quickly replaced by screams and cries of terror. We vanished into the night, but not before she siphoned blood from each victim.

I thought sure that would be it for the evening, that feeding on a dozen or so full-bodied men would satiate her bloodlust for the night even if she hadn't drained them all dry. I suspected that her words of the evening before were just idle boasts, just empty words to impress me. But alas, that was not to be. She had only begun her killing spree.

We wandered to the old quarter of the city, where a group of women and their children were sitting on a secluded side street. They were having a smoke and exchanging the gossip of the day. An old matron dressed in a flowered blue dress gesticulated excitedly with a heavy-set woman sitting in a chair. Two others, with cigarettes dangling from their mouths, stood in the doorway talking and cursing at their children. Half a dozen dark, pudgy bambinos played around the stoop or sat in lawn chairs chattering in high-pitched voices. As Rebecca approached the group, a fat little girl in a red dress and her pot-bellied younger brother, wearing only a blue undershirt, stopped and stared at her with their big cow eyes.

The old crone in the blue-flowered dress said something sharply to Rebecca. It was the last thing she'd ever say. The screams and commotion in the courtyard brought other inhabitants out to see what was happening. They too met their deaths at Rebecca's hands. She took a special delight in sucking the blood from the plump little boy while she looked at me smiling with a snarl.

I reeled from the carnage, sickened to my core, even after my years of witnessing her depravities. Where were the old ones? Surely they would not stand by and allow this butchery to continue night after night, not after hounding her for so long. Surely they would stop her. Yet they did nothing.

I don't remember much of that second evening, or the next. It all went by in one hideous blur, one day fused into the other. Whenever I thought it could get no worse, she would go one better. There is no end to the evil she can do when aroused.

Then last night Rebecca visited a small family factory in the basement of a rundown building not far from the catacombs where she and I stay until she can re-establish herself. She uses the caves as her base from which to issue forth at night to hunt.

The small factory employed ten women, young girls really, to make purses. I had met the two enterprising young brothers from Naples who owned the place, Gianni and Salvatore. I thought they would be helpful in setting up yet another new identity for Rebecca and me. She had something else in mind. They would have done better to have never left Naples.

She needed something close by and quick to satiate her bloodlust. I tried to tell her that I was working with these people to establish a new cover for us, but she would have none of it. She told me we did not need a cover. Just the opposite, we did not exist. I should have left her then and there. I shouldn't have helped her in her despicable deed. But what was I to do? So I went along like a donkey with a nose-ring. The factory was nearby. It was worse than I could have imagined

They all died horribly, the teenage girls with their pretty smiles, and the two young owners and their simple dreams, frozen forever in time in the harsh glare of the overhead fluorescent lights. We left it for all to see, their blood comingled and congealing on the cement floor. What I thought might serve as a cover would now lead the police right to our door.

And so the slaughter continues, night after night. She kills them as they ride in their motor-scooters and in their sleek sports cars. She takes them in their rented rooms and their swank apartment buildings. In pairs and alone, naked and clothed, in ancient hovels and modern skyscrapers, they die. Soon not even Rome will have room enough for all the dead.

Her plan has apparently worked, for Rome is sealed up as tight as a tomb. Where the streets were once filled with life, now only death stalks the night. A strict curfew has been imposed, which keeps everyone but essential personnel off the streets by nightfall. Police patrol every boulevard and stand on every corner. All public gatherings and entertainment have been prohibited or canceled, including movies, concerts, religious services, and sports events. It is as if a plague had hit the city, an epidemic of murder and mayhem, all caused by a single agent, my terrible mistress.

Terror rules the evening. Even the daylight is not safe. Few venture out even then and only for urgently needed essentials. She has made things difficult for humans and vampires alike. The authorities and news media, lacking any hard information, are rife with rumors. Every conceivable explanation has been brought forth from Satan worshippers to terrorists. Some think the rash of homicides is the result of an out of control drug war. Some think it anarchists trying to destroy the fabric of society. You name it, it has been brought forth as an answer, but you and I know, it's only little old Rebecca, the queen of the damned.

She stirs. I hear the weird howl she makes when she's hungry as I listen to stories of her handiwork reported on the news. She has changed races, my Rebecca, the result of her mad dash across the burning sands of Egypt and Arabia in the harsh light of day. Where before her skin was as white as ivory, it's now black as ebony. I've had to pass her off as a rich African heiress. She has regained something of her former financial status. It is not only the poor and destitute she has been feeding on of late, and we have been able to establish ourselves in some comfort again.

"Are you happy now, Mistress?" I ask, as she saunters up from her basement tomb. "The city is locked up so tight I can't even get a haircut."

"Your hair looks fine, Enrique."

"What purpose could all this killing possibly serve, Mistress? It only makes it harder for us."

"And for the old ones. They will not be able to move around so freely at night with the curfew. The murders are just the distraction we needed. The old ones have been taken off guard. They did not expect this, and don't know quite what to make of it all."

"Nor do I, Mistress."

"We have gained the initiative. While the old ones wait to see what we will do next, we will be outmaneuvering them. By the time they figure out what we're up to it will be too late."

Of course, I have not been idle. While Rebecca sleeps and Rome recovers from another night of butchery, I have been pursuing my search on her behalf. With the aid of the references I have managed to pick up on our journey through the Holy Land and Egypt, I have learned the whereabouts of the text she seeks, Belamarca's copy of the Tablets of Ur. The answer was found in dusty museums and archives; in words of broken Hebrew, Greek, and Latin sprinkled over the ages in ancient manuscripts. I now know where it is hidden, in the Vatican. Michelangelo was the key. Now all I have to do is get it.

Here is what I know: Belamarca was an ancient vampire of origin unknown, who took the name of the Count de Buffon de Navarre in 1076, one of his many pseudonyms. He became a master in the arcane discipline of alchemy and one of its leading exponents. He joined the Crusades in 1096 to learn the secrets of the Saracen soothsayers. Among these mysteries was the undisclosed whereabouts of the sacred tablets of Ur, which held the secret of creating a vampire. These he searched for and as if by miracle, he found them hidden under the floorboards in an ancient shrine in an even older desert oasis said to be the home of malevolent spirits.

At this point, in 1099, he allowed himself to be captured by the Moslems, presumably so that he could conduct his experiments away from the prying eyes of his fellow crusaders. For some reason, probably because his keepers were unknowingly under his vampire spell, he was allowed to keep all of his possessions while imprisoned, one of which was a long wooden box filled with strange tiles, the cuneiform tablets of Ur. These he studied in his years of fake captivity, for not only did he have skill as an alchemist, but he also had some understanding of Chaldean and other ancient tongues, so he was eventually able to understand and say the secret words.

After almost a hundred years of study and experimentation on his unfortunate fellow prisoners and guards, the old vampire perfected his pronunciations of the sacred text, and found the perfect vehicle for his mad scheme. Marco Teristi was a young nobleman from Italy, the count of Milan. He had been a raw recruit when he was thrown against the Saracen in a battle outside Jerusalem, in which his force was routed and several taken prisoner. Because he was a good-looking youth he had been spared the usual torture and death, and was being saved for the pleasure of the commandant of the fortress in which he was being held. The fat, perverted warden would never get a chance to break in the new infidel, however, for Marco was destined for greater ends. Without the commandant's knowledge, the youth was transferred to Belamarca's cell.

Then one night, as Belamarca and the young nobleman were about to retire for the evening, the old vampire gave Marco a surprise, an unexpected gift.

Macro must have looked in disbelief as the door of their cell opened. For there stood the most beautiful woman he had ever seen, a harem girl from the Master's own precincts, with soft, olive skin and large opal eyes, dressed in the skimpiest of dancing customs.

He took her on the floor as Belamarca watched from his writing desk, chanting the curse. At the moment of ecstasy, when Marcos was lost in oblivion, Count Buffon of the Nosferatu took him from behind, piercing his heart with the blade of his long dagger. As he did, he spoke the final words of the sacred Text of Ur. His voice rang out in the small confines of the room. It was over in an instant.

The ground trembled. The sky grew black. The walls of their tiny cell cracked with the strain. The locked door flew open and hung loose from its hinges. Dust and debris rained down on his head as Belamarca lifted the limp body of Marco and carried him up and out of their deep dungeon home, into the clear moonlight.

The whole earth shook in denial of Belamarca's terrible deed. When Marco opened his eyes and gazed up at Belamarca for the first time, it must have been a look of wonder and perplexity. And so a new vampyre was born. Thus began the wars of the Espiritus.

Belamarca hid the Tablets of Ur in his cell, creating two copies. One was lost during the chaos that followed the fall of Jerusalem. Only one copy remains.

Belamarca hid the surviving manuscript many times in the centuries that followed. On each occasion he recovered it just before it was located by his enemies. Eventually, unknown to them all, a human found it where it was last hidden in the middle of France. This was during the religious wars at the end of the 15th century. Henry IV had just come to the throne and had ended decades of bloodshed, not a little of it instigated by the strife of the vampires.

A reckless cavalier in the employ of Richelieu, the cardinal of France, attempted to use Belamarca's copy to make himself immortal. The authorities were alerted to the danger and imprisoned him in the dungeons of Andalusia. That is when they tried to destroy the document by sending it first to New Spain to be buried in the jungle, and again to North America and New France for destruction by Samuel de Champlain. Both attempts failed, and the manuscript was reportedly brought back to Rome to be hidden in the Vatican. This much I learned after endless research and long talks with Rebecca as we traveled.

Why didn't they just burn it? They probably didn't really know what they had. They may have been afraid of destroying it for fear of the consequences. Fear of the unknown is strong. People, even educated ones back then, were a superstitious lot. After all, they believed in vampires, didn't they?

What I did not know was the final hiding place of the Text of Belamarca here in Rome. This I have found!

Chapter 17

The deed has been done and the world will never be the same. Only a few hours ago I was walking along the seemingly endless corridors of Saint Peter's Basilica in the black and purple attire of a Prince of the Church. It was dusk as I approached the domed structure from the Tiber. The tourists had long since gone home. With the curfew and recent murders there were far fewer than normal. Not having time to be too selective, the clothes of the dead cardinal did not fit well, but they would do in a pinch. No one noticed the pant cuffs sticking out from under my cassock, nor the body stuffed in the rectory blast furnace. A crucifix dangled by my side. I never thought I'd be wearing one of those things, but then I have done many things I thought I'd never do.

From my study of the architectural drawings and readings of old Latin texts, I knew the document I sought was an ancient medieval manuscript written on thick sheets of vermilion, and that it was hidden in an arm of the crucifix, atop the lantern that sits on the dome of the basilica itself. It resides in an iron casket that also contains a fragment of the True Cross, a holy religious relic. The fathers of the church must have thought it the safest place in the world for a thing of such purported evil. Well, they were wrong.

The trail of clues was riddled with dead ends and false starts, but a hundred years of such investigations helped me unravel the maze-like path to its conclusion. Suffice it to say, you'd have to be an archeologist with a background in ancient religions, an expert in arcane languages, to follow even a brief summary of its discovery. I knew where it was, where it had lain untouched for almost four centuries, lost to the knowledge of man. It was soon to be rediscovered.

I moved quickly down a side aisle toward the main altar and Bermini's baldacchino, the giant bronze, four-poster structure beneath the even more gigantic space of the dome. Some cardinal and a few priests were saying mass in a side chapel. Otherwise, the place was deserted. No one seemed to take notice of my passing, just another prince of the church getting closer to the apostles. Beneath the altar sat the confessio and the entrance to the crypt. It was not to the tombs I was going, however, but to the roof.

I passed through the entrance to the elevator. Unhappily, it was closed, so I took the stairs to the dome instead, over four hundred feet above the ground. I did not stop to gaze at the enormity of the building from the gallery as most tourists do, but rushed through a closed door – after picking the lock - and up another flight of stairs to the roof. As I stepped out onto the viewing platform at the east side of the dome, I took a moment to catch my breath. The sights of the city glistened below me, as far as I could see, an endless array of glittering, colored lights. The stars above in the black canopy of the sky seemed so close I could almost reach out and touch them, just above the huge dome of St. Peter's. My target lay still higher, above the dome itself, atop the cupola that housed Fontana's Lantern.

I braced myself for the last stage of the climb, like one would before the summit of Everest. It seemed impossibly high for someone who hated heights, but facing Rebecca's wrath would have been much worse, so onward and upward I went. Unlocking yet another door, I ran up a flight of circular, metal stairs leading to the lantern at the top of the dome.

It was dark, but lights beamed out from nooks and crannies inside the cupola like search beams, making it seem like the middle of the day and almost blinding me. I would have to climb hand over hand from here on like a mountaineer. I have been in spots like this before, on towers and steeples for one reason or another in my hundred years of service, none by my own choosing. Still, I paled at the thought of trusting myself five hundred feet above the pavement on the outside of the building.

I had been quite athletic in my time, and was still fit with Rebecca's secret nectar, but my recent exertions had left me spent. I was breathing hard and sweating profusely. By hanging out over the balustrade, I could see the cross above me. Leaning out further, I grabbed a pillar and stepped out onto the lip of the cupola. Then I began pulling myself up using the abundant outcroppings and buttresses for hand holds and footing. I looked straight ahead, neither up nor down, and climbed until I clung to the base of the cross like a penitent monk. I even found myself praying, even though what I was doing was the worst of sins and I had never prayed before.

There was a small service ladder, ancient and decrepit, leading up the side of the cross. I began to ascend. The night wind howled in my ears. Just as I was about to reach the right arm of the structure, the rung I was on, long rotten and brittle, gave way, leaving me dangling in the air like a limp flag. My heart leaped to my throat as I struggled to gain my footing. Swinging my feet up, I clung upside-down to the arm of the cross hundreds of feet in the air. By sheer determination, with adrenalin pumping through my system, I pulled myself to the top of the arm, breathing rapidly and hugging it for all I was worth. After gaining my composure, I noticed a small metal hatchway, an opening in the cross-beam, where the scrolls were presumably hidden. I started shimmying to it.

There was nothing but air for hundreds of feet beneath me. Growing numb to the danger, no longer caring one way or another, half hoping I'd fall, I quickly moved to the hatch and began to pry it open to expose the hollowed interior of a compartment. Inside was a metal casket about the size of a small chest, which I gingerly removed. It was locked. For a moment I clung there not knowing what to do. My hands were encumbered with the burden I held. It was the sole reason for my being there, but made it impossible to maneuver, yet if I did not return with it, I might as well not return at all.

I must have been there for quite some time, although I wasn't aware of the passing of the hours. My whole life passed before me, all 100 years of it. I pondered my predicament and the consequences of my acts. I tried to pick the crude lock and open the casket using my penknife, but it was too intricate for my clumsy attempts. All the time, I clung to the arm of the cross far above the illuminated pavement.

I stayed trapped on the arm of the cross like that, far above the basilica floor, for hours, not being able to return down the way I had come because of the broken ladder, even if I hadn't had a large chest in my hands. I would just as soon have jumped to my death hundreds of feet below as fail in my mission, and several times I actually contemplated throwing myself over the abyss. But each time I decided to wait just a little while longer, until finally, just as the sun was beginning to peek over the distant hills of Rome, she came to me, although she was less than happy. She had to brave the old ones to do so.

"So here you are, Enrique," she said from the top of the cross where she perched like a giant condor. "I thought you had gotten lost when you failed to return this morning. What are you doing, sitting up here like a dumb bird?"

"Mistress, I am trapped here and cannot get down. The ladder is broken and as you see my hands are full."

"Do you know what I had to do to get here?" she growled. "The elders of my race are out in force tonight. It took all my cunning and ingenuity to elude them. Now we are sitting out here for all to see. Is this how you obey my instructions?"

"I have done what you asked. I have located the stinking book with your stupid curse, now get me off this cross or I swear I'll throw myself and the damn thing over."

"Don't bore me with your idle threats. You will do nothing of the kind. Here, give me the chest and I will help you down."

"No, Mistress, I have come too far and risked too much to give it up now, not until you get me down from here."

"All right, Enrique, as you wish. You deserve it after all you have done for me these past few months. But first I will see what is in the box."

She descended to the arm of the cross as easily as getting off a couch, and swooped up the casket, opening it with one flick of her wrist. As she did so, she glanced into the chest and saw the sliver of wood, the piece of the True Cross. Almost dropping the box in shock, she recoiled in alarm.

"Take it," she hissed.

I never knew Rebecca to be bothered by crucifixes or crosses. After all, she had killed a priest with one and crawled about this large bronze cross like a snake. Something about this small piece of wood, however, stunned her completely. A low growl escaped her lips, which were pulled back in a vicious snarl.

"Get that thing away from me, you fool. Do you know what that is? I cannot abide its presence. Get it away!"

I immediately threw the holy relic far out over the lantern where it disappeared into the darkness. Looking into the chest I noticed a leather-bound manuscript with large pages of vermilion. Removing the book, I threw the casket over the edge of the copula, where it crashed onto the dome and rolled over several times to disappear over the lip.

Holding me around the waist with one arm, while I held the book to my chest, she carried me down the side of the cathedral to safety and home.

So here I am, once again serving my terrible beloved as she pursues her quest for vengeance and blood.

Tonight we are having visitors, dinner guests, for a very special occasion. We no longer abide in the catacombs like the living dead, but now reside in relative comfort in a crumbling, ornate, 19th century villa on the hills overlooking the city in the north. With the funds she's stolen from her many Roman victims along with their blood, she has again amassed a good-size fortune. It is not much by Rebecca's usual standards, but enough to live contentedly on. Buying this small villa where we manage to live in modest style was the first step in our recovery.

Rome is still in a panic, the authorities unable to explain the string of grisly murders, small massacres, and mass homicides. With the heightened alert and security, it's getting more difficult to elude detection. There were several occasions where we had to dispatch the authorities themselves to avoid capture. In spite of all this and her seeming insatiable blood lust, Rebecca is still free to pursue her deadly purpose. However, she has seldom brought her victims home to the villa. I suppose this night is going to be an exception, for she has something special in mind

Slowly but surely, the old ones have restricted her movement, encircling her so that it is no longer easy to hunt even just the neighborhood. It was all she could do to rescue me that night at the top of St. Peter's. The Espiritus are closing in.

I have done what I can under the circumstances to restore the inside of the villa, which after years of neglect was rather rundown. I'm finally starting to get it into some semblance of order, though I don't feel quite ready for guests. There is still much to do, sweeping and dusting. Cobwebs still hang from the corners of the upstairs rooms. The dining room floor requires another coat of polish, and the tiles in the kitchen desperately need to be replaced. Ah, but the view of the city below is spectacular, especially during sunset.

It has rained off and on all day, but the air is warm and the windows are open. A misty dampness permeates the house as evening falls. Rebecca appears in all her radiant beauty, her hair loose and hanging in long pleats over her lovely shoulders.

"We are having special guests tonight, Enrique."

"Si, Mistress, but what do you mean by special?"

"Blue bloods, Enrique, royalty. Their blood has flown in the veins of Romans back to the days of the great Medici."

"Si, Master, but what of it?"

"They are perfect specimens. I have studied the scroll. I am ready to pronounce the words. These will be the first of my creations, your Lieutenants."

"So you are actually going through with it? You want to create new ones like yourself, and start another war?"

"I am only defending myself. I have explained it all to you before. Do not be difficult. I need your help."

"Si, Mistress. Of course, anything you say. I was only…"

"What, Enrique, getting cold feet?"

"No, Mistress, only thinking of the consequences."

"The consequences of our failing are much worse, now do as I say."

"But surely the old ones won't let you get away with this?"

"They will have no choice. They still do not yet know for certain if I have the manuscript. But they are close and waiting for an opportunity to strike. This will force their hand. Then we can be done with it once and for all."

"Si, Master, once and for all."

Much has happened. Our conversation was interrupted by the chime of the bell. The visitors had arrived. I opened the door to an extremely handsome couple, probably in their mid-twenties, both olive-skinned and well-dressed. The girl had jet black hair tied in a severe bun that showed off her high cheek bones and long neck. The man was dressed in a dark blue Amani suit and blinding-white silk shirt. He flashed me a smile and introduced himself and his new bride. They were married just hours before and had come to the villa at Rebecca's invitation to stay the night before departing for Capri on their honeymoon.

Apparently, Rebecca arranged for this little romantic escape posing as the editor of a big New York magazine doing a cover story on the cream of Roman high society. Their names are not important. The fact that their family had the blood of kings is what counts to Rebecca. It mattered not at all to her that this was to be their last night on earth as humans.

I prepared one of my best dishes for the pair, something I had not done in over a year, since those last days in Boston when she entertained the Colombians. But I have not lost my touch. Their final meal was their finest.

Their bridal suite had been equally done up, with a large, four-poster bed, soft plush mattress, perfumed comforters, and silk sheets. The drapery was light yellow, the shaded lamps pale blue. Their last night together was blissful, that is until she tried to make them children of the night.

They ate by the light of eighteen candles set in gold candelabras, placed evenly along the long, oak dinner table. Rebecca joined them and seduced them with her voice, caressing them both with her eyes. They looked at her with admiration and awe, already fully under her spell. She could have done anything she wanted with them.

It was easy to see they were in love, the way they looked at each other and touched each other casually as they sat together at the table drinking spiked wine. After dinner, they politely excused themselves and went up to their room. Rebecca gave them only a short time alone before following. As she went up the stairs she removed her dress, a long, black, backless thing that she slipped off and dropped to the stairs like snakeskin. Then she slipped into the room. I waited at the table drinking the spiked wine, trying to block out the sounds that came unbidden to my ears.

They were all making love. Then I heard Rebecca's voice rising over the noises of the others, chanting the curse as she learned it from the text. Suddenly, there was a high-pitched scream, which was slowly choked off as my mistress fed. The sounds told me all I needed to know. I flung my arm across the table, knocking the wine bottle onto the floor, along with several glasses and plates. Standing, I reeled across the room toward the stairs. What had she done?

She called me in a shrill voice from the upstairs room. I went to her obediently, not knowing what to expect.

"He does not stir," she said, poking the naked body of the boy. "His eyes remain closed! Is he dead? Did the spell not work?"

I bent over the body and examined him. A large knife protruded from his chest. He neither breathed nor registered a pulse.

"He is dead," I announced. "What happened?"

"I chanted the words and did the deed as it is written, as it was done to me those 4000 years ago, but it did not work."

I knew something like this might occur, yet I said nothing. Even Belamarca spent years practicing and learning the correct pronunciation of the words. The odds of Rebecca getting it right the first time were slim at best. I told her this without giving away my prior suspicions.

She looked at me as if she wanted to cut off my nose, but said nothing.

"You could have told me that sooner, Enrique," she said finally in a velvet tone. "I hope for your daughter's sake that you can teach me how to say the words faster than you alerted me to this fact."

I can delay the inevitable no longer. What hope does mankind have now?

Chapter 18

As I expected, soon after that long night, we had to leave Rome. Our last evening in the Eternal City was the worst experience of my life, and my life with Rebecca is full of terrible events. We fled for our lives, but not because the old ones had come for us. They had been stymied by the buildup of security forces around the city caused by the unexplained killings. Unknown to us, the old ones had had to disperse and observe us from a distance. They knew by then that we had found Belamarca's text, but there was nothing they could do about it without bringing unwanted attention to themselves. Rebecca seemed to show no such caution, however, and with her careless behavior brought the police right to our door.

The recent young couple was the last straw. They had text a friend – using one of those new useful contraptions they have now – and told them where they were going. When they didn't show up as expected the next morning at a breakfast in their honor, the frantic search led directly to Rebecca's front door. How could she be expected to be aware of things like text-messages and video cameras? She is an ancient evil creature, no matter what her appearance. But it is a weakness that might prove her undoing. I will have to keep that in mind. As it is, I was lucky to escape with my life.

The authorities came for us in the middle of the day, with their full force - all the law enforcement agencies in the city. Even Italian military troops were unleashed on us. They came through the doors and the windows of the villa, up from the basement and down the stairs, guns blazing. I could not believe that so many shots could be fired off all at once and for so long. It was like a war zone and I was in the middle, alone and unarmed. I thought I had been hit ten times before I made it to the secret tunnel, but each time I found I was still untouched.

She is not totally invincible, my Rebecca. She could not withstand the full effect of so many high-powered guns shooting at her all at once. She is fast as lighting and can come up on you in an instant from across the room like she popped out of air, her skin is hard as steel, but she has her limits. In any case, no vampire, I don't care who they are, would want to put themselves through that kind of test.

She was ready for them, having long ago planned our getaway. We stole down a secret passage to where, a block away behind a deserted warehouse, a vehicle was waiting, and made our getaway.

As we drove from the villa into the hills, following the ancient Roman highway out of town, I could see all the different colored lights of the emergency vehicles in the valley behind us. Someone had set the place on fire, perhaps from all the gunfire. The whole villa was in flames. We drove north unobserved, as all activity was drawn in the opposite direction by the police.

Running in the sunlight is still difficult for Rebecca, but with her darkened skin and the partial filter of our tinted windows, she had no problem. We had planned for this expedient down to the last detail. I knew just what to do and where to go.

We drove north all that day, up the coast until we reached the steep cliffs of Civita, near Lake Bolsena. There we found the medieval bell tower of San Donato, a crumbling city clinging to the cliffs that had once long ago been Rebecca's home. Normally occupied by tourists during the day and bats at the night, it was now closed the entire season for renovations. We reached it on the morning of the following day, sitting like a gleaming, rusted ruby atop the cliffs in the early morning sun.

Rebecca shielded herself with her heavy cloak as we made our way on foot across an ancient Roman viaduct. The only entry point to the city, it spans the half-mile wide ravine that cuts it off from the surrounding countryside. The red sandstone buildings and bell tower stood menacingly over us as we trekked up the cobblestone walkway. The empty windows and doorways yawned at us in the dim light. A riot of stone masonry and stunted trees greeted our eyes as we moved up a rise to the grounds of the crumbling city. From here, with its single entry point, Rebecca could hold off an army of the damned if she had to. All around us, the ground dropped precipitously, down sheer cliffs to the rocks below. The lake gleamed blue in the distance.

"I will make my home in the bell tower," she said as we walked along the deserted streets, crowded with medieval buildings. The landscape was littered with large red stones and bricks fallen from the surrounding structures. Decay and rot were everywhere. "We can meet them here."

"Yes, mistress," I answered, like the subservient dog I am. "You can rest now. I will watch for you."

"Yes, Enrique. You have done well. You have proven yourself many times over, especially these last dangerous days. Now you must do one more thing for me, teach me to say the words of Ur so that I may say them as they should be spoken. In the meantime, we can stand them off here."

"Yes, master, but this seems more like a trap to me."

"You will be able to study the text here. There will be no distractions. Once I learn to speak the words, then I will seek my revenge. I will not stop until they all quake before me. Then we shall see if the old ones will grow any older."

She strode into the bell tower, while I lugged up a newly vacated coffin from the precinct's long-closed cemetery.

Now she sleeps. I walk the streets of the silent city and talk to the ghosts that haunt the place, but none of them can tell me what's to become of me.

During our stay in San Donato Rebecca has disappeared for days at a time, only to return to the crumbling city on the cliffs above Lake Bolsena when I thought she'd gone for good. She goes to gather information and blood. Perhaps she is building her army of street thugs and dock workers, using me as a decoy.

By day I study Belemarca's text to learn the ancient, arcane languages of people who vanished long ago. By night I teach Rebecca how to pronounce the words. It is a slow painstaking task, which I must do as quickly as possible. Time is running out. Yet I am loath to finish, for that would spell the doom of mankind, as well as yours truly.

Now I walk among the empty buildings and ruins, waiting for her return and for the inevitable attack. It has come tonight in the middle of a storm, amid the flashing of lightning and the peal of thunder, so loud it seems the clouds have come right down on earth to explode.

They are coming for me, for I am alone. I see them in the intermittent flash of the lightning as it streaks across the sky. A great cloud has opened up like a sieve to pour down raindrops as large as pieces of glass.

They come across the viaduct in a large disordered mob, like trolls, dozens of them. No one seems to be in charge, but they are terrible to behold nonetheless. The years have gathered on them so that they move slowly, stiff at the knees, arms locked at their sides, their shoulders hunched, eyes burning in their sockets. They look like they are possessed by the devil, so consumed they are with malice.

I run from window to window, door to door, looking out at them as they crawl across the causeway. I catch glimpses of them moving along the road from different angles as I look down in terror and dismay from one vantage point after another. I am trapped. There is no way down the cliffs except the way they are coming, all of them ancient vampires.

The rain has stopped. All is deathly silent except for the shuffling of their feet and the distant claps of thunder. I call Rebecca's name. I wail for her to help me, to save me from these demons, creatures dredged up from our inhuman past that should have been dead ages ago. But there is no answer. Rebecca has forsaken me.

They are all around me now, creeping up each crumbling street that snakes through the cliff top, sniffing the air. I run through the mud-splattered gutters toward the tower, and go up the winding stairs on my hands and knees.

Higher and higher I climb toward the silent bell itself, while below I can hear the gnashing of their teeth, hear them murmuring to each other in the darkness, in their ancient tongue.

They are on the floor below.

I am at the top now. Rebecca's box is empty. There was no place left to go.

It has ended. My ordeal is over. Let me tell you all that happened.

I steadied myself on the bell tower as they came, and looked out at the valley below, where cliff rose upon cliff from the level of the sea. All was brown and green, and hazy blue in the distance. Dozens of them were crawling up the side of the tower. I thought what a fitting place to die. I longed for the peace I never had, for all those who had passed away so long ago like my young mother, who I never knew, and my dear wife, the love of my life. Only my child, Emily, remains, and who knows what will become of her. I longed to be with her.

I was preparing to fling myself over the balcony and down the cliffs to certain death, when suddenly out of the night Rebecca appeared. She hissed and grabbed me by the back of the collar. She had come from the roof of the tower itself, like a spider. Throwing me on her back, she proceeded to crawl up the outside wall of the structure, using her fingers and toes to grip the hardly visible cracks and crannies peeking between the bricks.

We scurried across the broken tiles of several decrepit rooftops, then down the cliff side to a copse of stunted trees covered with wide, green leaves. There we were partially hidden as she carried me further down the cliff, like a mother sloth with its baby on its back. Looking back and up, I could see dozens of black figures running along the streets and cliff tops above, like ants looking for the bug that got away. Soon they had our scent and came after us with one loud howl.

We were on the run again. The old ones had gathered into a considerable force, practically every old vampire left in Europe, all hell-bent on destroying Rebecca and her humble slave - me. As we made our getaway along the cliffs, she told me what she had been up to. Our dear Rebecca had not been idle.

"Tikana, the shaman, has gathered all the elders of my race from the great centers of Europe to come here and destroy me. But I have trapped them there. Now all you have to do is call the number. You know, the one that you used to summon the authorities. It was a good joke, Enrique, and I remembered it well. I may be old in years, but I can learn knew tricks. Now, quickly, before they get away, call the number."

"Yes, master. You are very astute. That is why I would never try to cross you. I've learned my lesson. A lot is at stake for both of us, but you must never leave me again."

"Yes, we must cling to each other like vines, you and I, if we are to survive."

"But Master, we cannot defeat all of them. They are an army."

"Do as I say," she bellowed. "Call the number."

That was a month ago. Her clever plan worked. Soon after the phone call, an army of paramilitary and commando teams swarmed the area, unleashing a virtual fire-storm of high-powered bullets. Although they were surprised and several shot, the old ones were able to get way down the cliff sides and into the surrounding countryside to blend with the local populace. They have had to disperse and cover their tracks. They won't be bothering us again, en masse, anytime soon, but there is still danger.

We made our way from Lake Bolsena heading south down the spine of Italy until we reached the southern coast of the country, where the heel begins, near the town of Matera, where Spartacus was trapped two thousand years ago.

In the old part of the city there are empty stone facades that mask deep cave dwellings cut into the sides of the steep hill. This is where Rebecca led me. There we made our new home. It's supposed to be deserted now, but in Roman times it was the overcrowded home of countless families, along with their goats and pigs. Now it is the haunt of silent memories and more.

In the slanting rays of the rising sun it looks like a bombed out village, pock-marked and cratered, gray and dirty with the filth of ages. The empty doors and windows look like a hundred black eyes silently staring down on us. What a fitting place for my Rebecca.

Chapter 19

Rebecca has learned the correct pronunciation for the text of Ur. Now here in the caves of Matera she practices the words to unleash the curse. After that I do not know what will happen.

We hide in the caves during the day. Dark, dank places inhospitable even in the best of times. They smell of ancient diseases. Leprous fumes reek from the fissures in the broken stone pavement. Dogs and rodents fight over their turf in the raw heat of the day, while at night Rebecca feeds on any lingering squatters who the police haven't chased away, a few pee-stained drunks and straggling gypsies, barely enough to get by on.

I know that she plans to turn me. I try to put it off as long as possible. I tremble at the prospect of becoming a malevolent force for unrelenting evil like Rebecca. If I had but the nerve I would end it all, but I delay, somehow hoping against hope for some last minute reprieve.

I know too well what my life with Rebecca would be like. Not to mention what would happen to the human race if her demented plan is carried out and she creates a whole generation of new vampires. Life as we know it would be changed forever. No, somehow I have to stop this madness, but how?

Something terrible has happened. It's all a blur. It occurred so fast it hardly registered, like a film in fast-forward, but this was no movie. We were at the table with the text before us. Suddenly, there was another in the room. The next thing I knew, Rebecca and Marco were in pitched battle, canines gleaming. Another one stood at the entrance to the cave. At the same time, a dozen of Rebecca's men – enlisted in her usual way - rushed into the cavern from its many side tunnels carrying knives and guns.

Rebecca's little force of humans confronted the old one. The carnage was terrible. Their heads and limbs were piled on the floor in a moment by the Espiritus, but it gave me the time I needed to get away, while Rebecca dealt with Marco.

As we had planned in advance, I ran back into the caves to a secret passage that led to the other side of the cliffs, where the 450-HP pickup sat ready for just such an emergency. Such is our lives.

Still it was a close call. The old one was right behind me.

"Going somewhere?" a suave voice said behind me. You will not get away from me."

At that moment, before I could reply, something burst into the garage. It was just a blur, low to the ground, but it slammed into the old one's stiffened legs and knocked him to the ground. He did a complete somersault and landed on his back. It was Rebecca! Jumping up, she got in the vehicle. I slammed the door and put my foot on the gas.

Accelerating down the dirt street in a cloud of dust, I headed for the highway where I could gather some speed and outrun them. I saw something approach in the corner of my vision. It was moving fast to cut us off - Marco. He leaped onto the hood of the vehicle and clung there as we drove down the highway. I sped up and tried swerving back and forth across the road to dislodge him, but he held on tight. Behind us, the ancient city began to crumble into the ground, falling in upon itself. Dust billowed after us as we drove away.

I fought desperately to keep the car under control as Marco broke the windshield and reached in for me. Rebecca grabbed him by the arm, and tried to fend him off as he began to pull her out of the cab. I could hear his fingernails dig into the metal.

"Brake!" yelled Rebecca sharply as she struggled with Marco, half in, half out of the vehicle. We were going almost eighty on a straight-away. I jammed my foot on the brakes. At the same moment, Rebecca pulled Marco toward her. Then she pushed him away violently, at the same time letting him go. He went flying off the hood like a clay-pigeon out of a chute and landed twenty yards in front of us. Without hesitating, I jammed my foot on the gas and accelerated, hitting him right in the face with the front bumper at forty miles-per-hour as he was sitting up, smashing his head back into the pavement. The right-hand side wheels bumped over him as we sped down the road. He was not dead, but he was slow getting up and did not come after us.

"That was close, Mistress," I said, once we were in the clear. "Have you had enough of this madness?"

"No, Enrique, I have not even begun. I have big plans."

"That's what I'm worried about, Master."

"Don't whine, Henry. This was only a minor skirmish, a last desperate test of strength. We have thwarted the old ones. I know what I must to do now."

"I did not sign up for this, Mistress, the old ones, the SWAT teams, Marco. I am not cut out for this. I only want to serve you in peace."

"There will be no peace as long as the old ones have their way." She said this then paused for a moment and looked at me hard. "What did you sign up for, Henry?"

"I don't know, Mistress. I don't remember. I thought you were so beautiful."

"Were?"

"You are still beautiful, more beautiful than ever. But now I know how utterly evil you really are."

"And how evil is that?"

"More evil then hell itself."

"How nice of you to say so, Enrique. I did not ask for my life. I only try to make the best of it."

"Oh, no. Didn't you ask for it that night you went back to see Urammu, Ibihil of Mira."

"Don't mention those names!" she yelled in a hollow voice that sent shivers up my spine."

"I don't ask for this either, Mistress," I persisted. "Why must you force it on me?"

"We have been over this before. Don't fail me now, Henry. Not now that I need you most. That would be bad for both of us, especially for those you hold dear. For my minions have your daughter now. You are not the only one that does my bidding these days. Not all my slaves have been killed, so beware. Now, take me where I want to go."

"Yes, Master, as you say. And where is that?"

"Why, back to America, of course. New York City. There we will turn you."

We made our escape from Italy after a torturous drive across the peninsula, through the south of France to Madrid, where we booked a flight to New York City under assumed names. She didn't even wait for the plane to land before feeding on a man she found in the first class restroom. Now that's what I call a mile-high club, sex and death at 30,000 feet. Luckily for everyone on board, he somehow went unnoticed. I assume he was found some time after disembarkation, but I have heard nothing of the incident. I'm not sure how she would have disposed of him through those tiny lavatory dispensers.

We have been in New York for ten days now and have rented a penthouse apartment overlooking Central Park, paid for courtesy of a full dozen European gentlemen and ladies Rebecca killed and robbed along the way from Matera to Madrid. Her experiments in Italy and our escape from the old ones have given Rebecca more confidence. She is now determined to make me her vampire slave - the first of many, I assume - and take over the city for herself, to make it into some sort of fortress. Let the old ones fight and scrabble over her leftovers.

I am now more indispensable than ever. My technical skills and ability to drive and read have proven to be just the edge she needs to survive her enemies. And of course, once she turns me I will be her great general, or so she says.

The last gray light of day is slowly fading amidst the bare, interlocking limbs of dark-gray trees. Oh, that I could hold back the night, deny the darkness, delay the coming of my terrible mistress. If only I could prevent more death and sorrow. But death and sorrow follow in her wake. Are they not the lot of us mere mortals? Who am I to change that?

I am a virtual prisoner, watched when she is here and locked in when she is not. I am no longer quite trusted, no longer quite free. I look out from my bare room onto a barren world and long for release. I am too valuable to leave unattended, but not important enough to care about.

I can kick myself for all those times I could have ended it, could have assured her destruction. If only I had acted a little slower, or not at all. If I hadn't stood by her when she was on the run; if I hadn't procured sustenance for her when she was weak and couldn't feed herself; if I had not driven her from their traps, it would all be over now. I did all that and more. Actions once taken can cause a lifetime of sorrow.

New York is the perfect habitat for a vampire. I'm surprised we've never lived here before. Oh, Rebecca would visit the place from time to time, as she would countless other cities, to feed. After all, in this modern day and age, traveling 600 miles for a business lunch is considered normal. New York, a city that truly never sleeps, is also a city where you can find a dark secluded corner on the brightest of days. It is a perfect spot for Rebecca. For some reason, perhaps because of their recent setback, the old ones have not shown their faces.

She has her pick of a variety of ethnic flavors here, from white Anglo-Saxon executives to Navajo steelworkers; from black professionals to Pakistani taxi drivers; from Norwegian doctors to Spanish waiters. Young girls wearing the latest fashions, suave men cruising the streets for action, tourists gawking at the tall buildings, hookers and pimps, they all compete for Rebecca's attention.

New York has become her playground. She has defeated the old ones in the Old World, now she's going to conquer the new. She can go a long way in this city before attracting attention, there are just so many people to account for, doing so many crazy things.

Since we've come here Rebecca has roamed the city like a reptilian carnivore, frequenting the many singles bars and night-clubs in the tinseled town, some swank and sophisticated, some rough and tumble, but always filled with men and women eager to take a chance. The kind of people who drive too fast, drink too much, and take too many dares, who are always looking for a thrill. This is the kind she feeds on. So far we have not appeared to have disturbed an old one's territory. Maybe the Big Apple is a common ground, who knows.

Rebecca learned many things in her last effort. She will not make the same mistakes again, but my days are numbered. She is out looking for the perfect mate for me. Then she will turn me. I suppose it really isn't so bad. I can think of worse ways to die than in the arms of a beautiful woman. It's the aftermath that worries me, an everlasting slavery under Rebecca. For I know, even with vampiric-powers, that I could not withstand her.

So I do nothing. I bide my time and wait for the right moment, hiding my intent in phantasmagoric fantasies and erotic daydreams, though sometimes it all seems so hopeless. Where are the old ones and the Italian police when you need them?

In my virtual captivity I have contemplated my fate, tried to reconcile myself to the prospect of being one of the undead. As I've said, perhaps it isn't so bad. I wonder what it would be like to have superhuman strength, to be virtually invincible. I would be like a god. But something in me recoils at the thought. Perhaps some sliver of human decency given to me as a child by the mother I barely knew. God knows, I haven't had much of an example of human kindness in my life. My only role model is a merciless vampire. Yet I cling to my humanity like it is a precious heirloom. I am loath to give it up, but I know I have no choice. I see no way out. I'm afraid I will be even more in Rebecca's power once she turns me.

"What are you brooding about, Henry?" Rebecca says from somewhere behind me. "You have been so morose lately. Why so sad?

Things are getting good. All I see of your thoughts are your foolish daydreams. It is almost time for us to do what we must do."

"I do not think I can go through with it. Please Mistress, spare yourself the trouble."

"No Henry, it has to be you and it has to be the night of the full moon. But I will let you pick your own partner. You will have no excuse this time."

"But Mistress, I want to die in *your* arms"

"You will, my dear, but your partner must die too to maximize the spell."

"But…"

"No buts, Henry, you must do as I say. You will live through eternity with me and serve me."

"You are an evil master."

"Don't push your luck with me, Henry. I will set you free to pick your mate. Choose quickly and choose well. Don't disappoint me in my hour of need. Serve by my side as you have been doing these past hundred years, but as my equal, my general, my lord."

"I would always be a slave to you. That's what you really want."

"Henry, think of it. You said yourself so many times you love me. You will be invincible by my side."

"Yes, Mistress, that is true, but to become like you, one of the undead to haunt the night hunting human blood, no, I just can't conceive of that."

"You must. You have no choice. The weariness you feel, the pain and boredom will all leave you like dead leaves from a tree. You will be born again anew, stronger, with powers beyond your reckoning. Perhaps I have not spoken of these things enough."

"But of course, Mistress. I understand. You are right. It is for the best, and part of me wants it, too. Yes, let me seek my own mate, the perfect sacrifice to initiate my way to the dark life. I want to be yours for eternity, but what of my daughter?"

"Do not worry about her. What happens to her depends on you, Henry, and rightly so, for you are her father."

"I will not let you turn her."

"You will have no say in the matter, but don't fret. I have not yet decided. As I said, it all depends on you."

"As you say, Master, I am yours to command."

"That's my precious, Henry."

She stood and stroked my head for a few more moments before leaving through the front door like a normal person to take the elevator to the street. She almost caught me off guard, with my mental shield down, but luckily it is almost second nature now to divide my mind, compartmentalize my thoughts, so that she can never see what I am truly thinking. This knack I have could be all that separates me and my daughter from the most terrible of fates. I don't know why I dread it so. It's mainly my mistrust of my terrible mistress, whose word is as good as her bite. No, I would sooner be torn apart by wolves, which is my likely fate, than be a doormat for her to step on for eternity.

At least looking for the perfect candidate will give me a chance to get out of this penthouse prison, and once free I might find some way out of my predicament. I will search for the perfect woman to sacrifice. What better place to find her than Manhattan and its boroughs, with its dance spots, movie houses, theaters, and clubs, just the types of places aspiring young females frequent. I will have my pick of the city's best, and in the process perhaps find the key to my dilemma. Only time will tell, and time is running out.

Chapter 20

Today, in a particularly depressed mood even for me, I have been permitted to leave my prison to hunt for the perfect sacrifice. As I understand it, the killing of the girl will be used to increase the power of the curse and bring forth stronger demons from the pit, but the words will not be spoken over her death, only mine moments before. So only I will be turned. I have been thinking about that moment quite often.

Rebecca has been true to her word, though I know she watches me, or has one of her minions do so. I am wearing the disguise Rebecca has devised, a beard and wig, acting the part of a middle-aged bachelor. I have frequented all the hot-spots of the city, night clubs and discos where the most beautiful people are said to go. I've even haunted the back stages of Broadway and the theater district, looking for young female talent, but so far I have turned up nothing. All the women I see are so vacuous and empty-headed, filled with the most inane nonsense. It's hardly possible to strike up a decent conversation let alone become passionate about one of them, not that the young men are any better, not a cultivated one in the bunch. They all seemed the same.

I've thought about what beauty really means, and I've seen much of it in my 100 some-odd years, but it seems the beauty that lies beneath the surface is the type that will last the longest. I was looking for something deeper. If I am to live an eternity that is the type of beauty I would be tied to. Not the spell-induced, superficial attractiveness of a vampire like Rebecca.

How do I find such a one? How will I distinguish her from all the rest, determine she is the one? Do I even want to, considering the reason? Then I realized it didn't matter whether she was beautiful or not, I was luring an innocent young woman to a hideous death. I am nothing but a sick, rabid cur, not fit to walk the earth. Yet I am about to walk the earth forever. The poor innocent soul I find today will help me.

It was at that point that I realized I might be looking for an ally, someone to aid me in my battle against Rebecca. If that was the case, who would I choose? Someone older perhaps, an old soul, a soul mate? I was looking for a person of another time, an older age where strength and endurance were counted more than good looks, a time when things were simpler yet deeper-felt. How was I to find someone like that in the center of modernity?

In despair of finding anyone who I wanted to spend eternity with, I visited the Metropolitan Museum of Fine Art, hoping to find on canvas what I could not find in life. Instead of finding beautiful women, however, I found only death. I stood and stared at paintings of naked saints being pierced by arrows, shirtless sailors being chewed by sharks, wingless angels being hurled from heaven and impaled on stakes. Then I saw her, not in oil hanging on a wall, but in the flesh.

While I was looking at the painting of St. Sebastian, tied to a post and pierced with arrows - one of my favorite pictures for its pathos and eroticism - a young woman with long blonde hair ran up to me, threw her arms around me, and kissed me.

"David!" she said. "What are you doing here so early?"

I was momentarily at a loss for words. My hesitation made her take a step back and look at me more carefully.

"David, is that you?"

"No, madam, my name is Henry."

"Oh, gosh, I'm sorry. How embarrassing. You look exactly like my boyfriend, Doctor David Benjamin. And I mean identical. He's a professor at NYU. He comes here often. That's why I thought you were him. The resemblance is absolutely amazing."

She was young, much too young and good-looking for a guy my apparent age, roughly fifty on a good day. He must be quite the stud, very rich or well-endowed. She was pretty in a wholesome kind of way, with a narrow waist and full figure. She had a flawless complexion and smiled at me pleasantly. It was an old fashioned beauty that captivate me instantly

"I'm flattered," I said. "I don't get that many beautiful women mistaking me for their boyfriends."

"Now I'm the one being flattered. David's a little older than I am, but he's the most intelligent, sensitive, and energetic man I know, a lot better than most of the guys my age."

"Then there's still hope for me."

"You bet. Anyone who can pass for my David should have no trouble with women."

"That's so nice of you to say. Do you like this painting?" I asked, pointing to the St. Sebastian. "It's one of my favorites."

"Oh, I don't know. It's kind of morbid. He looks so sad and hurt. The way he's looking up to heaven like that with those eyes. Poor guy's practically naked."

"Anything to show off a good physique," I said, trying to make a joke, something I had not done in seventy-five years.

"Well, I'm sorry for bothering you. You just looked so much like David I could have sworn it was him. Sorry. Nice meeting you. Bye."

With that she was gone.

I stood there for some time after she left, staring at the painting but seeing only her. There was something about the fresh look of her face, something innocent and free of evil, something strong and good. She captivated me like no one had ever done before, the very opposite of Rebecca.

I went to a bench in another part of the museum and sat down. I felt drained, spent as if I'd been standing at attention for hours. As I sat there, amidst the artwork and sculpture, a germ of an idea started to play in my mind. Something about a man in an iron mask.

This evening, on her way out to the night's butchery, Rebecca asked me what I had done today. I told her I had gone to the museum to look at all the pictures of the dead. I told her I wanted to be like them, captured for eternity in my starkness, blameless and purified of my failings. She told me I was being melodramatic, that things were just getting good and that she had other plans for me. She told me I would be the most potent vampire yet.

"Did you find anyone worthy?" she asked.

"Yes, as a matter of fact I met the most promising young woman. I am going to try to get to know her better."

"Good, but you'd better hurry. We must act soon. The time is upon us."

Then she was gone.

I can't help thinking about that lovely girl I met today at the museum. I don't even know her name, but somehow I feel she's the key to all my problems.

She has a boyfriend that looks like me. She has a face like an angel and a body that would drive a saint to distraction. Yes, Rebecca would love to despoil a lass like that. I banish the thought from my head. How could I think of seducing a wholesome beauty like this to her death? And yet that's exactly what I am planning to do. Still, there is something about her boyfriend's resemblance to me that tugs at the corners of my brain. There may be something there that I might use to thwart Rebecca.

There is a definite pecking order among vampires, something I have learned only recently. Age determines everything. The oldest are the strongest and most powerful. Rebecca can hold her own and then some with Marco, who is centuries younger than her. But she could not survive an attack of one twice her age, as most of them are. However, what she lacks in strength, she makes up for in speed and agility.

It is now morning and Rebecca has yet to return. She has been out on one of her rampages. I thought they would stop after she stymied the old ones in Rome, but she continues to indulge herself. It has only gotten worse, the bloodlust habitual. The Early Bird news team reported another series of gruesome murders occurring late last evening at a private dance club in Spanish Harlem. Forty people, an equal mix of men and women, all found early this morning dead on the dance floor, as if torn apart by wolves, while the disco machine continued to play the latest Latino hits. She must have started killing them slowly and unobserved in the chaotic, ill-lit, smoke-filled room. Once she had thinned out the room, she finished off the rest with a flurry. The city is in an uproar, much as the Romans had been, but nothing can be done. So far there are no clues. No one has lived to describe the perpetrators of the grisly crimes taking place around the great metropolis.

Today, without my disguise on, the first thing I did was go to the museum, where I spent all morning wandering among the paintings and statues, the exhibits and relics, looking for that girl. Then on a whim, I went to the campus of NYU and searched the faculty register for professors with a first name of David. I'd forgotten his last name, my short-term memory disappearing with my hair and teeth. There it was - Dr. David Benjamin, Ph.D. Archeology - my look-alike, some young woman's old boyfriend. Using a computer in the lobby, I was able to get his class schedule.

My skill at applying make-up and disguises, honed through years of practice, allows me to blend into any situation. I can be a hobo or an executive, a cabbie or a jeweler, so I wasn't worried about attracting attention. As it turned out, as luck would have it, the wig of thick gray-black hair I had worn, and the fake beard, together with the tweed jacket and brown turtle-neck, made me the spitting image of Professor David Benjamin. Who could have believed it, just plain dumb luck. Or was it more than that?

I staked out the entrance to his building from the sidewalk across the street and waited. Without the disguise I was bald, and for this occasion wore glasses. Before long I saw a familiar face, the girl from the museum.

I could have spotted her in a crowd from the Good Year blimp. Her bright smile radiated from across the street amidst a flash of blonde hair like a sunburst. She was leaning against the side of the building near the entrance. A short time later my look-alike came out and arm in arm they headed back up the street. I followed.

I couldn't believe it. She was right. The likeness was uncanny, my height, my build. Except for my premature baldness, we were identical in almost every respect, same facial bones, same hands, same eye color, same nose, same frown, same smile. It was just my good fortune to have been wearing the right color wig and mustache that day we met.

I followed them for some blocks, until they entered a delicatessen on the Upper East Side. I noticed that even his gait was like mine, the way he carried his head, the way he held his hands. It was like seeing my reflection in a mirror standing there before me in the flesh. It was surreal. Perhaps there's only so many bodies, so many faces, so many souls to go around, and if you live long enough you're just liable to meet your double. Or maybe I've been cloned somewhere along the line. I wouldn't be surprised by anything at this point. Would you, after hearing my tale?

I took a booth at the rear of the deli, where I sipped coffee and watched them. She certainly seemed fascinated with the guy, the way she looked at him. I could only dream of having someone smile at me like that. I have to admit, he seemed robust and energetic for his age. He certainly had an air of sophistication about him, kind of like a poor man's Sean Connery. By the time they left, the sky outside had begun to darken perceptibly, and a detailed plan had begun to form in my head.

Now I sit in the darkness looking out the window at the streets below, alive with colors and people. She's out there, hunting. Somewhere at this very moment she's seducing some man to his death or stalking some female just out of puberty. I hide my thoughts in images of the past, images of Rebecca's more colorful escapades. It always helps to have a ready stream of false pictures, easily conjured up, to deceive a mind-reading vampire.

Chapter 21

The terror continues. On New Year's Eve she hunted in Time's Square, killing thirty-five in front of the TV cameras and a hundred million viewers, all without anyone noticing. The following morning when cleaning crews swept the area, they turned up more than debris and litter. There were bodies stuffed in garbage cans, corpses behind dumpsters, cadavers under parked cars, all drained of blood and otherwise mutilated.

The following week a theater full of concert goers was the scene of still another massacre, when twenty-four were killed, half during the ensuing panic and resulting stampede. Yes, Rebecca is on the rampage. At this rate she'll suck her way through the entire city in no time. New York is closed up like a spinster's legs at a barn dance. All public events have canceled until further notice.

I have seen one of her new servants, a handsome young man with evil eyes and a sneering smile. He looked at me as if he'd just as soon slit my throat as talk to me. I'd just as soon join a pack of hyenas.

I confronted her that night when she returned all blood-gorged and heavy from the recent carnage.

"Master, what are you doing? At this rate you will dry up the city in no time. If you're not careful we'll be on the run again."

"It is they who will be on the run this time. Are you ready, Henry? How are things going with your love life?"

"Very well. The girl is only half my age, so pure, so sweet and innocent that I will get great pleasure despoiling her."

"Well, if she is as good as you say she is, this will be just the special ingredient we need."

All is ready. I have been busy these past few days, scurrying here, sneaking there, making arrangements and sending out invitations, seeing to all the details of my elaborate plan. It has to work. It is my only hope, mine, my child's, and humankind's.

Whatever is to be done has to be done soon. The first new moon of the New Year occurs in a few days. In the meantime, the carnage is getting out of hand as Rebecca continues her butchery. Yesterday morning, just before returning home from her hunt, she came upon a bus full of inner-city children going to school. Their parents and New York went through great lengths to bus these kids to this particular upper middle-class, white neighborhood. Unfortunately, Rebecca happened to be prowling in that neighborhood, and the bus full of children ended up being a yellow hearse.

Now that I'm once again in her good graces and have somewhat earned her trust, I can come and go whenever I wish and have the complete run of the house, although she doesn't let me stray too far in case the old ones should reappear. She wants me close at hand, but so far we have seen no sign of them.

Last evening she summoned me to her tomb and gave me final instructions.

"I want you to invite your new friend, the wholesome one with the large breasts, to dinner tomorrow evening," she said, after rising from her crypt, ready for another riot through the streets of the city. "We're going to have a dinner party for her. Ask her to invite some of her friends as well, exactly ten of them. You will take care of Mister David Benjamin and take his place."

"Yes, Mistress, very good. As you wish."

"Good. I think we have reached a new level, you and I."

I looked out the window for a moment, lost in thought, and when I turned back she was gone, vanished into the night to hunt. I shuddered at the thought of it and turned on the lights.

There is not much time. I have learned a lot about Samantha Smith and David Benjamin since that day I followed them from the NYU campus. I know their habits, their friends, what they like, what they don't like, everything I need to know for my purpose. I contacted them and invited them and their friends to the penthouse under the guise of a dealer of rare and expensive antiquities, who represents a very wealthy collector. If anyone knows about antiquities, it is I, the keeper of an ancient succubus.

I checked the guest list. There were some on it that Rebecca would not care for, some who would be a big surprise. Their presence is necessary, however, if Rebecca's ravages are to end.

Obviously, she plans to substitute me for the NYU professor, then kill me and turn me as I make love to Samantha in his guise. I am to get rid of him while bringing him to the party, but I have other ideas. Not that I have scruples or anything. Not when it has anything to do with something as important as my survival as a human being. But I am not going to play into Rebecca's hands.

A rich collector like she is posing as, with deep pockets and a penchant for ancient art objects, is an archeology researcher's wet-dream, especially if that researcher has to manage a tight budget. An elegant dinner in a magnificent Park Avenue penthouse, hosted by one of the elite of New York's art world, was just too much for Samantha and her friends to pass up. Everyone accepted the invitation, including Doctor David Benjamin.

I readied the dining room for the banquet, a magnificent room with gold and crystal chandeliers, and a long cherry wood table decorated with polished silver and exquisite china surrounded by high-backed antique chairs. I knew Rebecca would bring a few of her young servants for appearance's sake. I just hoped they weren't going to mess up my plans. But I had accounted for all this. Failing was not an option.

The night of the dinner has arrived. I spent the day preparing the meal and its accompaniments - fresh Cornish hen, vegetables still fresh from the field, crab and lobster wet from the sea. It was good to be in the kitchen again, preparing a feast for an appreciative audience. But every time I thought of what was going to happen to them, my mood plummeted and my contentment went into hiding.

The image of the girl's pretty face keeps haunting me. The way she smiles, the way she moves, her hair, all bring back the innocence of my youth and remind me of the way my mother looked, with her blond hair tied in braids. Her complexion is as flawless as the most perfect master's rendering. How could I be luring this exquisite creature to a fate worse than death? How could I knowingly let Rebecca get her hands on this pure soul? But that's exactly what I'm doing. Yet, if my plan works as I hope, all may not be lost.

Darkness has descended like a curtain on a half-done play. How I've learned to hate the night, to loathe each sunset, like I abhor my everlasting soul. The evil I've done in Rebecca's name has made me damned for eternity. Too bad I don't believe in such things, just in the living hell my life has become. Who is to thank for that? Shall I blame God for letting this happen to me? Or perhaps it's the devil. No. I blame no one but Rebecca, that evil whore. She shall pay. The play is about to begin.

I left the house on my appointed rendezvous. Rebecca stayed in to receive our distinguished guests. Samantha was coming with her friends. It had been arranged that I would pick up David Benjamin at the university where he had late classes. On the way back to the apartment we stopped to get some cigarettes at a small motel. Once there, I knocked him out in the parking lot and tied him up in the room I rented earlier. Then I put on my wig and mustache, drove back to the penthouse, and joined the party as the professor. Not even Samantha noticed it wasn't him. Only Rebecca was in on the ruse.

She would have plenty to feast on this night. This was the first time since we'd been in New York that she'd be dining in. The logistics of room service for someone such as Rebecca should not be underestimated. Townhouses are not the most convenient places for disposing bodies. However, our apartment is in an old brownstone that still uses a coal furnace to heat the place, all cranked-up to ward off the January chill.

Samantha looked beautiful in a white satin evening gown, strapless and clinging. Her hair, loose and hanging below her bare shoulders, and her long neck, made her look like a princess in the moonlight. Her bare arms were well-defined and her breasts swelled invitingly beneath the low-cut fabric of her dress. We made quite a handsome couple, if I do say so myself.

The rich surroundings and priceless artwork of the penthouse impressed Samantha and her friends, all of whom I've watched and studied over the past few weeks. They talked animatedly about the many expensive paintings and rare antiques that graced the apartment, most of it taken with us when we fled Europe. Rebecca had planned her escape well.

Dinner was announced and the guests moved to the spacious dining room, specially prepared just for the party. There was an even dozen guests, including Samantha and her date. I, the faithful butler and chauffer, had the night off.

Rebecca sat at the head of the long table in all her regal splendor. Sitting to her left was young Michael Baines, an art dealer from a swank upper-eastside gallery, underdressed as usual for such a formal occasion in a turtleneck sweater and brown corduroys. Next to him was his current companion, a young Japanese art student whose name was Ken Sumo-wrestler or something. His thick brows frowned noticeably while his flamboyant partner jabbered away with Rebecca, ignoring him completely, as if she were the only person in the room. She had great plans for these two.

Next to Ken sat Charley Summers, a professor of art at Columbia University. A tall, attractive Englishman in his mid-thirties, Charley could have been a star on the big screen, with his pearly white teeth and slim physique. Instead, he taught art to panting young girls fresh out of high school. On his left sat the rich and beguiling Judy Van Horn, patron of the arts, a tall athletic woman with a loud voice fogged by too many cigarettes and too much booze. She was older than her companion by half a dozen years, but could still turn heads.

Next to them was an African-American couple, Mister and Mrs. Andrew Peters. Angela and Andrew worked at the museum. Angela's silky, ebony skin and high cheek bones made her easily the most striking human female in the room next to Samantha. She had on a colorful dress slit down the front to expose a long V of dark skin reaching to her navel. Andy himself looked like a football player, with broad shoulders that filled his blue double-breasted suit.

Judy Van Horn held sway over the conversation in this area of the table, her fog-horn voice booming over everyone, while she nudged and poked the good-looking black man sitting next to her.

At the end of the table I sat impersonating David Benjamin, wearing his best tweed suit. I said little, and probably seemed preoccupied as I silently watched Rebecca monopolize Samantha at the other end of the table.

Next to him sat Shanti Santakanra, professor of archeology at NYU, and a peer of Professor Benjamin. Her dark eyes and delicate features speak of both Indian and English descent. She talked animatedly to me thinking I was Benjamin . I listened half-heartedly to her as she expounded on the latest findings in archeology, something I know a lot about.

Next to her was Julie Rosenbaum. The youngest Ph.D. at NYU at twenty-one, she has a face and body that could be on any fashion magazine. Instead, she's usually seen in scientific trade journals holding a beaker of some liquid. She wore a simple short black dress with pencil thin straps that clung and moved around her like smoke whenever she walked. Julie was being monopolized by a large Russian gentleman with graying brown hair and thick, dark-framed glasses. George Tsenko spoke with a rich accent made even more difficult to understand by a bad stutter that had plagued him since youth, but hadn't hampered his illustrious career as a painter.

Another man named Paul White was seated next to the stuttering Russian staring unabashedly at Rebecca, who was sitting at the head of the table. He had long blond hair, and had obviously once broken his nose. Despite the facial flaw, he was quite attractive, with sharp blue eyes and a trim build. He had on a white shirt with an open collar, black slacks, and cowboy boots. Next to Paul sat Samantha, deep in Rebecca's spell.

Rebecca doesn't have to drug the wine and food, although it was spiked with her usual mix of drugs. She can put you under her spell with just her laughter, with only the lilting wonder of her voice and the tilt of her head. She can seduce you with a word or a glance, own you with a touch. Who has a chance with one so beguiling?

The surprise guests had not yet arrived, but were waiting in the wings, at least I hoped so.

"If you don't mind me saying so, I thought you'd be much older," Samantha said to her hostess. "To have collected so many art treasures and antiques, I mean."

"My father collected most of these pieces when I was but a girl in Italy," said Rebecca, with an indistinguishable, slightly European accent. "When he died, he left it all to me, a priceless collection, which I enjoy sharing with my closest friends."

"That is so generous of you. David was so excited about meeting you and seeing some of your wonderful objects for himself. He's like a little boy when it comes to antiquities."

Rebecca looked across the long table at the man sitting at the opposite end, as if wondering how long I was going to be able to pull it off before I'd blow it and she'd have to go to plan B and kill everyone outright. Rebecca's Latino minions served each course, as the conversation turned to her collection.

"Some of the art that you possess is quite rare," said Summers, the art teacher. "I thought some of these pieces had been lost, but you seem to have found them."

"My father was a very skilled collector. He went places few others knew about to gather his treasure from all over the world."

"The Boadacia necklace is a special find. I didn't think such perfect examples of Celtic art existed outside a European museum. And that collection of Roman jewelry is absolutely incredible."

"Why thank you, Mister Summers. My father would be very pleased to see we have such knowledgeable and gracious guests to enjoy our humble home."

"I especially like the exquisite copy of Michelangelo's David," said Michael Baines, the art dealer. "It truly captures the essence of the great master's treatment of the human form."

"You mean the male form, don't you?" said Judy Van Horn in her husky voice, sitting three seats away on the same side of the table. "You certainly would know a lot about that, wouldn't you, Michael?"

"Don't be a bitch, Judy," said Baines.

"You don't seem to have many African objects," observed Andrew Peters, his proud Nubian princess nodding in affirmation by his side.

"No, my father never had the good fortune of visiting Sub-Saharan Africa, although I always wanted to go there myself, you know, on a safari, to hunt and kill big game." Although not the ivory white it once was, Rebecca's skin was no longer ebony, but a dark olive brown that went well with her vague Mediterranean accent.

There was an awkward silence at the table as the guests digested this last bit of information along with their Cornish hen entree.

"Your new exhibit of Asian art at the museum is quite interesting, Mr. Peters," said Shanti, the Indian archeologist, who was also a connoisseur of modern art, Western and Eastern."

"Thank you, Miss Santakanra," said Andrew's wife. "Andy was instrumental in getting that exhibit here. Presents a nice balance to the standard fare, don't you think?"

"I'm surprised I haven't heard of your father," said Andrew Peters, not waiting for a response to his wife's question. "With such a fabulous collection, I would think you'd be in all the trade journals."

"Yes," said Julie Rosenbaum from the other side of the table. "As Charley said, some of these items are rare masterpieces, priceless objects once thought lost, missing for decades."

"I'm afraid my father was a recluse and avoided publicity. I seem to have acquired his habits. I've been in the field, in Egypt and the Mid-east, and before that the Far East. I've been searching the globe acquiring fine and ancient objects like my father, and like him keeping a low profile."

"Someone as beautiful as you must have a difficult time staying unnoticed," said the young blond man with the broken nose. "I'm surprised I haven't met you around town before now."

"Don't listen to him," said Julie Rosenbaum from behind the bulk of the stuttering Russian. "He says that to all the girls."

Rebecca barked her chilling laugh, which to the room of half-drugged diners, sounded warm and full and vibrant.

"I've only been in New York for a short time, and have been avoiding all publicity. The less people know about what's here, the better. One can't be too careful, you know."

"I don't blame you," said Miss Rosenbaum, liking the attention she was getting from their host. She had never gotten all warm and tingly when a woman looked at her before, but Rebecca was different. "With all the terrible murders going on, it's just not safe. There's a maniac going around butchering people. Isn't it horrible?"

The conversation shifted to the series of grisly murders that had been plaguing the city for the past few months, each guest recounting a particular gruesome detail that stuck in their memory. Rebecca seemed to relish the discussion, and egged it on by recounting other mass murders of the past.

I remained quiet and watched Rebecca intently from across the table.

"G-G-God is g-g-g-good," said Tsenko suddenly, in his stuttering, halting, thick-accented English. "For b-b-bringing such b-b-b-bounty upon this table."

He stood up unsteadily with his wineglass in his hand and made an incoherent toast, something about time and eternity, space and the cosmos, a barely understandable tirade interrupted by hiccups, burps, and stutters. Rebecca looked at him with eyes of stone, as if she would vaporize him with her Methuselah gaze.

"Thank you, Mister Tsenko," she said graciously with a velvet voice. They were all heavily drugged now and under the influence of her spell. Their voices and manner were loud, their eyes wide and glassy. They were breathing fast and shallow.

Her boys served the strawberry soufflé desert, one bite of which would make them her slaves, open to any suggestion Rebecca might give. Like a character in the Marquee de Sade, she would seduce them and play them like instruments of torture. And after feasting on them one by one and two by two, she would use the wholesome one, the pure one, my sweet Samantha to turn me into a vampire.

As soon as dinner was finished, the guests dispersed throughout the spacious penthouse, set up like a museum, with long curving hallways and richly furnished rooms where paintings hung like a gallery. Some sat in the den on brown leather chairs and sipped cognac, while others lounged in the living room on sofas and reclining-chairs to watch the big-screen TV. A few slipped into one bedroom or other, to lie together on beds or thick pillows strewn across the carpet.

Michael Baines and his boyfriend, Ken, went with Rebecca into one of the bedrooms to satisfy an urge that had been burning in him since the second course. Michael was as gay as they came, but this woman, Rebecca, inflamed him like no female ever had. He couldn't take his eyes off her during the entire meal, and when she invited him and Ken to her room for a little snort of cocaine, he followed her eagerly. Ken, his partner, had been getting more upset as dinner progressed, as Michael fawned and doted over their host, showing off like a schoolboy. As Ken followed reluctantly to the bedroom he seemed to be having trouble focusing.

Judy Van Horn had led Charles Summers to the game room by his hand as soon as dinner was over. They had not been seen since, but it was easy to imagine what they were doing.

The blond in the cowboy boots with the broken nose accompanied the Indian archeologist into the den, where I joined them as Benjamin. Rebecca came in a short time later. I could tell she had just fed.

The rich, brown liquid in the cognac glasses sparkled in the glow of gold-colored table lamps, adding to the intoxication of Rebecca's presence. The young blond man for some reason couldn't seem to pry his attention from the Indian professor, which was odd because she really didn't seem to be his type, a little too plump and moon-faced I'd judge. But the way he stared at her, you'd have thought the little butterball was the Queen of Sheba. You could cut the sexual tension in the room with a knife. Soon the Indian girl was sitting on the cowboy's lap, while Rebecca sat in a divan across from them watching. I left at that point, saying I was going to find Samantha.

When I returned a half hour later, I found the others in the living room listening to soft jazz and drinking the rest of the well-spiked wine. George Tsenko, now inebriated as only a Russian can be, was all over Julie Rosenbaum, pawing her like a horny ape. She took refuge between Andrew and Angela, who protected her like two Sequoia trees. Eventually, the three of them left the room in search of the hostess, leaving a frustrated George to be consoled by Samantha and yours truly.

When I left the penthouse, I went back to the motel where I had tied up David Benjamin. Unfortunately, to my dismay, he had choked on the oily gag I used to keep him quiet. It did a better job than I had intended in silencing him; he had died of asphyxiation. Unperturbed, I wrapped him in a blanket and quickly brought him back to the house, hiding him in the master bedroom. I then found Samantha and the others in the living room.

Tsenko sat in a chair talking to himself in Russian. Samantha, under the influence of Rebecca's sly charms, was responding whole-heartedly to my advances, which was all part of the plan. Even this close and intimate she did not suspect that I was not really her lover. We were sitting on the couch. I was kissing her neck and touching her all over, not the least bit inhibited by the presence of the Russian, although I could tell he was starting to get perturbed. A short time later, Rebecca came in.

"How is everyone doing?" she asked. "I'm sorry things are so lackadaisical, but my man is away on business and I have only temporary help."

"Oh, no," answered Samantha, slurring her words slightly. "We are having a wonderful time." She giggled like a school girl.

"Well, it's a very large apartment. Feel free to use any of the rooms, or look at the collections in the gallery below. Or perhaps you'd like to lie down and rest after that big meal."

"What kind of f-f-f-fucking party is this, everyone s-s-s-sitting around s-s-s-screwing each other?" asked Tsenko rudely, standing up and weaving back and forth as he fought to keep his balance.

"Young blood has a way of boiling out of the pot," answered Rebecca smiling her deadly grin. "Young men are always looking for romance, for death is only a heartbeat away. It's death, you see, that makes the other so desirable. It's the fact that what is beautiful will soon whither and die that makes it so valuable. Life ends so that it can begin anew in someone else, through your blood."

I knew that look. It did not bode well.

"Sammy," I said, leading her out of the room. "Why don't we check out one of the bedrooms."

As I led her out, I heard Tsenko say, "W-w-what did you s-say? You c-c-c-crazy bitch. This whole p-p-p-party is c-c-c-crazy."

I stayed just outside the door and watched.

Becoming more agitated each minute, the Russian went to leave. He only made it half-way.

Striding across the floor, Rebecca grabbed the painter by the throat and ripped out his trachea with a single snap. The big man began to spasm. His body jerked around like a headless chicken. Then he collapsed in a heap with a gaping hole in his throat. Before he hit the ground, Rebecca was on top of him, covering the wound with her mouth, sucking it so that only a little blood spotted the carpet. It did not take long for him to die.

Samantha, waiting further down the hall, saw nothing. In any case, she was quite heavily drugged. I led her by the hand into the master boudoir, into the mouth of the beast. I was like Urammu, the high-priest of Marduk, leading Ibihil of Mari into the dark-temple at the top of the Ziggurat.

It was pitch-black inside the room. The drapes were closed and the lights were out. I left them off and asked her to change into the negligee I handed her. She complied and disappeared into a small adjoining bathroom.

I could tell Rebecca was weaving her spell, for the young girl was totally susceptible to my every suggestion. As she undressed, I dragged the naked body of her dead boyfriend from the closet and laid him in the bed. Then I crawled beneath it.

The double deception I was attempting would try all my skills of mental dexterity. I was about to throw my mind into a dead man.

The bathroom door opened, leaving a sliver of light. I saw Samantha's feet as she ran across the floor and jumped in bed, snuggling under the covers with her beau.

"Oh!" she exclaimed loudly. "You're cold. Here, let me warm you up."

She jumped on the body and hugged it.

"Hmm!" she said. "All stiff, are you? Is that a banana or are you just a dirty old man?"

She began moving vigorously, up and down on top of the body.

As she did so, I tried to imagine it was me beneath her having pleasure, and threw those thoughts to the dead man.

I knew Rebecca was in the room. Even if I hadn't seen her enter, I would have sensed her, felt her presence by the excitement coursing through her cold bloodless veins.

"Is that you, Henry?" she said telepathically. "Now is the time."

"It is I, Henry. It is I." I threw these thoughts into the body of the dead man.

That was all she needed.

Rebecca moved toward the bed, chanting the forbidden words of Ur as she raised the long obsidian dagger high in the air

Her voice rose to a fever pitch. Samantha, on hearing Rebecca and seeing her approach, threw herself off Benjamin and to the floor just as Rebecca brought the sharp blade of the knife plunging down into the dead David Benjamin's heart. At that exact moment, she spoke the final phrase of the curse.

By this time, I had gotten up from beneath the bed and had moved to Samantha's side. She was shaken but OK. I led her to the far wall where a dumbwaiter stood partially opened.

I wasn't quite sure what would happen when she spoke the curse over a corpse, and was relieved when nothing occurred. The corpse remained a corpse, but that didn't mean the heavens would not object just the same.

The ground started to sway. There was a loud splintering of plasterboard and wood as the wall behind the bed cracked down the middle. The foundation of the building shifted. Plaster fell. It felt like an earthquake. I stood at the dumbwaiter with Samantha. She screamed in terror as lamps fell from shelves and bookcases toppled over. Shoving her into the small elevator shaft, I jumped in behind her. Before shutting the hatch, I lingered.

Rebecca was lying astride Benjamin's body, shaking and striking it, crying, "Wake up, damn you, wake up!"

As she did, I saw my other guests arrive, the old ones, Tikana and Shanitar, Belemarca, with his creation, Marco by his side, all in their ancient vampire glory. The room filled with their tall, gaunt, silent forms, all clad in red robes.

"Henry, you have betrayed me," Rebecca cried, in disbelief. "What have you done? Do you know what they will do? They will destroy me! How could you?" Her voice trailed off into a wail. "How could you?"

The Old Ones, the Espiritus, descended on her like an enraged mob, beating her and striking her until she swooned on the floor. Others grabbed her feet and arms and lifted her to their shoulders.

As I closed the hatch to lower us to the basement, I saw the red-robed vampires carrying Rebecca's limp body away on out-stretched arms. It undulated like a snake with their movement.

I hope that is the last I will see of my terrible mistress.

Chapter 22

That whole terrible evening was like one long demented nightmare, vivid yet half-remembered. I break out in a cold sweat just thinking about it. More than that, much to my surprise, the absence of Rebecca has left me empty and numb, as if an arm had been torn away. I feel a great loss. Perhaps recounting the horror will lessen it in my mind.

Before the old ones carried her away, she had slaughtered all the guests, all except Samantha, who she planned to finish off after me. Perhaps she was to be my first victim as a vampire.

From the many news reports of the aftermath, it sounded pretty bad. When Samantha learned of what had happened to her friends, she became hysterical. Only now, as several months have passed, is she getting back to normal. That I was responsible for much of it, having lured them to their deaths, just makes it worse, but then I am used to self-loathing. After a hundred years I've learned not to scourge myself. I've learned to live with it, especially if it means the end of that evil queen, Rebecca.

The apartment was like a museum of death, a half-dozen rooms full of mutilated bodies, each one like a morbid painting, each more hideousness than the last.

The den was filled with some of the more precious of Rebecca's antiques and paintings, most of which were strewn across the richly-carpeted floor. Among the ruined art treasures were sprawled the bodies of Mister and Mrs. Andrew Peters, along with Julie Rosenbaum. It looked as if they had been used in some sort of ritual. Each was placed in an obscene pose, as were the mutilated bodies of Shanti and the cowboy.

Along the long, curving hallway, lined with well-lit paintings, was the game room. There, dangling by their feet from the low ceiling beams were the bodies of Judy Van Horn and Charley Summers. Their throats had been cut. Buckets had been placed beneath them to catch their blood.

In the master bedroom was the naked corpse of Doctor David Benjamin, a stone knife in his heart. This news I kept from Rebecca. If she finds out, I will claim it is some mistake.

In the guest bedroom, lying on a large, four-poster bed, were the headless bodies of Michael and Ken laying side-by-side. Their dismembered heads sat on the dresser next to the door. All of the victims, except Dr. Benjamin, had been drained of blood.

After lowering us to the basement in the dumbwaiter, I carried Samantha to Benjamin's car, which I had been driving all night. Then I drove her to his apartment on the Lower East Side where we are now. For all intents and purposes, I am David Benjamin.

Samantha's fragile mental state made it possible for me to carry on my deception. She woke a short time later with a start to see me, or rather David, who she thought was dead, kneeling next to her by the sofa. I wore a worried and anxious expression, and was dabbing her forehead with a damp cloth.

"I, I, I thought you were dead," she stammered, on seeing me. "She stabbed you in the heart. Oh, David, what happened?."

"Shhh, don't worry. Everything's all right. We're safe now. That wasn't me she killed. It was that man, the one you told me about, who looked just like me. I guess they planned to kidnap you by impersonating me and lured you to the house. She murdered everybody in the apartment. It was terrible. You were next. I found out and got there just in time."

"I saw her kill George Tsenko. She ripped his throat out. And those others in the robes, David, who were they?"

I was surprised she had seen so much in her drugged-up state.

"I don't know," I answered. "I was kidnapped by the lookalike and tied up in a motel. I managed to get away and come to you." I laid a web of lies to deceive her. "I didn't even know about the party. I was completely in the dark about the whole thing. One of your friends called me just before they died."

In her dazed state she didn't question me any further, but dropped back into unconsciousness, where she mercifully stayed for the remainder of the night. With the drugs I gave her to sedate her, she doesn't remember much of that evening's events.

I can hardly believe it's over. Each minute I expect Rebecca to come through the door, smile her chilling smile, and call my name.

Looking back on it, I'm amazed my little trick worked. Decades of practicing mental deception, until I could do it in my sleep, finally paid off. I was not only able to hide my thoughts from her and disguise my intent, I threw my mind like a ventriloquist throws his voice. Luckily, it worked when I needed it. It was a gamble, but it paid off.

As the realization that Rebecca is gone for good fully hits me, I am seized with an emptiness that threatens to choke me. I should be elated, but each breath is a torment. The image of Samantha, with her sparkling blues eyes and honest smile, helps fill the void. Not to mention that Rebecca's nightly depravities are finally over, even if there are still creatures of the night that walk the earth. At least I am no longer serving one of them. I am no longer the slave of a vampire.

If God is lost to me then I will make my pact with the devil. If I cannot save my soul then at least I will preserve my body. For I will surely taste the sulfurous fumes of hell for the terrible deeds I have done. In the meantime, before the devil claims me, I will taste a small part of that life that has been denied me these past 100 years, simple pleasures and enjoyment, things I have been deprived of all my days.

Because of my long experience in things ancient and decayed, and through my diligent homework and studying of the man, I have had little trouble taking over Professor David Benjamin's archeology classes, as well as his bed, although the latter has proved a bit more challenging.

When she woke late in the day the morning after, Samantha looked at me with suspicion. When I answered all her questions and offered explanations for all her doubts, she slowly began to relax. It is so easy to play the man. We had so much in common down to the way we brushed our teeth and trimmed our hair. He was a gourmet chef and a meticulous housekeeper. In many ways, her relationship with him – with me playing the part of an ardent lover – has grown even closer.

I've already concocted a story to avoid being intimate with her, a slight prostrate condition that should help keep me out of her bed for the time being. I'll devise something equally clever to cover my other obvious deficiencies in this regard. David Benjamin, among other things, was rather well endowed.

I don't know the span of days I have remaining to me. Without Rebecca's blood-potion it cannot be long, although I don't seem to be deteriorating like I did before without it, maybe because she's really gone.

Whenever I long for Rebecca, I caress Samantha. Whenever I miss Rebecca, I kiss Samantha. Whenever I pine for the feel of my mistress's cold skin, I touch the warm skin of my Samantha. She alone has saved me from despair.

Of course, my life can know no real joy. For I am a child of the damned, born and bred to burn in hell, an empty shell of a man, doomed and cursed. But while I can lift my weary head to scorn the sky I will not give in to despair. Each day gets a little better, a little further from the demons that chase me, demons I know I can never outrun, for each day I get a little closer to hell.

The old ones have crawled back into whatever holes they live in. I have seen no sign of Rebecca. No one will know how close we all came to destruction, how close she came to creating more vampires to rule the world. This soulless creature would have subjected us all to perpetual misery and everlasting slavery, a fate that was almost mine. Precautions have been taken to prevent such a thing from happening again, something that should have been done many ages ago. Now I bide my time, but until the end comes I will live each day to the fullest, this lie that is my life, and curse the memory of my terrible mistress.

Chapter 23

It has been almost a year since I last took up my pen to tell you about my terrible mistress, the vampire Ibilhil of Mari. Much has happened in that time. My love for Samantha has grown more each day, as has her love for me, and matrimony is in the air. Or at least the promise of it, for we are now engaged. It is hard for me to deny her anything, for she has freed me from an evil curse. Or has she?

Lately, I have been feeling my age, my real age that is, not the fifty some odd years I pretend to be. I feel old beyond my years, for without Rebecca's sustenance I am slowly deteriorating, declining faster as the days go by, my mind as well as my body.

My stamina is not what it used to be. I have all I can do to keep up with my younger mate, who's full of vibrant energy. It seems her Dr. Benjamin liked to dance to disco music and jog with her in the park. I put an end to that early on, feigning fatigue and overwork, which was no lie.

What I thought was going be an easy job teaching archaeology to a bunch of snot-nosed kids, turned out to be a tiresome burden. I was forced to pursue a crash course on the most modern techniques and findings in the field just to stay ahead of my average students. I have feigned a series of illnesses throughout the year. The result is that half of my classes have been taught by research assistants, which has not done well for my, or should I say David Benjamin's, career. That's the least of my worries.

Lately, some of my colleagues have been asking about me, as I often hear from Samantha, implying I somehow seem different and pre-occupied. I fall back on my usual excuses, my failing health brought about by years of research in the field toiling under the most trying conditions. From what I've learned, this wouldn't be the first time Benjamin suffered from physical ailments, with a medical history of cancer - in remission - and a heart condition.

My poor performance at school has obviously spilled over to my bed, where the once well-satisfied Samantha is now left less than happy, though she does not complain, bless her heart, and even wants to marry me. Her support for her lover in his hour of need is touching - if she only knew the real reason for his decline. She thinks this is just a minor setback, for Dr. David Benjamin has bounced back from adversity before. Why should this time be any different? She has such faith in me. I hate to disappoint her.

These past few weeks have been the worst. Now my short-term memory is starting to fail. I can hardly recall what I'm doing from one minute to the next. Worse than that, I seem to be losing time, only a few minutes here and there, not more than five or ten at most, but even that short period of blanking out is disconcerting.

It happened the first time only a few weeks ago as I stood shaving. One minute I was lathering up my face, looking at my reflection in the mirror. The next, I'm standing in a steamed-filled room, my image just a misted blur in the fogged-up glass, soap running down my neck, the water on full-blast. The hands on my bureau clock had moved further around its face than they should have. It has happened several times since then, the last episode in front of my class. I'm sure it's all over campus now that old Professor Benjamin is losing it.

When I freed myself from my bondage I vaguely wondered how long I would last without Rebecca's blood-potion to sustain me beyond the normal span of human years. I guess I was in denial, for my rapid deterioration has taken me totally by surprise, though one should never be surprised by what happens when one makes a pact with the devil.

In the weeks leading up to my escape I did as much as possible to improve my condition, betaking of Rebecca's blood-bowl as frequently as she would allow. Afterwards, I did all that was humanly possible to maintain the appearance of the real Dr. Benjamin. We even have separate bedrooms, a concession on her part to the lifelong habits of a confirmed bachelor. Although my hair is less than full it passes for the real thing.

My teeth were a different matter, and were only repaired after months of painful surgery, where new teeth were cemented into pegs screwed into my jaw, which had to be broken in several places. All of this I kept secret from Samantha, who thought I had been in a car accident. So all in all, I've been able to play my part without discovery. Until recently that is, for now all my work is being undone by the ravages of decay, which has caught up to me and seems to be making up for time lost, like a picture of Dorian Grey.

Those first few months of freedom were blissful. I could hardly believe it was true, and expected to see Rebecca come though the door at any moment, until one day, after the half year mark, I began to let myself believe she was gone for good. Samantha did much to help me forget my evil mistress, though a hundred years of memories are not easy to suppress. Samantha's loving caresses and the time we spent together were like a balm to my wounded soul. I basked in her presence like a sun worshipper after an eclipse. Life was good, and I experienced some of those simple pleasures I had been robbed of by my early life of slavery to that evil witch, Rebecca. Unfortunately, I was not been able to locate my daughter, Emily, for she was no longer at the orphanage where we left her, having turned twenty-one.

Samantha and I moved into a bigger apartment and got a dog. It was a big risk for me after what happened the last time with my wife, Caroline. I was loath to let myself be hurt like that again. Yet I knew I had to take the chance and give myself wholly to Samantha if I was to heal my wounds, which I did.

In the back recesses of my mind, however, the fear of Rebecca still lurked, ready to spring out at any time - around the next corner, in the face of the next stranger, at the next knock on the door. Then lately, seemingly in connection with my failing memory and health, things have begun to happen that make me wonder if all is not right with the world. Even more troubling is the thought that she may be behind it.

A few weeks ago, on a fine spring day on which I felt particularly well, Samantha and I took a walk in the park with our dog, Zoroaster. The dog, a German Sheppard, is particularly well-behaved or we would not be able to keep him in our sixth-floor apartment, but this day he acted like a mongrel in heat. We were sitting at a bench, a concession to me as I tire easily, while the dog romped around us at will. Suddenly, without any apparent reason, it stopped dead in its tracks, with one leg up and its tail straight out as if it were some kind of pointer. Its ears were standing up. Its teeth were bared. The next minute it took off across the grass, running straight through a thick bush and almost knocking down an old man on the sidewalk.

We chased him for several hours through the park, often spotting him in the distance. Just as we would get close, however, he'd take off again, as if following some silent command. Soon we lost of him altogether. It was after dark when we finally gave up and called the police, who told us there was nothing they could do. We put up several posters with his pictures around the neighborhood and park the next day, but have heard nothing. That was several weeks ago. Samantha was devastated. I began to wonder if there was more to it than just doggie wanderlust.

Now lately, along with my blackouts I have been hallucinating. At least that's all I can describe it as, horrible images that leave me shaking and perspiring with fear.

The first time it happened I was making love to Samantha, something we did infrequently owing to my ill-health. Samantha was on the verge of orgasm. I was having trouble holding off mine, which had been building as soon as we started - it had been so long. I was weakening rapidly, but determined to give her satisfaction even if I collapsed in the process. Suddenly, it was no longer Samantha beneath me, but the hard body of Rebecca, her black-streaked hair sprayed out like an aurora on the pillow. I screamed and threw myself off the bed, ending Samantha's climax and scaring her half to death. It was only a moment, only a fleeting image, but it was enough to ruin our evening and our love-making for many nights to come. Am I going mad?

It happened again only a few nights ago. I was sitting in my room reading when I heard Samantha come in from a day of shopping, though it wasn't her I saw enter the room but Rebecca. She walked through the door and smiled that evil grin of hers. I screamed as she strode right up to me, her hands extended toward my throat. I came to with Samantha shaking me and calling my name in alarm. I must have been sleeping and dreamt the whole thing, though Samantha said my eyes were open and looking straight at her. She said I looked like I was seeing a ghost. I had - the ghost of an evil dame I can only hope is gone for good. For how could she have escaped the old ones?

It is true that I do not know the details of what happened to her, but to see how helpless she was in their grip, how she lay unconscious in their arms as they carried her out, I have no doubt that she is truly gone. Who knows what they did with her. Perhaps she was torn limb from limb, the pieces burned and trampled on or scattered in the wind. One can only hope. She had aroused them greatly. They did not look in any mood to plea-bargain with. They were out for blood, Rebecca's. Yet I wonder.

Of course, I have not relied totally on Dr. David Benjamin's salary, as adequate as it may be for a college professor, to provide for Samantha and me.. I have supplanted it with a few baubles and bangles I snatched from Rebecca's penthouse as we ran away, several hundred thousands dollars worth of diamonds and rubies and emeralds. I sell them when needed through agents throughout the northeast, contacts built up over the years of doing business for my mistress. I've explained the sudden additions to our savings as inheritances from old and wealthy family members, who just happen to die every year or so back in the old country. We live well, although within the means of a senior academic and well-published researcher. The last thing I want to do is attract attention or leave a trail a vengeful vampire might follow, though I would be easy enough for her to find.

I remember the subtle hints when she returned and found me the last time I tried to escape her. I am on constant alert. Yet other than that weird incident with the dog, and my bizarre hallucinations, there has been no sign of her. Nevertheless, I am ready to flee at a moment's notice, and have my escape route planned down to the last detail. I will not be caught unprepared.

Today I met Samantha after classes. She looked at me in alarm.

"Honey, you look terrible," she said. "Are you OK?"

"Well, hello to you, too. Thanks for the compliment."

"I'm sorry, hon, but you look so pale, and your eyes are so sunken and bloodshot. I'm just worried about you, that's all. You have to take better care of yourself."

"I've told you, I'm sick. I'm seeing a specialist. He's trying to figure out why I'm losing weight and my hair's falling out, but so far they don't know a thing. I just have a bad headache. Classes went terrible. No one seems to want to do the required work any more. Kids are just so lazy now days."

"Maybe you should take some time off. The semester's almost over, you've been driving yourself so hard. Why don't we take a nice relaxing vacation upstate like we used to before that awful night."

"I've already taken enough time off this year. I haven't any more vacation or sick time left."

"The university won't mind. You can say you're doing some research."

With that she gave me a provocative smile insinuating the type of research I would be doing. It was a hard offer to turn down, and I promised I would think it over.

We went back to the apartment, where she nursed me back to health with tender loving care. I felt so good that evening I made love to her on the couch in front of the fireplace, where we sat sipping red wine. It was a perfect evening, except for when I tried to drive an iron stake through her heart. As before, in the middle of our lovemaking, she turned into Rebecca. One minute I was smothered in Samantha's lush bosom, the next I was embracing Rebecca's cold body, her chilling laugh reverberating through the room. I leaped to my feet and grabbed an iron spike from the heath, to jam into the evil vampire's black heart and put an end to her once and for all. I came to with Samantha struggling beneath me, the sharp metal point only a fraction of an inch from her soft flesh. I have moved out of the apartment and have not seen her since, though she has called several times. I don't pick up. I just can't take the chance. Not after what happened. Yes, I must be going mad - or worse.

It's the middle of the day, but it's dark outside, as large, gray clouds block out the sun. The sky rumbles with thunder that seems to go on forever, shaking the window panes as the rain slashes against the thick glass like pellets. I am back in Benjamin's old place near the NYU campus, while Samantha stays in the apartment. My health is at an all time low. I have not been to classes in weeks, having taken a leave of absence. The only research I do is in my room, looking for a way out of my dilemma. I know my days are numbered. There is no denying it, I am dying, and rightly so. Then why do I fight it? Why do I long to go on living, especially now that I have lost the only thing worth living for, my Samantha, the light of my dark life.

She would take me back if I could explain, but I can't. So I will suffer alone. Just when I need her the most I must shut her out completely. Benjamin's apartment is large and rambling, strangely empty for someone who should have possessions and mementoes of a long and fruitful life. But that is my existence, only mementoes I have are of burned bodies in the bottom of a furnace, of slaughter throughout the old and new world. Oh that I could forget. So it is fitting my end is near, yet I protest. There is yet so much to make up for, so much lost time to recover, decade upon decade of wasted chances and spent dreams. I so much want to experience life like it is meant to be, not some warped parody of it from the demented mind of an evil Mistress.

I try to concentrate as I write, yet I am having trouble thinking straight as I attempt to describe what happened last night. It stills seems like a hellish dream, but it was all too real. For the veil that separates reality and make-believe is thinner than you think. All I can hear is the wind outside, banging against my windows as if it wants to knock its way in, while the charged air thunders and crackles like a hundred freight cars rumbling overhead.

I was woken by the storm in the middle of the night, as it swept in from the west bringing high winds and hail. It wasn't the noise of the storm that woke me, however. Another sound, imperceptible, but there all the same, just heard over the din, made all the more noticeable by its novelty, a sound that should not be there. I sat up in the dark and listened. I almost gave up and lay back down at one point, when I heard it again, a soft sobbing. It was just perceptible above the tempest, as if someone was at the wall separating my room from the one next door. When I put my ear to it, however, there was nothing there, nothing but the rain pounding on the window panes and the thunder reverberating through the canyons of tall buildings in the city.

I lay back down, only to hear it again, a faint scuffling noise now coming from the back stairs near the laundry room, as if something was scratching the door trying to get in. Getting up, I put on a robe to investigate, using a cane in my weakened state for support. Pushing open the door, I entered the room where the washer and dryer stand, but it was empty. I checked the front door as well, and found it locked. Stopping, I listened intently with my ear to the wall, my breathing still, but the noise of the incessant rain and the peals of thunder covered all other sound. I began to think that it must be my imagination or perhaps just the wind, my fear getting the best of me. For as the anniversary of Rebecca's demise grew closer, my terror that she had returned increased in proportion. I was alone for the first time in my too long life, totally alone.

I searched each room again, turning on every light in the apartment, until one particularly loud thunderclap plunged the whole place into darkness. Now it was pitch black except for the occasional flash of bright lightning. Then I heard it again, between the peals of thunder, the distinct sound of scratching at the apartment door. This was no illusion, no figment of my imagination. This was real. The scratching grew louder and more distinct the closer I got to the doorway. Stopping, I instinctively looked around the room for a weapon of some kind, but there was nothing. All I had was my cane. There were no guns in the house, not that one of those would be any use against Rebecca. But she was gone for good, right? What did I have to fear?

I looked through the peep-hole but there was no one there. The sound had stopped, as had the thunder and rain, just as suddenly as it began. The wind was silent as well. All I could hear was the beating of my heart. I called out in the darkness.

"Hello? Who is it? Is someone there?" No one answered. Then there was a loud bump at the door. I jumped back in alarm. Then another one, harder and louder, as if someone was throwing themselves against the frame.

"Who's there?" I yelled with all the authority I could muster, which wasn't much. Fear was coursing through my veins. "What do you want? Leave me alone."

Again, there was a loud thump that jarred the door. I could stand it no longer. Throwing caution to the wind, I grabbed the knob and threw open the door. With my cane raised over my head as a club, I stood there ready to face whatever it was on the other side.

In leapt my dog Zoroaster, or at least that's what registered on my brain, as a large brown and black blur of fur barreled into my apartment taking my legs out from under me. He began running back and forth across the hardwood floor.

I called its name as soon as I realized what it was, but the dog was wild, frenzied from whatever horrors it must have experienced. How it found its way to me, up the stairs, through the stairwell doors, defied explanation. Yet here he was, my long lost dog, or what had once been my dog. Now I faced a wolf-like creature that hulked against the far wall, hackles raised, teeth bared, growling lowly as it looked at me with red glowing eyes, eyes that had seen hell.

I tried again to talk to the animal, to coax it back to some semblance of sanity, calm it down so I could approach and give it aid. It only grew more vicious the more I tried to calm it. It crouched and started moving toward me when I tried to approach it with an extended hand. I had all I could do to make it to the door and escape the room, closing it behind me as the crazed dog's jaws snapped at my heels.

That was twelve hours ago. I called the police, who in turn contacted the city dog catcher, who came but found nothing, not so much as a hair-ball in the apartment. They looked at me like I was crazy and probably chalked it up to someone hallucinating on prescription drugs. They asked me if I wanted to be taken to the hospital. I told them I was perfectly fine. I just had a rabid dog in the apartment. I explained that my dog, who I had reported missing several weeks ago, had apparently found its way home, but was crazed by lack of food and ill treatment. I don't know what had happened to it between the time it ran away in the park and when it showed up on the Lower East Side, but I doubt it was pleasant.

The police said the door to the rear stairs was shut but unlocked. I know for certain it was locked earlier. Either the dog unlocked and opened the door or the police are mistaken. Or is there another explanation? Poor Zoroaster, I hope he's OK. I shouldn't have panicked. I should have stayed and tried to help him, but the way he looked at me, with those weird red eyes and his teeth bared, drooling thick saliva, did not seem very encouraging.

I have not been able to sleep since. Nothing I eat stays down. I am down to a mere hundred and thirty pounds, which for my six-two frame is dangerously low, yet nothing I do seems to help. It's as if I am going through the final stages of lethal radiation sickness.

So be it, but let me die with dignity if it must be so, not like some mongrel by the side of the road. And let me take that evil witch, Rebecca, with me if she is back. These will probably be the last words I write.

Chapter 24

I was wrong. I live to suffer another day, although how I do not know. I am in a bed in a private hospital connected to an array of machines, each dispensing life-sustaining fluids, but none of what I really need - Rebecca's blood-potion.

I was brought here in a private ambulance by my physician, a highly paid specialist I hired a few months ago when my condition had deteriorated and I needed constant medical attention. I was in poor shape when they brought me in, and had suffered a stroke of some kind. I was totally paralyzed and having difficulty breathing. My weight was down to 110 pounds. If something drastic didn't happen soon, I would be a couple lines on the obituary page.

Before the seizure I was capable of only the least exertion. Every breath I took left me nauseous and dizzy so I could hardly lift my head, though lying down made the room spin. My head ached constantly, as if there were a dull buzz-saw silently vibrating between my eyes. I couldn't eat or sleep. Concentration was a thing of the past. Even my favorite music sounded like jack-hammers to my ears, so that I didn't even have that simple pleasure to lighten my distress. My misery was such that I wished I had died back there in that penthouse apartment like the rest of Samantha's friends. I was at my wit's end. It was at this point they rushed me to the hospital.

The many specialists that were brought in to consult in my case, all at considerable cost, were unable to diagnose the cause of my sickness and rapid decline. A few of the more astute of them liken it to a rapid aging process, as if I were growing old from the inside out. Of course, everything about me baffles them and makes any diagnoses all but impossible. They have never seen the enzymes that float in my bloodstream, nor the age of my cells, all of which I've explained as a rare genetic trait inherited from a long line of highly-inbred ancestors. Nothing they did could stop the deterioration process. I went from bad to worse, eventually slipping into a coma. I was expected to die that night, but here I am.

No one is certain why or what happened, but the next morning I was conscious and the morning after that sitting up and eating toast and milk. The experts are again just as baffled by my seeming recovery as they were by my rapid decline. Some still expect me to suddenly keel over and die, but I feel better than I have in weeks.

I had a dream, or perhaps it was a series of dreams, I am not quite sure, but it must have been when I was in the coma, though it seems to go on even now. I was lying in bed, delirious, calling out Samantha's name, when a night nurse came in to check on me. At least I assume it was a nurse. She had on a nurses' uniform of white with a scarlet cape, and a white cap lined in red. I thought her appearance a bit odd, for she looked as if she were from another time. She was worn-looking but not unattractive, with yellow-black hair tied in a tight bun beneath her cap, and dark green eyes sunken with years of care and toil. Her skin was as smooth as ivory. She looked like a forty-something hooker who had been with one too many johns, but she was gentle, and wiped my forehead trying to sooth my discomfort.

Then it was I knew I must be in a dream, for she slowly unbuttoned her white nurses' blouse and un-strapped her bra. Her breasts were hard and pointed, and seemed to grow as I beheld them, moving slowly toward my mouth. I closed my eyes and suckled them hard, but more for sustenance than pleasure, like a newborn babe goes instinctively to its mother. That's all I remember. The next day, as I've said, I was awake and talking.

Samantha and my associates have been told I have a rare form of leukemia, which is being treated by a specialist, whose name I have not divulged, at an undisclosed location here in the City, which not even Samantha knows the location of. My nurses have strict orders to admit no one. I feel more like a rare specimen than a patient, but that is only as it should be. No one must ever know the truth. If I die, I will die an enigma.

I told the doctors of my dream. They assured me there is no nurse in the facility - a private, swank, twenty-bed penthouse clinic above 5th Avenue - who matched the description of the person in my dream. They think it was some sort of unconscious survival mechanism in the form of a dream, which kicked in to give me the boast I needed to shake off the coma and gain consciousness again.

"It was just nature's miraculous healing process at work," they told me. But I know different. Rebecca is back!

I grow stronger by the day. Soon I will leave the hospital. If the dream has recurred I have no memory of it, for I sleep like the dead. The doctors and nurses look at me like the lab rat I really am. I should not be alive. My carcass should have been hauled out of here on a steel slab. They all know it, yet here I am. It makes no sense to any of them, but it does to me. She has returned to succor me. The thought both thrills and terrifies me. Or is it only a nightmare, a figment of an oxygen-deprived brain?

The New Year has come and gone, as has the anniversary of my freedom, while I still suffer in my sick bed. I cannot explain it, but I know the person in the dream was Rebecca. Then last night I had the dream again. I lay in my delirium calling for something to ease my pain, for the buzzing headaches were upon me again, this time almost audible like something pounding in my skull. The same one came again, the older nurse with the old-fashioned cap and red cape.

"Do you need something?" she asked. "You look so pale and thin."

I could not answer, but only moan in my misery.

"Here, you dear man, take this."

She handed me a bowl filled with a dark-red liquid. I drank it greedily, holding the cup tightly in my hands.

"This will make you strong again," she said.

"Who are you?" I asked, after draining the liquid, my mouth still smeared with the substance.

"Don't you recognize me, Henry, after all we've been through together?"

I must have screamed and passed out, or perhaps I woke up from another dream, for I cannot recall if I was awake or asleep when she came to me. I had tumbled out of bed to the floor. Another nurse was standing over me looking at me in alarm. They assured me there was no one else on duty that night.

So here I am again, writing, when only a few days ago I could not hold a pen. I feel stronger than ever, as if I've been shot with energy. The headaches and nausea are gone. If this keeps up I will soon be sent home.

Could it really be? Has she come back to me? Has my terrible mistress returned to claim her due? How did she escape the old ones? And if that is her, how come she has aged so? I thought they never grew old. Even the old ones look... Hmm, now that I think of it, they did all look a bit long in the tooth, stiff and rigid.

If it is Rebecca, why has she brought me back from the brink of the grave, especially after what I have done to her? Or was that her plan all along, like last time, to string me along, only to bring me back at the last moment so she could make me suffer even more? What evil has she in store for me? I can only hope against hope it is only a dream and my recovery, even though miraculous, has some natural cause, though I know in my heart it must be her. Nothing else explains the dreams and how I feel. It is some vampire spell she has woven.

I am more helpless now than ever, but for some reason I don't care. After what I have been through these past days, even to draw a single breath is a sweet sensation that makes it a joy to be alive again. Whatever she has in store for me, I care not as long as the sickness has left me.

Am I sorry to be here, back in the land of the living? I cannot say, but even though I was dead to the world, I was not dead to all thought. My dreams were vivid and real even though I cannot remember them. A hundred years of subconscious thoughts and desires, long repressed, will bubble to the surface like air from a drowning man. I have a feeling they would have kept on going, these thoughts and sordid memories of too many sins and suffering, from a past too long to forget peacefully. They form my own kind of hell. But then I am from an old superstitious age. I know the devil will get his due. Perhaps that's why I fight it so. But who can outwit the devil?

Tomorrow I leave the hospital. I am almost back to full health. My weight and strength slowly improve each day, although no one knows why. They will be glad to get rid of me, for strange things have been happening around the clinic since I've been here. From what I have managed to learn, there have been more unexplained deaths than usual among the rich patients that occupy the place. One of the head nurses has also disappeared while on night duty and has not been seen since. Her husband thinks she's run off with one of the doctors, who has also disappeared, but some of the other staff think it could be foul play. I will be glad to leave, although I am less than eager to go back to Benjamin's apartment alone.

It's funny, the better I feel the more dread I have of Rebecca. I haven't had the dream since that last night she spoke to me, but sometimes, when I first awake, I have the vague sensation of the half-forgotten taste of blood.

I am now destitute. All Rebecca's jewelry is gone. My sojourn at this private clinic and the expensive doctors, have all but left me penniless. I am no longer collecting Dr. Benjamin's salary, and his insurance didn't cover the private clinic or the unnamed disease I didn't have. I am lucky to have a place to go.

Some of the doctors are still skeptical and expect a relapse as soon as I leave the hospital, but I know my own body, and I know I am well again. I can't explain it, or at least I don't want to. I don't think anyone would want to hear that I am being fed by a vampire, but I fear it's true.

Is Rebecca there waiting for me, waiting to give me my just reward for betraying her? I deserve no less, though the thought of how cruel she can be leaves me terrified. The woman in the dream was so tender and gentle. Lately, I have been wondering if maybe it was my mother. Though as I remember vaguely after so many years, she had blonde hair with braids, and freckles that covered her nose, and she was much younger. No, it was not my mother I dreamed of, but someone who was mother-like, not like Rebecca, who had mothered nothing but suffering and misery all her long life. Yet what other explanation is there for my miraculous recovery? The timing, right at the anniversary of my escape, is further evidence in the inescapable conclusion I try to deny. She is back. Rebecca has returned from the grave.

I should have known I could not defeat her. She must have escaped the old ones, or struck a bargain with them. If that is her, she shows the torture and torment they must have put her through, for she has aged much even for a human in such a short time.

I should try to flee but where can I go? I have little funds and few options. I'm tempted to just get up and run blindly into the night, but who can outrun a demon? Who can flee from someone who can carry a full-grown man up the side of a building and run as fast as a speeding train? She could smell me out of whatever hole I crawled into within a hundred miles. And let us not forget, I would not get far without her potion. No, I am tied to her, at least until she decides to dispose of me, which I'm afraid will be soon. Then the devil will get his just dessert.

Chapter 25

I am back at the apartment. Where is Rebecca? Is she just stringing me along for fun, or is she really gone? The uncertainty is driving me mad. If she is back, she is keeping her presence a secret.

I confine myself only to the three front rooms, and my activity to reading and listening to music. I love classical music. I would have loved nothing better than to play violin in an orchestra, but in all my hundred years I never learned to play an instrument. Rebecca could not abide music. I could only listen to my records when she was away, which was often, but not often enough. This past year of freedom has been a paradise, although only an oasis in the desert of my life. I fear I am destined to serve my mistress for eternity. Where can she be?

I am totally alone. I find it impossible to make friends, even if I wanted to. I have too much to hide, too many secrets. Even with Samantha I lived a lie, for she knew me only as Dr. David Benjamin, not Heinrich Fredericks, that hundred and one year old monstrosity from Berlin, the real me. I lived, as it were, in another man's body, lived another man's life this past year. I'm not sure I could have gone on living the lie, though I would have done anything to keep Samantha. I am glad she is gone if Rebecca has returned.

I have not heard from Samantha since I entered the hospital. She probably thinks I'm dead. I've had the phone disconnected. My physician agrees I'm completely cured. I don't think he really wants anything more to do with me, and who can blame him. His practice seems to have fallen apart since he's had me as a patient - subordinates and colleagues disappearing without notice, patients dying on him overnight after operations, family troubles. It's as if he's been cursed for knowing me.

I no longer even bother to peek through the peep-hole when someone knocks, but ignore it completely and pretend there's no one home. I shun all company, though my loneliness seeps out of every pore. I sleep in the day and sit awake at night like the vampire I served for many years, reading or playing my records. I usually eat out at all-night delicatessens, where I can get good German food cheap. And I wait.

Then last night she came. I was sitting on the couch listening to Bach's B-minor Mass, a piece with a passion that always seems to match my darkest moods, when between the strains of the violins and voices I heard a knock at the door, light and tentative. I turned down the music, which had just reached a crescendo, and listened again, looking at the clock on the mantel. Who could it be at this late hour? Instead of turning up the music to drown out the knocking as usual, I got up and went to the door. The knocking continued, but even more lightly and hesitant than before. I peeked through the peep-hole. Whoever it was had their back to me, their head hooded to keep off the rain, which was coming down hard this evening. I opened the door.

"David!" she screamed. It was Samantha. She turned as soon as the door was opened and rushed in to hug me. "I thought you were dead! Is that really you? They wouldn't tell me anything down at the hospital. I had the hardest time trying to find you, now here you are at your old apartment. What happened? Are you OK? You look fantastic."

"I got sick and went into a private clinic," I replied, still shocked at seeing her. "I was pretty bad off. I didn't want anyone to know."

"David, being sick is nothing to be ashamed of."

"I'm better now, especially after seeing you." I hugged her tightly.

I felt like telling her the truth and saying, 'no, I'm not your precious David,' but I was unable to utter a sound. For some reason, Samantha was the last person I expected to see at the door. I thought for sure she had given me up for dead, but she had never stopped searching for me, despite all the obstacles I placed in her path.

"Samantha, what are you doing here?" I finally stammered when I found my voice again. "It's not safe here. You must go."

"What's the matter? Why have you been hiding from me? I want to help you."

"I don't need your help. It's not safe around me. Don't you remember what happened last time? What I tried to do?"

"You would never hurt me, David. You couldn't last time. You won't hurt me now, I know it. Please let me help you."

"I'm not David, don't call me that."

"David, what are you saying? What are you talking about?"

"My name's Heinrich, Heinrich Fredericks. That's why no one at the clinic knew who you were talking about. Your precious David Benjamin died back there in that penthouse with all your other friends. What you saw wasn't a dream. It was real. I'm the man you mistook for David that day at the museum. Remember, you were looking at the St. Sebastian picture?"

She looked at me hard, then shook her head. "David, I know what you're trying to do, but it won't work. I'm not going to let you turn me away again. I don't care what you say. I'm going to help you."

"Get out of here, you stupid fool," I said, shoving her toward the door violently.

"David, stop that!" she yelled, slapping me hard across the face. She kept on hitting me with the flat of her hands, moving me backward. I did not raise my arms in defense, but let her strike me until she split my lip and drew blood.

"Oh, David," she wailed, tears in her eyes. She threw her arms around me and held me tight. I could feel her trembling next to me. I sobbed and hugged her in turn, all my pent-up emotion bubbling out of me like lava, searing my soul. It felt so good to hold her again, to feel the warmth of her body, the sweet smell of her skin. We clung to each other like lost lovers, our whole beings consumed. I called out her name over and over again, as I did in the delirium of my dream. Then I remembered.

"Sam, you've got to go. It's not safe here. She may come at any time."

"Who, what are you talking about, David? Who's coming?"

Despite my confession, she still clung to the belief I was David Benjamin. After all, what other choice did she have? It was either that or madness.

I knew I had to somehow convince her Rebecca was real and that her life was in danger, but I knew she would never believe the whole truth. She would have enough trouble dealing with Rebecca's existence, without trying to cope with the fact that she was a vampire. I realized I would have to feed her half-truths to convince her she was in danger, to convince her of the real truth. Her trust was critical to my success.

"The woman whose party you went to is a murderer. She killed your friends. She was going to kidnap you and hold you for ransom. You never told me your family is rich."

"It's not. I'm an orphan."

"Hmm, perhaps it had nothing to do with money then. I don't really know her motives. All I know is that lookalike knocked me out and tied me up in a motel room after luring you to the penthouse."

"None of this makes any sense."

I told her more lies and half-truths.

"We were on our way to the party when he said you were hurt and was going to take me to see you. He hit me on the head and tied me up, but I got loose. I didn't know where you were. Then your friend, Julie Rosenbaum, called me in a panic from the party, saying the hostess was killing people. She told me where she was and to get help. I called the police and rushed over. I got there just in time. She would have killed you, but I got the knife away from her. There was a struggle and the imposter was stabbed. She got away before the police arrived."

"I don't remember a thing about that night. It's all so confusing."

'You were heavily drugged. It's lucky you can remember anything after what she did to you. Now she's come back to finish the job. It's not safe for you to be near me. I'm afraid she is close by and could come at any moment."

"No, David, I won't leave you."

"Yes, you must. She won't harm you as long as you're not with me. It's me she's after."

"I'm not leaving you. Not after just finding you again. Whatever it is, we'll face it together."

She threw her arms around me again. I held her close.

Samantha not only believed me, she was ready to help. Now I knew why I had fallen in love with her despite all my intentions to the contrary. Here was a love so complete, so trusting, she was ready to believe and do anything for me.

"Samantha, Samantha," I said repeatedly, as I held her and rocked her in my arms. We were standing in the middle of the floor hugging each other, turning in a slow circle. In spite of my fear, I did not want to let her go. She turned her mouth up to mine and we kissed, long and passionately. I started to caress her. She probed the front of my corduroys. Soon I had her blouse off and her bra hiked up to her throat as I kissed and fondled her breasts. Throwing her onto the sofa, I began to take off the rest of her clothes.

"David," she panted, as she felt me react to her. "Oh, David."

Our feelings had been denied for so long that we tore at each other like animals, forgetting everything else. I had never felt like this before. I had finally found true love again.

We were totally lost in each other's arms until we both screamed in ecstasy. Neither of us noticed a third person slipping silently into the room, a slight female with long, tangled yellow-streaked hair. She had sharp features, and was not unattractive, but too cruel to be called pretty. In her hand she held a long obsidian spike. She was chanting something unintelligible under her breath.

Even if the phonograph had not been on, we would not have noticed her. We were so taken with each other. It wasn't until the blade pierced my back that I knew something was wrong. It pieced my heart a split second later stopping my breath in mid inhale. The last thing I saw was the look of horror on my lover's face as I slumped on top of her. At the same instant, the stone-age spear protruding from my chest penetrated her heart as well.

I could still hear Rebecca's chilling laugh echoing against the high vaulted ceiling, could still feel the last drops of blood dripping from my shrinking heart. Somehow I was still alive, though my brain did not seem to be working. My vision was clouded, my sensations dampened as if stuffed with cotton. Everything was going in slow motion. I could hear a loud, hollow booming, like a base drum in an echo chamber - boom-boom, boom-boom - one loud, one soft, which beat in a steady rhythm, but slower and slower until I realized it was my own heart slowly stopping. Then someone called my name as if from a great distance. I strove to open my eyes and respond. It felt like I was in a bottomless pit, trying to get to the top where there was light and air, but I could barely open my eyes let alone scale the immense height.

"Henry, Henry. Awake, my Henry and join me. It is time."

My eyes snapped open as if on springs and I beheld Rebecca staring down at me. She looked radiant, like she had appeared of old, shimmering in the moonlight.

"How does it feel to be one of the immortals?" she asked laughing.

'What have you done?" I groaned, looking at the still body of Samantha lying beside me. "What have you done to her?"

"She is not dead and will share your immortality. You will be my slaves for eternity, father and daughter.

"What are you saying?" I yelled.

"Samantha is really your daughter, Emily. This has been my plan all along, to trick you and turn you both into vampires, the first father-daughter pair. You will be my slaves. This is the cost of betrayal, for how you turned on me after all the years I cared for you. See how long you lasted without me? What bargain did you make with the old ones for turning me over to them?"

"I will serve you no longer," I said, ignoring her question, "and neither will my daughter.

"You have no choice. The old ones have agreed. You and your daughter will comfort me for eternity."

Naked and covered with blood, I rose to confront her, feeling the power growing within me. Rebecca was right. I was no ordinary vampire, for I had been fortified for a hundred years with her blood-potion, a concoction of ancient magic and modern science. I felt young again, younger than I had felt in decades, and stronger than a normal man.

"No," I yelled, throwing myself at her.

Leaping from the sofa where I lay with Samantha, I flew across the room at Rebecca in a single bound, throwing her into the wall. She landed with a loud crash, cracking the plasterboard. I was on her in an instant, moving like I was on an elastic band that pulled me through the air. She was ready for me. Grabbing me by the arm, she spun me around, and crashed me into the wall, splitting it right down the middle. A stand and lamp went flying. Instead of cracking my bones, it was the wall that split. I wondered at my new abilities.

Rebecca slashed her nails across my face, aiming for my throat but hitting my chin instead. I grabbed her arms and tried to fend her off, but she was still a force to be reckoned with even in her weakened condition. Whatever the old ones did to her to make her so docile to their wishes must have taken a lot out of her, for even with my newfound strength, I would have been no match for her otherwise. As it turned out, I still wasn't.

Pinning my arms to the wall, she kneed me in the groin. Even in my state of super-strength, the pain made my knees buckle. I hardly had time to register this when she slammed my head back against the wall.

"I see I will have to kill you after all," she said. "I will tear you limb from limb."

She began to pull my arms in different directions, as she impaled me further into the wall with her knee. Her face was only inches from mine. I could feel my arms being pulled from their socket though I fought with all my strength against her. Then suddenly, I saw a shadow move behind her. It was Samantha, risen from the dead. Her blonde hair stood out straight like a frenzied halo. Her eyes blazed with an angry light. Her shoulders hunched, she moved toward Rebecca, who was still unaware of her.

As Samantha came toward us, I pulled my arms down with a final tremendous effort, and held Rebecca tight. Samantha grabbed her by the neck and tried to twist her head off. She looked like a wigged-out shock treatment patient, but said nothing. Suddenly, Rebecca burst from our grasp and threw us to the side. We both stood there defiantly, staring at her.

Rebecca looked at us in shock.

"It appears I have miscalculated," she said. "You are both stronger than I thought you'd be, both having my blood in you. You make a formidable pair, father and daughter. I will have to discuss this with the old ones. You would be more trouble than you are worth. I will find others. This is not over between you and me."

With that she was gone.

To my utter amazement my terrible mistress has left us. She hadn't considered the effect of us both having her blood. Her mistake was her undoing. Samantha, my love, was my daughter, Emily, the child I never saw again after that terrible night my Caroline died. No wonder I loved her so at first sight. I thought it was chance that brought us together, but it was that demon witch, Rebecca.

So there you are. These will be the last words I write. I am no longer one of you. What else is there to tell? The two of us were too much for Rebecca in her weakened condition. Hopefully it will remain so, and she will not bother us again. If she does, we are ready.

I'm surprised the old ones let her go after how angry they were, but Rebecca has a silver tongue. She is a queen of debate, but I doubt she will be able to sway them to bother us, even if she has the nerve to tell them what happened. I doubt they would be happy.

I am finally free - totally, completely free, freer than any human. I have the freedom of virtual invincibility, the liberation of unlimited strength and powers. I can never grow old or die. I can read your mind, put you under my spell, and yes, kill you and drink your blood. My un-death may be an eternal torment to me, trying to quench a thirst I can never satisfy, but so will it be for those who cross my path. I am bound to a demon that has no love of your species. I serve no one but myself and the devil.

Samantha is traumatized by the whole thing, not realizing what has befallen her. I will teach her all she needs to know, though her powers amaze me. We will be a force to reckon with. Beware, for I am Henry the Espiritus, and I am hunting for you.

The End

To Kathleen, my friend, my wife, my life's inspiration.

Made in the USA
Middletown, DE
02 October 2017